The
SEA
NURSES

BOOKS BY KATE EASTHAM

An Angel's Work
When the World Stood Still

THE NURSING SERIES
Miss Nightingale's Nurses
The Liverpool Nightingales
Daughters of Liverpool
Coming Home to Liverpool

KATE EASTHAM

The
SEA
NURSES

bookouture

Published by Bookouture in 2022

An imprint of Storyfire Ltd.
Carmelite House
50 Victoria Embankment
London EC4Y 0DZ

www.bookouture.com

ISBN: 978-1-80314-596-9
eBook ISBN: 978-1-80314-595-2

This book is a work of fiction. Whilst some characters and circumstances portrayed by the author are based on real people and historical fact, references to real people, events, establishments, organizations or locales are intended only to provide a sense of authenticity and are used fictitiously. All other characters and all incidents and dialogue are drawn from the author's imagination and are not to be construed as real.

For Joe

'I can't stop while there are lives to be saved.'

Nurse Edith Cavell (1865–1915)

PROLOGUE

HMHS BRITANNIC, THE AEGEAN SEA, NOVEMBER 1916

A nurse ran towards the deserted dining room, her feet skidding on the wooden deck as the ship continued to tilt into the sea. An untethered wheelchair hurtled towards her; she leapt out of the way, grabbing hold of a deck bench to stop herself from falling. The ship heaved and slanted even further. Panting, she reached up with one hand to rip off her starched cap which had slipped forward, obscuring her vision. She felt something shift beneath her and somewhere, deep inside the vessel, came a loud crack that sounded like an explosion. The hospital ship was breaking apart.

Seeing an injured young man, a crew member clinging to the ship's rail, she threw herself forward. 'Hold fast, I'm coming to help,' she yelled, sliding helplessly towards him. By sheer luck she landed heavily against the rail right beside him. He turned his head in her direction, but his eyes were wide with terror, unseeing. One arm hung useless at his side – it was badly broken. Gripping the metal rail with both hands she looked over to see the water rushing up to meet them. 'We need to jump!' she screamed, but he was shaking his head. Her heart clenched. Whatever she did now would be crucial. He was in shock; she would have to drag him with her. 'Come on!' she shouted, grabbing his good arm. In the moment he loosened his one-handed grip a wave washed over and swept him out of her grasp. His mouth opened in a scream as she lunged forward, almost touching his hand. But she was a second too slow, and she saw the look of horror on his face as another wave came and took him over the side.

Still clutching the rail, drenched to the bone, she felt as if someone had punched her in the gut. Sucking in a deep breath, she tried to straighten up, spurred on by the terrified screams from injured men in the water below who desperately needed help – crew members who hadn't made it to a lifeboat, some of them thrashing around, others slumped in their lifejackets. The water was rising faster now – she needed to act, but hollow dread started in her stomach and rose to her throat, for a moment she was paralysed. Then a blood-curdling cry from the sea made her gasp. Loosening her vice-like grip on the rail, she scrambled over the side and plunged into the waves.

Water rushed in her ears and salt burned her nose, her lungs felt like they were bursting – she was in so much pain it made her angry, angry to think that this might be how she would die. *No. Never.* Kicking as hard as she could, once, twice, she started to move. Something sharp scraped against her leg but she felt no pain. With one more effort her head broke the surface and she was bobbing in the water, sucking in air. Her sodden uniform was heavy, dragging her down. She used all the power in her limbs, but she was hardly able to swim. Her chest seared with pain as she kicked with her legs, and at last she was able to make some progress. Frantically she glanced around, her vision blurred, but then she saw the injured men and the sea stained red with their blood. She tried to move towards them but still her uniform impeded her. There was no other choice but to lie back in the debris-strewn ocean with her arms spread wide and try to stay afloat.

If the sea took her, it was meant to be – there was no more that she could do now. The pale face of the young crew member who she'd tried to rescue flashed against her eyelids; she felt disorientated, struggling to grasp the enormity of what had happened to the ship from the moment of the explosion – whether it was a mine, or a missile fired from a U-boat. She glanced from side to side, looking for other members of the nursing crew... Most had got away in lifeboats.

If she hadn't stayed to search for her best friend, she would have been with them.

She drew in a ragged breath, feeling the air stinging her throat and down into her lungs. The injured men were still shouting, they were in terrible pain, they must have been caught by the blades of the ship's propeller... If only she could reach them. In a split second she felt her legs sinking. She lay further back and forced her body to relax, exhaling deeply as she levelled up in the water. *Stay alive. Just stay alive.* She closed her eyes, aware of the gentle waves rocking her body. The warm Aegean sun caressed her upturned face as she lay floating, her unravelled hair fanning out like a halo around her head.

PART ONE

CHAPTER 1

RMS OLYMPIC, AUGUST, 1914

TWO YEARS EARLIER

Iris Purefoy closed the door to the first-class stateroom with a firm click. She needed to find a piece of chicken for Miss Amelia Duchamp's Pekinese lapdog or there would be hell to pay. Miss Duchamp had embarked at Cherbourg already impatient because her personal maid had fallen ill. Iris was so busy, it irked her to be delayed by the needs of a dog, but if she didn't fulfil Miss Duchamp's request quickly it would cost her even more time. The lapdog had guzzled lamb till it came out of his ears on the outbound voyage from New York in the spring, but now Miss Duchamp had declared that he simply could not have red meat. Chicken would have to be found.

The first day at sea was always a hectic time, with the crush of boarding passengers, room bells ringing constantly, and the porters dragging trunks around the decks and hurriedly sorting luggage. And the stewardesses had to deal with hundreds of boxes of flowers that were sent aboard by well-meaning friends and relatives as a bon voyage gift. There were never enough vases to go round and often some of the flowers had to be quietly strewn in the wake of the ship. At least Iris was spared that problem – Miss Duchamp was a bad-tempered elderly spinster who never received flowers from well-wishers. But she was the ultimate challenge when it came to cabin service and it was a relief to all of Iris's fellow first-class stewardesses when she had taken on Miss Duchamp last year, after her regular White Star stewardess had left to join the P&O line. As Iris was also a qualified nurse, she had the advantage of being familiar with the array of pills and potions that Miss Duchamp travelled with. However, even with her breadth of experience, it had taken all of Iris's poise and determination to keep Miss Duchamp's demands under some degree of control.

Iris had heard there were some chicken leftovers in third class, so she made her way swiftly down the crew staircase. The ship was alive with activity – from the uppermost decks where those in first class were dining in a crystal-chandeliered restaurant with an orchestra playing into the night, down through the realms of second and third class and into the deep belly of the vessel where soot-stained men, stripped to the waist, were feeding coal into the huge boilers that drove the ship onward. It sent a thrill through her body, being a part of all this. As she reached the third-class deck, she could hear a woman singing a lively ballad in a European language that even Iris, with all her years of travel, couldn't quite place. A fiddle was playing a brisk and merry tune that gave the whole lower deck a festive air. Two small boys with shiny, pink faces and shirts hanging out of their britches came hurtling towards her and as one caught up with the other, they fell wrestling to the deck, shrieking with laughter. 'Sorry, miss,' the biggest boy called with a cheeky grin as she squeezed by them.

As she continued to make her way through a warren of corridors it pleased her to hear lively voices and feel the buzz of expectation. A gaggle of Swedish women were chatting excitedly in the passageway. Iris smiled and said hello to them. The numbers down here would be increased markedly tomorrow as more Irish passengers came aboard at Queenstown, and Iris knew there would be even more revelling and banter. Sometimes she wished she'd had the opportunity to work in steerage; joining as she did as a qualified nurse, she was automatically given a position in second class. And once she'd proved herself in both roles – stewardess and nurse – promotion to first class had come quickly.

When she'd sourced a slice of chicken, wrapped in grease-proof paper, Iris made her way back through the third-class dining room with its patterned linoleum and long wooden tables, then up the decks to the first-class pantry to collect the supper tray for Miss Duchamp. She was relieved to arrive back at the stateroom without any spills. Balancing the tray deftly on one hip, she tapped at Miss Duchamp's door, and above the yapping of the little dog, she heard the murmur of a 'come in'.

'Hush, Marco,' urged Miss Duchamp, in the gentle tone of voice she reserved solely for the dog. Iris stood poised with the tray, as Miss Duchamp reached down and scooped up the Pekinese. 'What's all this silly noise for,' she said, kissing the top of his caramel brown head and waving a hand towards a side table for Iris to deposit the gilded tray. Iris then waited by the table with her arms neatly by her sides. She was very used to this particular routine. Miss Duchamp approached the table with the dog under one arm, reached for the creamy hot chocolate laced with brandy and took a tiny sip, immediately scrunching her face. 'Much too hot,' she said. And then, glancing at the toast, 'Is it *always* necessary to put so much butter on every slice?' Lastly, she pursed her lips as she picked up the piece of chicken between finger and thumb. 'Far too dry,' she pronounced, dropping it straight back onto the silver salver. 'You'll need to cut it into tiny pieces or Marco will *not* manage it,' she insisted, fixing Iris with her sharp gaze.

Iris remained calm, but she detected an extra note of

tension in her passenger this evening. She hoped that Miss Duchamp hadn't overheard any of the agitated gossip amongst the victualling crew. It had reached a new level since Germany had declared war on Russia. She'd even overheard a kitchen steward saying he thought he'd seen a U-boat in the Atlantic, just waiting to fire on anything that moved. Iris had been determined to ignore the disquiet that nagged in her head, but still it whispered away. She felt a trickle of sweat run down her back as she stood waiting for the next instruction from Miss Duchamp. She needed to fill her head with other thoughts.

When Miss Duchamp was ready, she placed Marco gently down in his fur-lined dog bed and indicated for Iris to lay out her nightgown on the exquisite lace bedspread. As Iris pulled the gown from the drawer, the smooth, cool silk slipped through her hand. It soothed her, thinking of how it would feel to have the same luxurious sensation against her body. She imagined herself in an elegant robe with a peacock pattern, reaching for a glass of champagne—

'No, Miss Purefoy, not that one, the pale blue,' Miss Duchamp's voice snapped Iris back to the reality of assisting her out of her close-fitting bodice and full skirt. Once Miss Duchamp was seated in front of the dressing table, Iris removed the ruby necklace and matching drop earrings that her passenger always wore when boarding. It had puzzled Iris at first; these jewels were ones that should be worn at dinner, in the evening. But once she'd heard Miss Duchamp mutter something about making sure they weren't lost amongst her luggage, she understood that she was wearing them for safekeeping. When the necklace and earrings were secure in their velvet-lined case, Iris brushed and braided Miss Duchamp's dyed black hair and smoothed the special cold cream over her parchment skin.

'The ruby necklace was given to me by a young man,' Miss Duchamp said unexpectedly.

Iris drew in a breath. 'Oh,' was all she managed in return.

'I was late to find love, in my thirties... he was a handsome French army officer, and we had a wonderful year together. He was killed in the Franco-Prussian war, blasted from his horse by cannon fire... I thought I'd never recover. In many ways, I haven't...'

Iris heard the raw emotion snag Miss Duchamp's voice. Even with the distance of time, she was still grieving.

'I am so sorry, Miss Duchamp.'

Her passenger nodded and then she heaved a sigh. 'It was and is the cold, heart-rending reality of armed conflict, Miss Purefoy. And now, here we are again, contemplating another war. The politicians on both sides have absolutely no idea what they are doing. They are rushing headlong into a catastrophe... the reality of which will only truly be understood by the injured men and the women who have to deal with the consequences.'

Iris placed a hand on Miss Duchamp's shoulder and the elderly woman reached up to rest her own there, just for a moment. But in the next breath her passenger pointed to the pill bottles lined up on the dressing table, querying the dose of digitalis which she took each morning for her chronic heart condition. Iris pulled out her pocket watch and checked Miss Duchamp's pulse, paying attention to the fullness and the rhythm of the beat.

'Your pulse is strong and steady, there is no need for any concern,' she said confidently, knowing that her tone of voice was key to providing the level of reassurance that Miss Duchamp needed. The arthritis in Miss Duchamp's knees required nightly application of an expensive embrocation recommended by one of the best doctors in New York. Iris applied it sparingly, making sure that no drops smudged the silk nightgown.

'You know that cough I had in the spring, it's still there each

morning... My physician in Paris – Monsieur Bourdieu – he is
useless, all he has to say is that it is probably related to the few
cigarettes I smoke after dinner.'

Iris cleared her throat, 'It is true that smoking can exacer-
bate a cough—'

'Nonsense, Miss Purefoy. I was recommended to smoke
years ago to help *clear* my chest.'

Iris had had this same conversation many times with Miss
Duchamp, and she knew there was no chance of persuading her
to change her mind about the cigarettes she smoked so elegantly
from an ivory cigarette holder. But given that Iris also enjoyed a
smoke, she was more than happy to listen and make sympathetic noises here and there. By the time she had her passenger
resting back against the goose down pillows, the hot chocolate
was at a perfect temperature and the little dog was licking his
lips, having already jumped up onto a chair and scoffed all the
chicken on the silver salver, even before Iris had had time to cut
it up. All Iris was left to do was fuss over the position of sheets
and a wrinkle in the silk eiderdown before she could, at last,
leave her passenger lying in state, her bird-like frame lost in the
grand double bed.

Bursting out onto the deck, Iris's breath quickened as the
salt air met her. She drew it in hungrily, starting to let go of the
tension at the back of her neck that had grown steadily during
her confinement in the cabin. Walking briskly to the side of the
ship she clutched the rail and leaned out so that she could see
the white spray rhythmically lapping against the hull. It always
gave her a thrill, especially on these giant liners which were so
high and felt so solid. Looking down to the sea, aware of the
depth of water beneath her, feeling the energy of the ship as
they forged ahead, sent a ripple of sensation through her,
cancelling out all thoughts of U-boats and impending war.

The sea could always refresh her and had done ever since
she was a child returning to England from Madras to live with

her maiden aunt in Birkenhead, after both of her parents had died from cholera. It was the ship and the sea that had saved her on that voyage home alone, and the Indian steward of the P&O line who'd brought her food and escorted her out on deck to see the stars and the magical spectacle of flying fish skimming the blue ocean. Once she'd learned to trust the ship as it rode the waves, it had become her security as her mind started to process exactly what had happened to her.

When she'd become ill from a septic finger during her work at the Liverpool Royal Infirmary, and needed to take some time off, going back to the sea to recuperate had seemed a natural choice. Something so minor as a slip of a scalpel as she debrided a nasty wound had led to blood poisoning, that's why she was here now. They'd tried to pack her off to Southport for convalescence, sea air and all that, told her she might need six months off. But Iris had always wanted to work on one of the luxury liners she'd loved to watch in and out of Liverpool docks. So when she was strong enough, she'd applied for a nurse stewardess position with Cunard out of Liverpool. They had no vacancies, but, determined, she'd written to the White Star Line and got her posting to the *Olympic* out of Southampton.

On day one, she'd been struck by seasickness. Already in a weakened state, she'd found herself struggling, but once she'd heard that the ship's surgeon was thinking of putting her ashore at Queenstown, Ireland, she'd pulled herself up out of bed and made him change his mind. Dr O'Malley had been a friend since that day. They still laughed over the memory of her stamping her foot, insisting she stay on board. It had been hard, that first voyage, but Iris had made her mark with the crew. Dr Mayhew, the assistant surgeon, was a neat, serious man with a sharp eye, his pale brown hair and softly spoken voice at odds with his exacting, scientific demeanour. Only three years qualified, he'd been grateful for Iris's breadth of knowledge and hospital experience. Out in the middle of the ocean, the medical work was a law unto itself, relying solely on the expertise of the staff. Matron Beckett was a tower of strength though; she'd done twenty years at sea, and she'd delivered babies, stitched up wounds, chased after deranged passengers and even once saved the life of Miss Duchamp's Pekinese when he'd started to choke on a piece of meat.

One day, Iris might go back to a hospital on dry land, but right now this adventurous life at sea suited her, and there was something else... She'd fallen completely in love with New York. Even after four years of service, passing the Statue of Liberty still made goosebumps prickle on her arms. And in the evenings, when the low sun reflected on the glassy expanse of the thousands of Manhattan skyscrapers, it made the city sparkle. Each time, as the *Olympic* inched into her berth in the harbour, Iris felt a ripple of pleasure, and she always went ashore with her cabin mate, Roisin, during the long turn-arounds. Walking through the city, visiting the department stores to buy make-up, silk stockings or jewellery, calling by a cocktail bar later on... these were moments when Iris existed more fully, when it felt as if everything new was opening up to her.

Leaning out now, bathed in light from the brass-framed windows of the staterooms behind her, she listened to the sound of the ocean for a few more moments before gulping in one last mouthful of salt air. She knew that she needed to get moving; she had her final check to make on an elderly gentleman who had been suffering a bad bout of stomach pain and indigestion after a lavish lunch and too much wine. Dr Mayhew had prescribed a hefty dose of bicarbonate of soda plus a lead and opium pill, and her passenger did seem to be settling, but she just wanted to make sure. Then she would go to see her friend, Sam King, in the second-class smoking room where he worked as a bar steward. He often had a hot toddy ready and waiting for her. She'd known Sam since her first voyage on the *Olympic* and they'd struck up an instant rapport. When she'd visited his home in Southampton, his French wife, Francine, desperate for female companionship after living with a husband and two grown-up sons, who had now left home, had welcomed her with open arms and offered her onshore lodgings. Iris now felt like part of the family.

Sam was wiping down the glossy wooden bar when Iris walked in, passing the lavish oak-panelled walls and the green leather club chairs. A junior steward, sweeping the chequered linoleum tiles, lifted his head and offered a shy smile as she walked by. Iris gave him a nod. She had already noted a scattering of ash that he'd missed under one of the card tables, but she didn't say anything. Her friend Sam might be a big, good-natured fella with a seemingly casual approach to his work, but Iris knew that when he did his final inspection he would be just as eagle-eyed and exacting as she was.

Sam looked up and gave her his lopsided grin. 'Are they all sleeping like babies?'

'Probably not,' she replied. 'No doubt the bells will be ringing on and off throughout the night. You know what it's like on the first day.'

'I do indeed,' he said, as he poured two glasses of whisky, topping Iris's up with some steaming water from a flask. 'They were really going at it in here tonight... I'm surprised there's any liquor left.'

Iris leaned with both elbows on the bar, feeling the damp through the sleeves of her uniform where Sam had just wiped. She straightened up and ran a hand down each arm in turn. 'I sometimes wish I could work in the bar or wait on tables. I don't know why they won't let the women do it... It would make a nice break. I'm used to all my first-class passengers, I know them well and – as you are aware – I have the patience of a saint, but sometimes...'

'Get that down your neck, you'll feel better,' grinned Sam,

lifting his glass in a toast. 'Here's to the *Olympic* and all who sail in her.'

'Cheers to that,' said Iris, picking up her glass and tipping it back, taking a good swig. 'Ahh, that's so nice,' she sighed, feeling the warm toddy hit her stomach and give her an instant glow.

Checking that the bar was dry, she leaned forward on her elbows once more, cradling the glass in both hands. Sam had turned to wipe down the counter behind him, leaving Iris to study the ornate wood carving and the shiny brass rail.

'What do you think about this war talk?' she breathed.

He inhaled deeply. 'I think it's just talk... and even if it isn't, what's the use of worrying ourselves sick about something that might never happen?'

Iris was nodding but when Sam turned around, she noted the concern in his eyes. At his age, he wouldn't be called up if it came to war, but his two sons, who worked as stewards on the Cunard Line's *Lusitania* out of Liverpool, were both in their twenties. Iris took a breath and made herself smile, trying her best to give Sam unspoken support. Her aunt had been her only family and her friends on board the *Olympic* were all that she had.

'Here's to you, Sam, the best bar steward in the whole of White Star,' she offered, raising her glass.

Sam gave a mock bow and ran a hand through his greying hair, sweeping it back from his forehead. He straightened up to raise his own glass in a toast. 'Cheers, Iris... here's to life on the ocean waves, and may the war forever stay away.'

Later, as she walked back to her cabin, Iris thought of all the men, women and children on board settling for the night or already sleeping in their bunks. After the *Olympic*'s sister ship, *Titanic*, had sunk with such terrible loss of life two years ago, Iris had never taken safety for granted. She knew that the talk of

U-boats was only a rumour, but imagine what would happen now if the ship was struck... She quickly ran through the evacuation procedure in her head, taking a deep breath to stop the panic that caught at her throat.

Back at her cabin, Iris found Roisin already sleeping soundly on the top bunk, her red curls spread out over the fresh white pillow. A rosy flush on her cheeks made her look almost like a sleeping child. Just the sight of her friend sleeping peacefully without a care in the world calmed Iris. Earlier, Roisin had laughed off the talk of war, said they were more likely to strike an iceberg on a summer crossing. For now, in this intimate shared space, Iris made herself believe that her friend always had an instinctive feel for things...

Moving quietly, Iris removed her white starched cap, collar and muslin apron and then slipped out of her navy-blue serge uniform, hanging it up so that it would be in perfect shape for the morning. Unpinning her dark blonde hair, she felt it cascade over her shoulders, then with her tortoiseshell brush she slowly went through every section until it was completely tangle-free. She ran some water into the porcelain sink and wiped her face with a flannel – she never wore any face powder or make-up for work, only when she was ashore. Smiling into the mirror she whispered goodnight to herself, before slipping into her bunk and easily drifting off to the deep thrum of the ship's engines. She had heard it for so many years it was like a lullaby, making her feel that she was in the safest place in the world – like being back in the womb.

CHAPTER 2

On the White Star quay at Queenstown, Jack Rosetti watched the black steel hull of the *Olympic* cut an arc through the ocean as she manoeuvred into the outer harbour. It was a hot summer's day, the sky was blue, the sea calm. Light reflected off the glossy white upper structure of the ship. The sheer size and the lines of the vessel were dramatic, crowned as they were by four huge funnels painted cream and tipped with black, emitting sooty smoke. The presence of the *Olympic* on the water was instantly breathtaking.

Standing to the side, in a protected area, Jack picked up the bustle and excitement of passengers waiting to board and the vendors with their baskets of souvenirs. He could see men in their best suit and tie with newly polished boots, women in their finest, some in plaid shawls and scarves, others with large hats decorated with bows and silk flowers. They were a gaggle of expectation – all chatting and laughing. At the screech of a herring gull, Jack felt a stab of anxiety and began to feel on edge. He ran a hand through his tousled black hair, feeling exasperated. He should have been standing with the passengers, a ticket with his name on tucked securely inside the breast pocket of his jacket. Instead, he was beside a photographer who was waiting to board the tender that would take them across to the *Olympic*. He had no idea how to use a camera and the one slung around his neck was broken, given to him by a friendly young fella from the pub who'd offered him a way of getting on the ship.

As Jack stood, bleary-eyed, a surge of acid came up from his stomach. Patrick Casey, a stocky man with a pink face and short-cropped hair, grinned in his direction and shouted, 'How you feelin' this morning, champ?' while punching the air with both fists in a show of pretend boxing. Jack offered a tight smile, feeling a stab of pain around his bruised eye. It was hard enough to face his own stupidity without having to deal with the gleeful man who had won his ticket and most of his money during a drunken cards game. Seeing Casey sparked a flash of memory – swinging a punch, only to be caught by a heavy return blow that knocked him down to the ale-soaked floor of the pub.

He suppressed a groan, shifting his weight from one foot to the other, glad of the distraction that the *Olympic* provided for all those gathered on the quay. He had no idea if his plan would work but he had to try. After his extended visit to his Irish family in Galway, he was heading home to New York for his sister's wedding, and he couldn't bear to think of his mother eagerly awaiting his arrival only for him not to turn up. Thankfully, in the few days he'd been staying in Queenstown he'd met and made friends with the photographer. At least he now stood a chance of getting on board, and if he managed to hide out long enough, he was sure he could make his way down to third class and find somewhere to lay low.

The tenders *America* and *Ireland* were puffing out black smoke and starting to load passengers; it wouldn't be long before they were making their way to the *Olympic*. He fished a silver hip flask that his mother had given him for his twenty-first birthday out of his pocket and took a good swig of Irish whisky to steady his nerves. Loosening his shoulders, he struck up conversation with the pressman next to him, easing himself into his role. After all, he'd grown up on the streets of Brooklyn; ducking and diving was a way of life.

As the *Olympic* dropped anchor, Iris took a few moments away from her morning schedule of bed-making and cleaning cabins to look over to the quay. She'd made this stop at Queenstown many times and had always longed to go over to the small town with its colourful houses huddled close to the shore. And she enjoyed seeing the lively women who came aboard to sell their fine lace and Irish linen. Miss Duchamp had asked for assistance out of her cabin so that she could be the first to look through the lace samples. Iris knew she would have to time it just right, so that the elderly lady wasn't left standing around too long and therefore wouldn't get impatient. She hoped that she wouldn't need to make too much small talk, or worse still carry Marco, the little dog – the beast had nipped her on the arm on more than one occasion.

Seeing Roisin waving from the second-class promenade deck above, her face shining with excitement, Iris waved back and blew a kiss. All their chat this morning had been about New York, what they would wear to go ashore and the stores they would visit.

The vendors were already coming aboard, sturdy women carrying large baskets loaded with clean white fabric. Each had a regular place on the first-class promenade deck. Iris saw Bridget, a tall woman with a determined expression, leading the way. She was heading to the covered walkway, to claim her spot that none of the other sellers dare take. Iris saw the tenders well on their way, packed with passengers and mailbags. It was time to collect Miss Duchamp.

As she made her way back to the lace vendors – with Marco

tucked under one arm and Miss Duchamp, in a pale green linen suit and matching hat, on the other – Iris struggled with the weight of the little dog. He might look delicate with his black-nosed face peeping out from a ruff of pale brown fluff, but his body was solid, and he felt strong as he squirmed against her. She clung to him as Miss Duchamp made a beeline for the covered walkway. Iris guessed her sharp sapphire-blue eyes had spotted the piece of lace with particularly ornate detail that had been enticingly displayed.

Iris could see two photographers heading in their direction. One of them she recognised, as he regularly came aboard at Queenstown, but the other was a tall young man with dark curly hair who Iris had never seen before. As they came through the walkway, she saw the young photographer stop and raise his camera in Bridget's direction. The lace vendor stood erect and straight-faced while the man found the right angle for his picture. Iris waited with Miss Duchamp. Once he'd clicked the shutter he peered above the camera and looked directly at her. He had a purple bruise along his left cheekbone, but his gaze was bright, and his eyes were deep brown. Even as he stood still, there was a sense of urgency about him, so much so that, for a second, she was transfixed. Then the man strode away, and she stared after him, only shifting her attention back to the little dog when he started to squirm beneath her arm.

After the purchases were made, Miss Duchamp took hold of Marco and placed him squarely on the deck. But as she reached to attach the red leather leash to his velvet collar, a steward along the deck dropped a wooden trunk with a clatter. Marco yelped and shot off. Iris was in pursuit before Miss Duchamp could even open her mouth to issue an order. Her feet pounded the deck as she dodged her way around passengers and benches, still she couldn't see him and had to assume that he was heading back to the cabin. As a group of people moved aside to let her pass, she caught a flash of his tail straight ahead. 'Come here, you little beast,' she gasped, to spur herself on. She couldn't go back to Miss Duchamp without him, she just couldn't.

She was sure she could see the shape of him up ahead and he seemed to be slowing, but then she heard a yelp and he shot off again. Iris took a deep breath and picked up her skirt so that she could run even faster. They were close to the side of the ship now; she couldn't bear to think of the hapless creature somehow scrambling over and falling into the ocean. 'Marco,' she shouted, beginning to feel desperate. She stopped running and glanced around her, then she saw him cowering behind a stack of deckchairs. She moved swiftly and launched herself at him, flinging herself down almost on top of the little dog. He yelped and nipped her arm, she felt it sting through the sleeve of her uniform, but she didn't care; she had him now and she wasn't letting go. She could feel him writhing against her, but she used her voice to soothe him as she got up and then, one step at a time, she began to walk, murmuring, stroking his fluffy pale brown fur. His tiny heart was pounding against her and for the first time in the years since Marco had first come aboard with his owner, she felt protective of the creature. 'Hush now, hush,' she said gently.

Miss Duchamp stood like a statue with a hand pressed over her heart. 'You found him!' she cried, her voice breaking on a sob. 'You found my darling boy.'

'Please give me the leash,' Iris advised, holding out her hand. 'We don't want to lose him again.'

Her passenger complied without a word and as Iris snapped the clip onto the velvet collar, she received a small smile of gratitude. 'Thank you, Iris,' Miss Duchamp said – the first time she'd ever used Iris's first name in all the years they'd been acquainted.

'All part of the service,' Iris replied, reaching down to give Marco a stroke. In the next breath, Miss Duchamp had straightened her shoulders and regained her usual tone of voice. 'Take the lace back to my cabin,' she said, waving a bejewelled hand in the direction of her stateroom.

Iris moved swiftly, bustling along the deck with the folds of bright fabric. Taking care, knowing that as soon as Miss Duchamp returned to her cabin after lunch, she'd be fussing over it, finding the tiniest fault in the way it was folded or where it was stowed. Iris would have loved to have taken the whole lot down to third class to distribute amongst the women so they could trim their collars and make lace bonnets for their babies. Miss Duchamp probably had enough lace in her New York apartment to open her own shop.

As soon as she exited Miss Duchamp's suite, Iris heard the three customary blasts on the ship's siren, immediately echoed by a reply from one of the tenders. They were weighing anchor and ready to steam out of Queenstown harbour. She briskly climbed up to the boat deck, wanting to catch a final glimpse of Ireland as the *Olympic* began to turn back out to open sea. They had a straight run now; there would be no more land before New York.

Plenty of passengers were crowded on deck, and Iris only had a moment's glimpse between a portly gentleman wearing a linen jacket and a tall woman with a broad-brimmed straw hat. She could hear the strains of 'Erin's Lament' being played on the pipes from one of the lower decks. The haunting, melancholic notes, combined with the sound of the sea against the ship's hull, made her breath catch. She knew that all the Irish immigrants who had boarded would be crying their eyes out as they left their homeland behind.

As she turned to walk up the deck towards the lifeboats, she caught a glimmer of movement and a young man with dark curly hair stepped out from between two boats. She recognised the young photographer she'd seen earlier, but he no longer had his camera. All thoughts of him having inadvertently missed his way back to the tender were completely dispelled when she saw him glancing furtively from side to side before mingling with the passengers making their way down the deck.

She walked quickly. Clearly he didn't have a ticket or he would have boarded legitimately with the other Queenstown passengers. She stood to the side so that he wouldn't notice her and then she stepped out in front of him, grabbing his arm. 'Excuse me,' she said authoritatively, 'I believe that you should have disembarked with the rest of the press.'

He gasped and tried to pull away, but Iris was holding fast to his arm, and they were attracting attention. He stood still then with his head bowed. When he looked up his face was beseeching. 'Please, I beg you,' he pleaded, his voice warm and distinctly American. 'I did have a ticket but I lost it... and I have to go home, my mom is very sick, I have to see her.'

Seeing what looked like genuine tears springing to his eyes, Iris instantly felt sorry for him. But even though she had never encountered a stowaway before, she knew what her training had told her: she needed to report him straightaway, while there was still time to have him removed before they were out in the deeps. She pressed her mouth into a firm line – the expression she used for disciplining more junior staff – and was about to speak when he fixed her again with those deep brown eyes and repeated, 'Please, I beg you.' The timbre of his voice sent an ache through her heart. She knew what it was like to lose a parent without ever having the chance to say goodbye; what if his mother died and he didn't manage to see her one last time?

Iris swallowed hard and let go of his arm, glancing around to make sure that she hadn't been seen by any other crew members. 'You don't know me,' she said curtly. 'If they pick you up, you never saw me.'

'Of course,' he said, leaning close, lowering his voice.

Iris felt a tightness in her throat. How could she be letting this man go free? Seeing the flash of gratitude in his eyes, she knew that it was already too late. She spoke again, making sure that her voice was steady. 'If you follow along a few paces behind, I'll take you to the stairs that lead to second class. I'll distract the steward, you keep going down and you'll come to third class... there will be lots of activity with the newly boarded passengers and mailbags being stowed; mingle with the others and then find yourself somewhere out of the way.'

'Thank you,' he breathed.

Iris turned and strode briskly along the boat deck with her head held high, the tiny hairs at the back of her neck prickling with sensation at the thought of him following along behind. She felt guilty and excited at the same time, and part of her prayed that she never laid eyes on him again. But another, greater part wanted to be sure that she would see him before they reached New York.

Now that the ship was on the move, Iris needed to check that all the staterooms were clean and in order. As she bustled about her duties, she knocked at every door and listened before entering. At Mr and Mrs Buchanan's suite she was shocked to see a young woman wearing a pale grey skirt and white blouse lying prostrate across the red silk eiderdown of a four-poster bed. Iris knew the couple well – Mr Buchanan was a wealthy New York banker and they regularly travelled to Europe for pleasure. This was the first time they'd been accompanied by their daughter, Astrid, who was sixteen.

'Are you all right, miss?' Iris spoke softly, walking towards the bed.

The girl sniffed and tried to sit up. Her face was sheet-white and her straight blonde hair had begun to straggle loose.

'Are you feeling unwell?'

'I will be fine,' the girl muttered. 'Nanny checked me an hour ago and she is a qualified nurse.'

Iris nodded, she knew the nanny in question – she had all the qualifications but she was very easily distracted by the first-class cabin stewards.

Iris walked to an elegant side table and poured some iced water from a cut-glass decanter. 'Take a sip,' she said. 'It might help.'

The young woman shook her head. 'I feel nauseous,' she said, her voice catching as she clutched her abdomen. Iris felt a stir of unease.

'You look rather flushed, Miss Buchanan,' Iris offered, placing the back of her hand against the young woman's fore-head. It was burning. The girl was trying to sit up and she was swinging her legs to the side of the bed. As she did so, she doubled over in pain. Iris crouched beside her, starting to feel the urgency of the situation but keeping her voice and demeanour perfectly calm. 'I am a trained nurse as well as a stewardess. Just lie back and let me have a feel of your tummy.'

The girl started to shake her head but then she clutched her abdomen and cried out in agony. Iris spoke gently, easing the girl back. It wasn't seemly to ask the young woman to pull up her skirt, so she examined through her clothing. As soon as she pressed, she could feel the tension of the girl's abdomen and as she carefully moved her hand down to the lower right quadrant, the girl screamed out. This was the clearest case of acute appendicitis that Iris had ever seen. They were heading out to open sea, the only resources they had were here, on this ship. Without showing any concern in her voice, Iris said, 'I'm going to use the bell to call for the cabin steward, so he can bring the ship's doctor to examine you, and it might be best if we find your parents...'

Dr Mayhew quickly confirmed Iris's diagnosis and ordered a transfer of their patient to the first-class ship's hospital. As Mrs

Buchanan stood teary-eyed beside the iron-framed hospital bed, Iris tried to offer reassurance, but her daughter's face was as white as the pillowcase. Dr Mayhew, meticulous as always, was already preparing the instruments for surgery when Dr O'Malley bustled in, out of breath, with his white hair slightly dishevelled.

'Now, what do we have here?' he asked kindly.

Mrs Buchanan tried to speak but her voice was breaking, so Iris quietly gave the surgeon all the information.

He narrowed his eyes and walked to the side of the bed. 'Has she vomited?' he enquired.

'Nausea, but no vomiting,' Iris replied.

'In that case, Nurse Purefoy, I think we should treat conservatively in the first instance – give her some pain relief and peppermint water and see how she goes. Undertaking surgery out here in the middle of the Atlantic isn't the best option, if we can settle her until we reach New York.'

Iris could see the relief in young Dr Mayhew's eyes. Mrs Buchanan exhaled deeply and reached for her daughter's hand. Once the girl was more comfortable with an injection of morphia and she had begun to drift off to sleep, Iris left her patient under the watchful eye of Dr Mayhew and returned to her stewardess duties. It was a relief to be back in the fresh air. Most of the time the ship's hospitals stood empty, so when an emergency came it meant quick-thinking and a sudden change of tempo. Hopefully, the girl's condition would continue to be stable till they reached New York.

It was too early to make her visit to Miss Duchamp, so Iris continued her check of the first-class cabins and then, noting a stain on her usually spotless apron, she headed to her cabin to change. Enjoying the peace, she was tempted to rest on her bunk for five minutes, but something still niggled her about

Miss Buchanan's condition and she knew she wouldn't be able to settle until she'd been back to check on her. The girl was sleeping peacefully with her nanny stationed on a chair beside her, reading a magazine. 'How has she been?' Iris asked as soon as she walked in. The nanny looked up, mildly affronted. 'No pain, no fever... the same as she was when you left her, just over an hour ago.'

Iris picked up the chart from the bottom of the bed to make her own check of the observations. The last two readings showed an incremental rise in temperature, not enough to elicit undue concern but it was there all the same. Although she had fewer years of nursing practice than the Buchanan's American nanny, Iris wasn't one to hold back. 'I can see the beginnings of a low-grade fever and the pulse rate is slightly elevated, please record at least half-hourly throughout the night and keep the chart up to date.'

The nanny's eyes narrowed. 'Yes, of course I will do that. It is routine procedure.'

Iris gave a nod and withdrew, not worried one bit by the nanny's reaction. If something needed to be said regarding a patient's welfare, she would never hold back. She didn't care how many nurses were put out; the patient always came first. She would go and find Matron, Dr O'Malley or Dr Mayhew and express her concerns... make sure that all the team were aware of Miss Buchanan's condition.

Moving swiftly down to the second-class infirmary she found Henry, one of the hospital stewards, making up a bed.

He rubbed a hand across his chin, 'Well, Matron Beckett's gone down to third class, we had word that a woman was going into labour, so she was straight there, you know what she's like. And Dr Mayhew, he's been seeing to a fella with a bad headache... he's gone off to the dining room now, I think... And Dr O'Malley, I've not seen him for ages, he could be anywhere... he's as likely to be down in steerage with the great unwashed as he is up in first class treating some rich woman with a touch of the vapours.'

'I'll just keep looking,' Iris smiled, stepping forward to straighten the starched white sheet at one side of the hospital bed that the steward was making up.

Almost as she got to the door, Henry called, 'You could try the crew hospital, I've heard there's been some minor incident down in the boiler room, it might be he's gone there.'

Iris moved quickly; as soon as she got close to the hospital, she could hear a man groaning in pain and then Dr O'Malley's gravelly voice. Once through the door she stopped a moment, catching her breath. A member of the boiler crew, his face scrunched with pain, lay on the stark white bed, his head and naked torso black with coal dust. The doctor was stooped over him, scrutinising the hand that lay helplessly on the sheet, raw and bright pink with peeling flesh.

'How bad is it, Doc?' the man croaked.

'Superficial layers,' Dr O'Malley replied. 'You'll live.'

'Thank Christ for that... I've just had word that me missus has given me another son, I 'aven't even seen him yet.'

Dr O'Malley was laughing. 'This won't hold you back, and once I've got the wound cleaned up and dressed, we can raise a glass of whisky to wet your baby's head.'

Iris walked straight over. 'Need any help?'

'Iris,' the doctor called, the deep lines of his face creasing into a smile. 'Right in the nick of time. Our man Jim has been at the wrong end of a jet of steam from one of the boilers. I'm about to give him a dose of laudanum before I treat the wound, are you able to assist?'

Iris scrubbed her hands and donned a cotton gown and then tended to the peeling flesh on Jim's hand while Dr O'Malley prepared a dressing. Determined to clean the wound thoroughly, she swabbed and swabbed until the water in the bowl was thick with soot. Iris wondered how the stokers ever managed to get clean. She'd visited the boiler room once or twice, it was like hell down there, she had no idea how the men coped.

'I'll get some clean water,' she said quietly.

Jim flinched a little when she came back, and she checked that he was bearing up before she continued. His red-rimmed eyes were closed now as he lay back against the pillows, smearing soot on the bright white linen. When Dr O'Malley approached with a clean tray and the dressing ready to apply, Iris peered closely. 'I would use an iodine soak,' she said, 'it works well on these superficial burns.'

Dr O'Malley tilted his head and then retreated with the tray, and in moments Iris detected the pungent smell of iodine being poured from a bottle. Once he was back at the bedside, she spoke again. 'We'll have to pad it well and put a firm bandage on, you know what these stokers are like, he'll be back to work in a few hours.'

Iris saw Jim's chest heave with a deep chuckle. 'If we stop the ship stops,' he croaked.

While Dr O'Malley held the dressing in place, Iris applied a bandage. 'Fine job there, Iris,' he smiled, as they both stepped away to wash their hands and let Jim have a short rest on the bed. Iris had almost forgotten the reason why she'd sought the doctor out, but when she relayed her concern about Miss Buchanan's rise in temperature, he listened very carefully, rubbing the back of his neck for a few moments as he considered his response.

'It does sound like something might be brewing... but Matron has offered to supervise the night shift, so she'll soon let us know if there's any change in the girl's condition.'

Iris nodded, beginning to feel reassured.

'Pray very hard, Iris, that this one doesn't develop into full-blown appendicitis... it would be drastic indeed if we needed to perform surgery out in the deeps with no chance of a return to dry land... and the other thing is, I've not done an appendicec-tomy in years.'

Iris felt a stir of unease. She hadn't fully considered the outcome.

'I'll pray,' she breathed.

CHAPTER 3

In the early hours of the morning there was a firm knock at the cabin door. Roisin groaned in her top bunk, muttering something about why she had ever chosen to share with a nurse. Iris, instantly awake, was already at the door, standing in her nightdress, blinking in the light. It was a young cabin steward with bleary eyes and dishevelled hair, out of breath, his brow scrunched with concern. 'Matron Beckett sent me to fetch you, she said to tell you that Miss Buchanan is vomiting now and she's in a lot of pain... they are going to operate.'

Iris gave a single nod. 'Tell Matron I'll be ten minutes.'

Her heart thudded against her ribs as she quickly sponged her face and slipped into her uniform. She had always worked on surgical wards and in theatre and had assisted with many appendicectomies at the Liverpool Royal Infirmary, but never before in a ship's hospital on the Atlantic.

Iris could hear Miss Buchanan crying out in pain as she walked swiftly along the alleyway towards the first-class hospital. The sharp rhythm of her stride gave her confidence, making her feel capable, professional. When the girl gave a bloodcurdling scream, however, Iris's heart lurched and she instantly broke into a run.

Entering the hospital Iris saw Matron's broad back was turned as she lifted shiny instruments out of the steaming steriliser, deftly placing them on a stark white surgical cloth. Dr Mayhew was at the head of the bed, desperately trying to calm the patient's distraught mother. There was no sign of Dr O'Malley, and the American nanny was grappling to keep Miss Buchanan in bed.

'Let me take over from you with the patient,' Iris insisted, the tone of her voice causing the nanny to step back. She saw the visible relief on Dr Mayhew's face as she grasped the girl's hand and started to speak firmly. 'Astrid... I know you are in terrible pain right now, but I promise you, if you squeeze my hand and take some deep breaths, it will start to ease...' Iris felt the girl crushing her hand. 'Breathe in... and out,' Iris said quietly. 'That's it... and again... there you go. Dr Mayhew will give you some chloroform in a minute, it will put you to sleep and when you wake up, it will all be over.'

The girl's greenish-white face contorted with agony, and she pulled up her knees, but she nodded as she clung to Iris. Iris used her free hand to sweep the strands of blonde hair back from the girl's sweating forehead. 'Please fetch me a damp cloth,' she asked the nanny, 'and then it might be best if you take Mrs Buchanan back to her cabin and stay with her... we will send word when the operation has been completed.'

The nanny nodded. Mrs Buchanan spoke softly and bent down to kiss her daughter's cheek before withdrawing, the nanny supporting her.

Once Iris had more space around the bed, she had better control of Miss Buchanan and Dr Mayhew was able to prepare the chloroform anaesthetic mask. In moments, Matron Beckett had the instruments laid out and two enamel receivers ready and waiting. She was scrubbing her hands with carbolic soap at the sink when Dr O'Malley appeared at the door – he looked tired and dishevelled, his hair sticking up at one side and a tea stain on his bushy white moustache.

'We're almost set, Doctor,' Matron called over her shoulder, making way for him to scrub up.

Iris and Dr Mayhew shared a concerned glance. Iris had never seen Dr O'Malley perform anything other than a minor procedure.

When Dr O'Malley turned from the sink, Iris was relieved to see that the hand-scrubbing and the scent of carbolic seemed to have revived something of the surgeon in him. His eyes were bright now, focused, as Matron helped him into a surgical gown and rubber gloves.

Iris held Astrid's hand, spoke soothing words and then, when Dr Mayhew was ready to deliver the anaesthetic, she explained to her patient that they would place a gauze mask over her face and the smell would be strong from the drops but when she breathed them in, she would fall fast asleep. The girl clenched her jaw and nodded.

The chloroform worked instantly, and it was such a relief to see the patient free from pain at last. While Dr Mayhew carefully tied back the girl's tousled blonde hair with a thin strip of bandage and carried her over to the wooden operating table, Iris went to the sink to scrub her own hands and don a surgical gown and gloves. Matron would act as scrub nurse, but Iris would be ready to assist as required and collect the used swabs in an enamel bowl on the floor. When Iris came to the operating table, Matron had already fixed surgical towels around Miss Buchanan's smooth, pink abdomen and sprayed with carbolic acid solution. Dr O'Malley stood poised with his scalpel to make an incision but to Iris's horror he appeared frozen and his hand was shaking.

Dr Mayhew cleared his throat. 'Are you thinking of a midline or a transverse incision, sir?' he called nervously from the head of the table where he was monitoring Miss Buchanan's level of anaesthesia.

Dr O'Malley looked up as if he'd been woken from a dream and his hand began to shake even more.

Iris spoke up. 'I'm just wondering, Dr O'Malley, wouldn't it be better to let Dr Mayhew get some experience of surgery... maybe he could swap, before you make the incision?'

'Oh yes, that's an excellent plan,' Matron piped up from behind the table laid with instruments.

Dr O'Malley swallowed hard. 'How does that sound to you, Mayhew?'

'Yes, that's fine by me, I could do with the practice,' Mayhew replied vigorously, already at the sink scrubbing his hands. In moments he was ready to take the scalpel from the senior physician.

Iris drew in a deep breath, her head a little swimmy.

Dr Mayhew's slim, steady hand made a confident transverse incision and as Matron dabbed expertly at the bright red blood, Iris began to feel a sense of ease.

'Ah, I can see the difference already,' Dr O'Malley murmured. 'You young doctors and your new-fangled procedures... McBurney's muscle-splitting incision...'

Iris knew that the incision had been in use for many years, but she made a quick comment to support Dr O'Malley with his interest in technique, all the while making sure that his attention didn't wander from monitoring their patient's anaesthesia. When a bloodstained swab missed the enamel bowl, she stooped to retrieve it and felt the floor of the hospital tilt ever so slightly. 'The ship's rolling a little,' she said. 'It must be getting a bit rough out there.'

Dr Mayhew's eyes widened but he merely leaned against the operating table to help steady himself and continued with his work. It felt like they were all holding their breath as the gentle roll of the deck continued. Iris was relieved to see that Dr

Mayhew was an adept surgeon – quickly and precisely he pulled out the loop of bowel to expose the red and inflamed appendix. Thankfully, it hadn't perforated, so the girl stood an excellent chance of making a full recovery. Once the ligature was applied and the appendix removed, Dr Mayhew started to close up. As he sutured the skin, Astrid groaned and shifted her position on the table. 'I don't want to give her any more chloroform if I can help it,' Dr O'Malley said. 'It will only make her groggy... let's see if she settles.'

Dr Mayhew nodded and continued his suturing without any further event.

Iris could have fallen to her knees with relief when it was time to assist Matron with the application of an abdominal dressing. The ship had started to roll even more strongly now, and the enamel bowl of used swabs was sliding back and forth across the linoleum.

As soon as their patient started to rouse, Iris spoke softly to her, telling her that all was well. Astrid opened her eyes and gave a drowsy smile and then began muttering jumbled words. The girl drifted back to sleep, and Dr Mayhew stripped off his surgical gloves and carefully lifted her from the table to carry her back to the hospital bed. Once the patient was settled in position, he smoothed a stray lock of blonde hair off her forehead and then spoke softly to Matron: 'Might be best to give Miss Buchanan a tiny dose of morphia via hypodermic injection to keep the pain at bay... and just sips of water at first. Fluids only for at least forty-eight hours.'

Matron nodded, smiling as she gently swayed from side to side in time with the rocking of the ship.

Dr O'Malley patted his colleague on the back, congratulating him on a good job, but Iris could see how Dr Mayhew held back. He knew, as they all did, that they needed to wait and see what happened in the next few days. If suppuration set in, the girl could still lose her life. It always felt brutal, to cut through someone's skin, especially if the patient was young, but it was a miraculous feat if the patient was cured. Iris loved surgical nursing for that reason. She sighed with relief, turning from the bed to press the buzzer to summon a steward to take a message to the Buchanan's cabin, telling them that all had gone to plan and they could visit their daughter in an hour's time.

When the steward arrived, it was the same young man with dishevelled hair who had knocked on her door in the early hours. His eyes were wide with apprehension, but when he received the news he appeared jubilant and ran off at speed to deliver the message.

Later, after Iris had spent time monitoring Miss Buchanan's post-operative recovery, she headed out to the side of the ship, clutching the rail and leaning over to breathe in the salt air. Only now could she start to unwind. But with three more days at sea till they reached New York, they would have to remain vigilant for signs of infection and make sure the wound was healing. Iris sucked in another deep breath, she had learned years ago that the best way to deal with anxiety was to keep busy, seek diversion. It was too early to go along to the smoking room to see Sam, but she would be in time to attend her favourite American couple, Mr and Mrs Fontaine. They always loved a chat, and right about now they would almost certainly be in their cabin enjoying pre-dinner cock-tails. Even though it was another warm evening, Iris felt a shiver run through her body, and she wrapped both arms around her body as she started to walk briskly with her head down.

'Whoa, whoa, where're you going in such a hurry,' a familiar voice said, and in the next second she walked smack bang into a tall figure wearing a too-large grey jacket with a straw boater pulled down low over his eyes.

Iris almost shrieked out loud but she could hear the man laughing, and when he pushed back his hat to reveal his face, she gasped. It was her stowaway.

'You shouldn't be out here,' she hissed. 'You might be seen.'

'I don't think anybody will recognise me in this straw boater,' he grinned. 'I've been strolling around all evening. I even descended that grand staircase with its carved wood and fancy glass dome... No one batted an eyelid.'

Iris shook her head. 'You shouldn't have been up there... I'm amazed that you weren't spotted.' She wanted to step around him and go swiftly on her way, but she couldn't resist his smiling face and, against all her better judgement, she felt her shoulders drop and she almost returned his smile.

'Where have you been staying?' she asked, trying to make her voice formal, as if she were interacting with any other passenger.

'Down in the depths of steerage... I've made some mates and even buddied up with the fella who has my ticket.'

Iris scrunched her brow, trying to make sense of what he'd just said. 'Look, you can't go roaming around the ship, you shouldn't—'

'I can and I will,' he said. 'I've been looking for you. I wanted to come and say thank you.'

'Well, you've said it now,' mustered Iris. 'I need to get on with my duties.'

She tried once more to step by him, but he leaned in and brought his face up so close that Iris could see the fading bruise on his cheekbone and smell the fresh tobacco on his breath. 'I can't see properly in this light,' he said, frowning, 'but I'm sure from the other day on the boat deck, that you have the most beautiful blue-green eyes...'

He smiled again, as if they'd shared something intimate.

It seemed as if they were breathing the same breath, it sent a shiver through her body. She angled her face away, shaking her head.

He reached out, his fingers lightly touched her cheek, and there was an undeniable frisson as he gave her a slow smile. Then his arm curled around her, brushing the small of her back and she realised that she was lost, helpless, unable to resist. He pulled her close and as she rested against his body, the sound of the orchestra playing for the first-class passengers drifted over them.

'I wish we had some champagne,' he murmured, starting to sway from side to side in time with the music.

Within moments they were moving together, catching the rhythm of a dance. She looked up and saw his dark eyes reflecting light. She knew that she was taking a huge risk but there was a prickle of excitement deep inside her belly. She sighed when the music ended and, as if it was the most natural thing in the world, he bent his head and kissed her gently on the lips. His stubbly beard scratched her chin, but his lips were soft and warm and tasted of salt. She had no choice but to kiss him back.

'Do you go ashore, in New York?' his voice was breathy and she could feel his heart thudding in his chest.

'Yes, always... but I thought your mother was ill, surely you—'

He twisted his mouth. 'Ah that, well, the thing is – and this is still important – my sister is getting married, so I do need to get home... But what I said about my mom, I kind of made that up...'

Instinctively, Iris pulled back from him. 'But you gave the impression that she was dying, I thought that—'

'I'm sorry, I was just so desperate... and I did have a ticket, I just... lost it, that's all. And it wasn't all a lie, if I don't turn up for my sister's wedding, my mom's going to make herself sick with anxiety.'

Iris shook her head but he was smiling again, his eyes burning into her. He was absolutely infuriating. Turning his mouth down in mock sorrow, he moved close once more. 'Please give me a chance, blue-green eyes...' he said, sweeping his hand towards the ocean, 'we've been drawn together by the wind and the sea and the stars above... you can't abandon me now...'

Iris knew she should walk away. This man was unreliable, foolish, overly excitable, and he told blatant lies. But when he pulled her close and she breathed in the smell of him and they were kissing again, her body reacted, overriding any concerns that her mind still screamed.

The sound of footsteps behind them further up the deck made her step back smartly. Clearing his throat, he said, 'Thank you very much, stewardess, I'll make sure to book a table for the restaurant...' And then he mouthed, 'I'll see you later,' as he backed away with a cheeky grin, raising a hand in farewell before the young honeymoon couple in evening dress, taking a stroll out on deck, could think that there was anything amiss.

Iris could feel her lips still tingling with sensation and she pressed a hand to her chest to steady herself. Making herself walk, she started to smile, suffused with warmth as she continued on her way to the Fontaines' suite.

Passing the first-class passengers inside the gilded glass world of their à la carte restaurant, she saw men in white shirts and dinner suits, women in brightly coloured silk gowns and extravagantly feathered hats, their diamonds and rubies and pearls glinting in the golden light. Theirs was a separate existence and most of the time she was content with her own lot but, after what had just happened out on deck, seeing the couples dancing to the orchestra and sitting at tables sipping champagne, the intimacy of it all made her yearn for something other. She paused for a moment, watching her fellow steward

Michael, who was pouring wine at a table close to the window. He rolled his eyes and with a tiny movement of his head indicated the grim-faced middle-aged couple who were sitting straight-backed in their padded chairs closely examining the menu. The woman's sour expression contrasted sharply with her yellow sequined gown and wide-brimmed hat with a festive silk band. Clearly, they weren't the life and soul of the party this evening. Iris clapped a hand over her mouth and started to move away as Michael pulled a comic face. He had a slapstick sense of humour and he could always make her laugh, but she didn't want to get him into trouble with the chief steward.

Fancy having all that money and access to such a fabulous restaurant and just sitting there with miserable faces. Iris was sure that if she ever got the chance, she'd grab it with both hands. Life was precious; she knew that, especially after what had happened to her parents. It had always niggled her, knowing that she could have had something different. She'd been born in India, the daughter of an ambitious British army officer and his beautiful wife. They'd lived very comfortably in Madras and Iris even used to have her own ayah. In a single day, her parents had fallen seriously ill, and everything had been taken away from her. Heartbroken, she'd been shipped back to England to live with her father's grieving sister, Aunt Edith Purefoy. She'd cried herself to sleep for months, missing her parents, her ayah, and the colour and the warmth of their life in Madras. Nothing would ever replace that love.

Aunt Edith had been formal, strict, but never unkind and had actively encouraged her to eschew the advances of young men and find herself a career. When Iris had come up with the idea to train as a nurse, Aunt Edith had been reticent at first, advising that maybe teaching might be a more suitable choice for a young lady of Iris's disposition. But Iris had been set on training as a hospital nurse. The need to care for the sick had slowly kindled inside of her from those few days in Madras when she'd witnessed a gently spoken Indian nurse take charge of her dying parents. Although Iris had gone on to do the rest of her growing up in a house almost devoid of human contact apart from a cook and a part-time maid, her aunt had loved cats – so much so that she'd left most of the money in her will to a cat sanctuary. The house had always been full of their meowings and their need for comforting or nursing through sickness and giving birth to their many litters of kittens. Iris had adored the cats and she had cared for them meticulously.

Aunt Edith had died from a sudden illness during Iris's year of hospital training and therefore had never known that her niece, who she'd always referred to as a bit of a misfit, had begun to blossom, maybe not always at the centre of a group of friends but the other probationers appeared to enjoy her company. And then, of course, when she'd gone on to nurse on the ships, she'd been thrown together with a mixed bag of crew who could be bad-tempered but were mostly loyal, friendly and full of fun. That's where she'd truly flourished and become the woman that she was now, still with her self-contained core, but good with people, someone who actively cultivated friendships.

That's why now she was earning her own living she was determined to experience all that life could offer, and she'd established a distinct onshore life for herself, something warm and beautiful that she could enjoy with her fellow stewardesses. She'd also had her share of romance – a relationship with a junior doctor at the Liverpool Royal which, when it had come to a choice between continuing her work as a nurse or accepting his marriage proposal, she'd instantly chosen the former, and a brief relationship with a handsome ship's officer who'd long since left the ship. He'd been keen on her, she might even say besotted, but he hadn't held her attention for longer than a few months.

Already though, it felt like there was something different about the stowaway – despite him being entirely the wrong type and most definitely beneath her level of expectation with regard to social class. Infuriatingly, she had never been attracted to any other man so strongly before. Their instant connection vibrated between them like a plucked string.

Iris found herself outside the Fontaines' suite. She couldn't remember having covered the distance but now she was standing at the door. She had to take a deep breath before she was ready to knock and wait to be admitted. As soon as the young maid opened the door with a polite nod, Iris smiled as her senses picked up the sweet smell of freesia and gardenia. As always in this suite, there were at least a dozen vases of flowers all sent on board by well-wishers. Iris moved straight to the bedroom and bathroom area to start the cleaning and tidying – glad of the physical activity, needing to take up a rough cloth and give something a good scrub to try and stop her mind from whirring with what had just happened out on deck.

While she worked, she could hear a low murmur of conversation from the sitting room. As predicted the young American couple were enjoying pre-dinner drinks; she could hear the rhythm of their conversation punctuated by Mrs Fontaine's tinkling laughter and the gentle clink of ice against cut glass. Mr and Mrs Fontaine and their four-year-old daughter, Vita, had boarded in Cherbourg after travels through France. They were from San Francisco, a fact that Iris loved, she always listened out for any detail of a city that one day she was determined to visit. Little Vita was a sweet girl with blonde curly hair who was now sleeping peacefully in her cot bed, her cheeks flushed pink after the exertion of chasing up and down the promenade deck all day.

Once Iris had finished her cleaning, she went through to the sitting room to check if the Fontaines needed anything. The couple were relaxing on their brocade sofa with their cocktails. As Iris walked through, her eye caught the delicate detail of Mrs

Fontaine's red-beaded evening gown set against her glowing complexion and black hair. She was a very handsome woman.

They'd hardly noticed when she'd entered the suite, but now Mrs Fontaine looked up with a smile. 'Iris, how are you this evening?'

'Very well, thank you... can I get you anything before I go to my next cabin?'

'No, thank you... we will be going for dinner in a few minutes. Why don't you sit down here with us? Maybe you could sneak a sip of cocktail... This Tom Collins is remarkably good.'

Iris shook her head. 'No, I couldn't possibly, we have a surgical patient in the hospital, I need to go back and check on her.'

'Yes, of course,' Mrs Fontaine said. 'I heard about poor Astrid Buchanan... and the person who told me remarked upon the adroitness of the nurse stewardess who had her swiftly diagnosed and removed to the ship's hospital. I didn't need to ask for a name, I knew it was you, Iris. One day I'm hoping to persuade you to come and stay with us in San Francisco – it's always reassuring to have a capable trained nurse as part of the household.'

Iris felt a burst of pleasure at her passenger's kind words and her cheeks flushed pink. 'Thank you,' she said, 'but most nurses worth their salt would have done the same.'

'Mmm,' breathed Mrs Fontaine. 'I don't think they would have been quite as quick off the mark as you, Iris... And I won't forget, the next time we're back on board the *Olympic*, I may well have a proposition for you... I know what an adventurous spirit you have.'

'Thank you,' Iris beamed, unable to contain her pleasure.

'Let's hope this war talk doesn't come to anything though,' Mr Fontaine muttered.

Mrs Fontaine held up a hand to make a dismissive gesture

but then paused, a line of worry creasing her brow. 'Yes, let's hope so.'

At the forlorn sound of her voice, her husband reached out to take her hand. 'I'm sorry my dear, I didn't mean to alarm you... I've just been bogged down with it all day, the talk amongst the men in the gymnasium and out on the deck has been not whether, but when, war will be declared.'

Mrs Fontaine sighed and then she rallied, making herself smile. 'Whatever happens, we will not be daunted, and we will be back to our beloved Paris for the spring.'

No reply came from Mr Fontaine, he simply gave a tight nod and squeezed his wife's hand. Iris felt a stir of unease in her stomach as she turned to leave their suite. It seemed that her plan for distraction hadn't worked quite as well as she'd hoped.

Later, when Iris called by the first-class hospital to check on Miss Buchanan, she was pleased to find her sleeping off the chloroform and making a good recovery. Roisin had tried to persuade her to join the first-class stewards for drinks, but Iris hadn't wanted to go – she felt too restless and on edge. It wasn't only the tiredness from her extra duties in the hospital; she hadn't been able to shake off her anxiety. No matter how many times she overheard her educated, well-heeled passengers – those who should know better – dismiss the threat of war, she could tell by the look in their eyes that they were bluffing. They were just as aware of what was coming as the young stewards who constantly showed off about marching to war and doing their bit. It was all getting too much.

Back in her cabin, she picked up a magazine from the stack at the bottom of Roisin's bunk and stood flicking through the pages. The new fashions were mildly diverting, and then a

piece on San Francisco caught her eye. It interested her, especially after the invitation that Mrs Fontaine had offered earlier.
Kicking off her shoes, she settled on her bunk and lay engrossed
in the article – imagining herself riding cable cars, seeing the
Golden Gate Bridge, exploring San Francisco Bay. It would be
a wonderful opportunity to extend her experience of America
beyond New York. Who knows, maybe she would settle there,
find work in a Californian hospital...

With a loud bump, the cabin door flew open and Roisin
tumbled through, her red curls dishevelled and her cap askew.
Iris shot up on her bed, the magazine sliding to the floor. Her
cabin mate stood swaying and grinning.

'One day, you are going to give me a heart attack,' Iris said.

'Shorry, Iris...' Roisin grinned tipsily and then she started to
giggle as she told the story of the first-class stewards and the skit
they'd performed making fun of the chief steward.

'What you been doin?' she asked, sitting down next to Iris
on the bottom bunk.

'Just reading a magazine to stop myself from worrying about
the war.'

Roisin snorted with laughter. 'What war, silly? There won't
be any war, it's all a load of cock and bull.'

Iris wasn't going to argue with her drunken cabin mate. She
retrieved her magazine and let Roisin lean against her while she
flicked through the pages. 'When we go ashore, Iris, I want to
get myself a new outfit from that store we went to last
time... What will you be wearing, have you got something new?'

Iris got up and pulled out the outfit she'd been saving for her
trip during turnaround – a pale blue skirt and matching jacket
with a splendid red velvet collar. Roisin stroked the collar and
asked if she could try it on. This was a familiar routine – they
were both the same size – but Iris drew the line at lending out
her clothes to her cabin mate. Having witnessed the many spills
and marks that came back with Roisin on her apron, she firmly

rejected anything other than supervised 'trying on'. The pale blue did suit Roisin, setting off her red hair, and when she reached for the matching hat decorated with red silk flowers and a veil, Iris gasped with delight and started to smile... 'You look incredible in it, Roisin, it really suits you.'

'Really?' Roisin's eyes were wide as she stood there, swaying.

'Yes, really. Now, slip it off before you do something to it... I need to wear it to New York.'

Roisin started to giggle. 'If I'd have been wearing this tonight in Michael's cabin, I'm sure he would have proposed marriage to me there and then.'

'You can do a lot better than Michael, Roisin, you know you can.' Iris felt her cheeks flush as she realised that she was one to talk, dancing with a stowaway on the promenade deck for all the world to see.

'Maybe so, but he has a fine sense of humour. All a girl needs is to be with someone who can make her laugh.'

Remembering her stowaway's sense of fun, the feel of his body, Iris felt her breath catch and began to feel irritated with herself. 'Mmm, Michael won't be making you laugh when he's off to sea leaving you with three screaming children.'

'Iris! You always throw a dampener on everything... You have to admit though, he does have lovely blue eyes.'

'I've never even noticed Michael's eyes, he's always fooling around.' Iris remembered his antics in the dining room earlier and couldn't suppress a giggle. 'He was serving this miserable-looking couple this evening and he pulled a face through the window—'

'See, Iris, you're smiling now,' Roisin grinned as she slipped out of the pale blue skirt. 'I think he's the one for me,' she said, standing in her cotton petticoat with an embroidered pink rose on the bodice, one stocking unravelled around her ankle.

'Don't get carried away. Remember the last one...'

'Now you're making me head spin,' Roisin said, dramatically clutching the bunk. 'I need to lie down. Help me, Iris, help me!'

Once Iris had her cabin mate in her nightgown and sleeping soundly beneath the covers, she quickly got ready for bed and took up the magazine again. As she lay for a while longer, leafing through the pages, her eyes grew heavy and even the gloss of San Francisco dimmed. She kept turning the pages though. On days when she'd attended an emergency, she always found it harder to switch off, and she needed to do all that she could to ensure that she got a full night's sleep... just in case there was another call to the hospital in the early hours of the morning.

CHAPTER 4

No knock came to the door during the night, but Iris was awake at five thirty anyway and quietly slipping into her uniform as Roisin gently snored on the top bunk. Always an early riser, she loved to be up and about, her heels tapping along the deserted deck while all except the night crew were still sleeping in their bunks. This time, she had a set purpose: she was heading to the first-class hospital to check on Miss Buchanan.

Even before she entered the small ward, she could sense calm, and once inside the clean, white space she was further reassured. The girl was sleeping peacefully, her cheeks flushed pink but not fevered. Her blonde hair had been carefully brushed and lay spread out across the pillow. Matron was at the bedside, and she looked up from her knitting, her round face fully alert and offering a smile. 'Your patient is doing very nicely,' she said, keeping her voice low. 'She had a mild fever in the early hours and I sponged her down and changed the sheets, gave her a sip of water and a small dose of morphia and she's been sleeping beautifully ever since. She'll need another drink soon, but after surgery, the body needs to rest, don't you agree?'

'Yes, of course,' Iris murmured, approaching the bed,

pleased by the clean white sheets and the clinical smell of carbolic. She reached out and laid the back of her hand against Miss Buchanan's forehead. 'No fever.' Gently lifting the corner of the bed sheet, she glanced at the dressing pad... her sharp eye detected no sign of seepage. 'Yes, I agree, Matron, all seems to be well.'

Iris quietly withdrew, feeling pleased. It was satisfying when these surgical patients made progress. She prayed that youth would be on Miss Buchanan's side, and she would go on to make a full recovery. She felt lighter, with this new day all of the gloomy thoughts that had hung over her last night seemed to have dispersed like the morning mist.

On her way to the galley to scrounge a cup of coffee, she encountered a young woman in a green silk evening gown scattered with silver sequins, stealthily making her way back to her cabin. Her hair was mussed and two decorative ostrich feathers were wildly askew, but the girl smiled delightfully and placed a finger to her lips. 'Don't tell a soul,' she giggled, still a little tipsy. 'Your secret's safe with me, Miss Darlington,' Iris replied, and the woman gasped with surprise that the stewardess knew her name.

Giggling, Miss Darlington continued back to the stateroom she shared with her elderly maiden aunt, someone who would definitely not approve of her niece creeping home unchaperoned at this hour. However, Iris also knew that the aunt took a heavy sleeping draught and she was usually knocked out cold until eight or nine a.m. She smiled, thinking of Miss Darlington sneaking into bed, holding her breath in case she disturbed the grumpy older woman. Iris would have loved the luxury of being able to sleep off the night before, but only when she was ashore could she allow herself the opportunity to fully relax. A stewardess could usually get away with being heavy-eyed and less attentive, but for a nurse it could mean the difference between life and death for a patient. She thought of the stowaway, remembering the secret dance and the kiss... but the strict voice in her head reminded her that there was work to be done and she had passengers to look after. Perhaps if she saw him in New York during turnaround, it would be a different story.

Once she had her coffee, Iris walked to the side of the ship and rested her elbows on the rail, gazing out to the horizon. It was another delightfully warm morning; this summer had been a scorcher and she knew it was set to continue. Tossing the coffee grounds down into the ocean, Iris turned and started to make her way back down to the staff quarters.

Sam was marching in the opposite direction. He looked preoccupied and didn't see Iris until she gently called, 'Where are you going in such a hurry?'

'Iris,' he gasped, his eyes wide, 'have you heard the news?'

She felt her heart jump. 'No...' she offered, tentatively.

'We are at war. Britain issued an ultimatum for Germany to withdraw from Belgium and it expired last night... the ship has received a telegram, war has been declared on Germany.'

Iris couldn't speak, she was dumbfounded – even though the whole world had been expecting this to happen for weeks.

Sam's voice was heavy with emotion. 'There's going to be so much bravado among the men, but none of them even know what war means, it's outside of their experience, and I know for a fact that my two sons... Phillipe and Louis...'

His voice started to break and Iris reached out to grasp his arm.

'But they are stewards, Sam, surely they won't have to join up?'

'All ships will be requisitioned for war purposes – battle-cruisers, troop carriers, hospitals – they might be stewards now but inevitably they'll be caught up in it.' He ran a hand through his hair, making it stick up on end, 'I can't bear to think of Francine waking up alone in the house, to this news.'

'I'm so sorry, Sam... but you know Francine, she's the calmest person on earth.'

'Not when it comes to her boys, she's not.' Sam drew in a ragged breath and tried to offer a smile and then he began walking away. 'I need to go and speak to the other stewards... See you later, Iris.'

As she watched Sam stride away down the deck, it felt as if something had shifted beneath her feet. All the crew and passengers waking up this morning would be entering a new world. Iris pressed a hand to her chest and glanced down to check that her apron was straight. 'All we can do is soldier on,' she said out loud, weighing the coffee cup in her hand for a moment before she started to walk briskly along the deck, already forming in her head the exact words that she would use to tell Roisin about the declaration of war.

'War! Holy mother of God!' Roisin screamed from the top bunk, pushing back her dishevelled curls and instantly swinging her pale legs out of bed. 'When? Do you mean now?'

'Yes,' Iris replied. Even though she'd shared with Roisin for a full year, she'd never seen her this agitated. Her cabin mate sounded like she was gasping for air and her eyes were wide like saucers – with shock or excitement, or a mixture of both.

'So, what will happen now, will we still go to New York?'

'Yes, of course, we're not at war with America.'

Roisin was pacing now, up and down the confined space. 'I'm thinking that we'll both be out of a job, then?'

Iris was struck by the remark, she hadn't really considered it.

'You're a nurse, so you'll be all right... but what use will a stewardess be during war?'

'Let's not race ahead, hey,' Iris said firmly, trying to get a hold on the situation for herself as much as Roisin. 'Get yourself dressed and ready for work as usual, and let's see. There's bound to be some official announcement by the captain, and then of course, we'll have to deal with any shock or upset amongst the passengers.'

'Yes, that's right, the passengers... Oh, and the staff. What about Michael? Will he be joining up? I'd love to see him a different uniform... all manly...'

Iris thought about sallow-faced Michael in an army uniform, and it just didn't seem plausible. But Roisin was all dewy-eyed now, she seemed to be making a rapid recovery from the shock, so Iris left her alone to get dressed while she went back to the hospital to speak to Matron about the news. Hearing cheering voices from the male crew quarters, closely followed by a rousing rendition of 'God Save the King', it was easy to interpret how the turn of events had been received there. She thought again about what Sam had said – *they don't know what war means* – and it made her heart clench with fear for the imminent future. She desperately needed a cigarette, but her shift had started now and there was no way she wanted to be found at the side of the ship smoking. She had to get on with her duties... but she was racking her brains for what the routine was, her thoughts were jumbled. Start with the early breakfast trays, that was it.

The ship's crew and passengers absorbed the news like a sponge with a range of responses from terrified to thoughtful and silent. The victualling crew went about their routines with a semblance of normality, but some passengers were anxious, others were agitated or even excited and the whole process of morning duties took so much longer. Iris had already attended the Fontaines and the Buchanans – both American families who wouldn't yet be directly involved with the war but were nevertheless shaken. It was now time to pay her morning visit to Miss Duchamp – a French national by birth, she still kept an apartment in Paris but she had been raised in New York. Iris didn't think that Miss Duchamp would even be aware of the issue, she spent her mornings firmly in the cabin with the deck steward calling by at nine to take Marco for a walk to perform the 'necessaries', and then, at nine thirty on the dot, Iris would appear with the morning breakfast tray. Miss Duchamp was hers and hers alone. No one else would go in there.

Iris stood listening at the stateroom door for a moment with the tray balanced neatly on her hip. Other passengers were standing out in the carpeted passageway holding agitated conversation and Michael was currently trying to calm a distraught middle-aged British couple who were convinced that there were German spies on board. But there was no sound from inside Miss Duchamp's cabin. Iris tapped lightly on the door but no reply came. Unusual. Perhaps Miss Duchamp was anxious after all. She knocked harder and this time Marco started to bark but still there was no voice telling her to enter. She had no choice now, she would have to open the door and step in. As she did so, Marco leapt from the bed and came at her with lightning speed. Iris had never seen him move so fast and now he was growling and yapping around her legs in a fearsome display.

'What? What is it?' snapped Miss Duchamp, struggling up into a sitting position. 'Who are you? How dare you come into my room without permission?'

Iris could see her passenger getting out of bed remarkably nimbly for someone of her advancing years. She seemed undaunted by the prospect of meeting an intruder head on.

'Miss Duchamp, it's me, Iris, your stewardess,' she said, trying to raise her voice above the noise of Marco's yapping.

Iris was sure she heard her passenger almost growl and she was even worried that she might be accosted by her.

'Miss Purefoy,' she shouted. 'Whatever are you doing creeping around at this time of the morning? I haven't even had my breakfast yet, and what with this terrible news of war that the deck steward delivered when he brought Marco back from his walk, I just don't know where to put myself!'

'I'm sorry that the news has distressed you, Miss Duchamp, but we've been told to carry on as normal with our duties. I've brought your breakfast...' Iris felt her heart twist when she saw her passenger trying to stop her lip from trembling.

'What use is breakfast when we are facing such horror...' Miss Duchamp wailed. 'I've seen it all before with the Franco-Prussian war – it was awful, and now with modern methods we are able to manufacture even bigger guns. More men will be killed, more women will be grieving just like I have been all these years. These politicians are fools, they have no idea what they have set in motion. France will be ravaged by this. It will be terrible.'

Iris set the tray smartly down on the side table and went straight over to Miss Duchamp. 'I believe you are right, Miss Duchamp, but we have no choice now, war has been declared.'

Miss Duchamp started to wail even louder. Iris passed her a lace-trimmed handkerchief from the wicker basket on her bedside table.

'I will have to stay in New York,' she sobbed. 'I might never see my beloved France again.'

There seemed little that Iris could say to comfort her passenger, though she thought it was indeed a good idea for Miss Duchamp to remain safely in America.

'This will all pass,' Iris breathed, keeping her voice steady. 'And one day you will be back in Paris.'

'If those fools, those warmongers, think this will all be over in a few months, they are very badly mistaken. Mark my words, Iris, this will drag on for years...'

Iris felt tears pricking her eyes. She was unable to speak, all she could do was put an arm around Miss Duchamp's shoulders as her passenger dabbed at her eyes and Marco shivered and quietly whimpered beside her on the bed.

'Hush now, hush,' the elderly woman said at last, reaching out to gather her dog against her silk nightgown. 'You are going to be safe with me, my precious, safe and sound.'

Iris inhaled deeply. 'Shall I serve you breakfast in bed now, Miss Duchamp? The porridge is going cold, I'm afraid.'

Miss Duchamp waved her hand in a dismissive gesture, 'I haven't got the stomach for porridge today, just bring me a slice of toast – scrape some of the butter off it first... That's it. You know me so well, don't you, Iris.'

Iris brought the porcelain plate over to her passenger and then returned to the side table to pour coffee. Miss Duchamp sighed heavily. 'Pour yourself a cup, Iris, and come and sit with me here on the bed.'

'But I'm not really allowed to—'

'Damn what you are allowed, these are extreme circumstances, and I am ordering you to do this.'

Iris had no choice but to comply, and once the two cups were poured, she perched awkwardly at the side of the bed. Miss Duchamp started to smile and then blurted out a laugh. 'You don't look exactly comfortable, Iris... for goodness' sake, we've known each other for years.'

Iris nearly choked on her coffee.

Miss Duchamp was smiling again. 'I know I can be hard work sometimes... no, not sometimes, all the time. But you have withstood all that nonsense better than anyone I have ever known. You are a very special person, Iris, you deserve a medal.'

Iris couldn't speak, she was so shocked.

Once the coffee was drunk, she helped Miss Duchamp wash and dress and their usual routine clicked into place. The bed made and Marco settled in his basket, Iris waited to be dismissed.

Miss Duchamp narrowed her eyes. 'One more thing, Iris,' she said, opening her dresser drawer. 'I've never really provided you with big enough tips, I'm aware of that, so given that I may not see you for a very long time, there is something that I've been meaning to do...' Iris saw her passenger remove a blue silk drawstring bag from the drawer. 'I want you to have this, as a gift, for all your excellent service over the years.'

Iris was shaking her head, 'No honestly, I couldn't...'

'You don't even know what it is yet! Take it, go on, take it!'

Iris reached out a hand. As soon as she felt the shape and the weight of the silk bag, she knew that it contained jewellery. Miss Duchamp's eyes were shining. 'I haven't worn it for years, I know it will be perfect on you.'

Iris undid the bag and pulled out a diamond choker that glinted in the electric light, like stars fallen from the heavens. She drew in a sharp breath, holding the necklace up to the light to see the flashing sparkle of the precious stones. 'It is beautiful,' was all that she could say. 'But I can't—'

Miss Duchamp held up a hand and Iris stopped what she was about to say. There was no point, she knew that the more opposition she put up, the more Miss Duchamp would insist. 'You can and you will,' Miss Duchamp said forcefully. 'As you are aware I have lots of jewellery and only an estranged nephew to inherit them when I'm dead and gone. It is important to me. I want you to have this one and there will be more to come in due course.'

Iris swallowed hard to stop herself from gasping out loud. She slipped the necklace back inside the bag.

'Put it in your pocket,' Miss Duchamp urged with a wicked smile.

Iris did as she was told. 'Thank you,' she stuttered, still thrown and fumbling now with the handle of the door. 'Will you need anything this afternoon, Miss Duchamp?'

'No, I can manage. I'll go out to the veranda café later, see what the ladies have to say about this awful news of war. I'll see you this evening at suppertime... maybe we can have a glass of wine together...'

Iris's head was spinning, she felt bewildered, struggling to make sense of what her passenger had just said. Pulling herself together, she replied, 'Yes, Miss Duchamp,' and exited the cabin, her head still reeling. She attempted to regain her composure at the other side of the door. Pushing a hand back into her pocket she felt the smooth silk and the shape of the necklace inside, and it made her feel uncomfortable, having such a precious item in her uniform pocket. But what choice did she have? As she walked away, she started to imagine what the necklace would look like on, and she let her mind wander to items in her wardrobe that might be a suitable accompaniment... none matched up.

Before she was able to walk the length of the deck, she heard a man's voice shouting behind her, 'Stewardess! Stewardess!'

Turning on her heel, she was surprised to see her stowaway striding rapidly towards her. Just seeing the excitement in his eyes gave her a jolt of pleasure. As he got close the orchestra in the restaurant began to play some classical piece and he started to laugh. 'They're playing their music again, just for us!' The man was so animated, Iris had to step back, she was sure he was going to take her in his arms, there and then, out on the deck in broad daylight. 'It's uproar down in steerage, the men are boozing and singing and some poor passengers with German accents have locked themselves away in their cabin... I wanted to check that you were all right, and I've suddenly realised I don't even know your name...'

'It's Iris, I'm Iris,' she stammered, 'and yes, I'm fine.'

He blew out a breath, 'Please tell me you'll still come ashore in New York. I want to see you, even if it's only for a few hours.'

'I will try, but the crew are already saying that we'll probably have to get the *Olympic* ready for the return journey. There's talk of blackouts on the windows to make sure the ship is darkened. Stuff like that.'

'Damn and blast this war!' he almost shouted. 'Well, meet me tonight, on the deck and we'll have a dance...'

Iris wanted to say yes, she wanted to grab hold of him right there and then, but she knew that it would only make things worse. 'I can't,' she breathed at last. 'I just can't.'

His head dropped, he looked devastated.

She could see passengers staring, she needed to calm him so as not to draw any more unwanted attention. Steering him to the ship's rail she started to explain. 'I want to see you, I truly do, but now with this war, it's unlikely we'll ever see each other again. Meeting briefly on the deck later... it's not enough and it's too much all at the same time, if that makes sense.'

He frowned, still shaking his head.

'Shore leave will almost certainly be cancelled, so tonight will be all that we have... it will make it worse for me, do you understand?'

He sighed and then he nodded. 'But at least give me your full name and address, then I can write to you.'

Iris pulled her pad and pencil out of her pocket and scribbled down the detail, giving Sam and Francine's address in Southampton where she boarded when ashore. 'What is your name?' she asked, glancing up at him.

'Jack Rosetti,' he replied, his voice flat and his shoulders slumped.

She hardly dared look back at him after she'd scribbled his name on the next page of her notebook, already knowing there was no need to write it down, it was sealed in her memory forever. Tearing the piece of paper bearing her address cleanly from the pad, she handed it to him. He folded it and pushed it in his pocket. 'Well then, unless we meet again by accident, I'm thinking this is goodbye and good luck for now.'

'Sadly, yes,' she replied, kissing the palm of her hand and placing it gently against his cheek.

'I *will* see you again though, Iris,' he said, his eyes starting to burn. 'One day, we will meet again.'

As he strode away, a dull throb of pain bloomed deep in her chest, wrapping itself around her heart. She took a breath to try and ease it.

'Stewardess!' a male passenger shouted, 'I can't find my daughter, she was here a moment ago.'

Iris composed herself and turned with a reassuring expression. 'Don't distress yourself, we will find her... children do go missing on board, but they always turn up.' Amidst the swell of passengers' voices and the orchestra still playing in the first-class restaurant, Iris began the process of losing herself in her work. It took a while but after the child had been discovered and she had visited the hospital to find Miss Buchanan making a vigorous recovery, she was fully focused – making herself believe that she needed nothing more in life than her work, the companionship of the crew and the occasional tot of whisky.

CHAPTER 5

GREAT YARMOUTH, EAST COAST OF ENGLAND, AUGUST 1914

News of war was broadcast unrelentingly around the world, it spread like wildfire from London to New York, Yokohama and back again. On the east coast of England the herring season was in full flow, and in the fishing port of Great Yarmouth, a man's rugged voice shouted above the rest, 'Germany have declared war!'

Evie Munro felt a shiver run down her spine, as if someone had walked over her grave. She looked up from the wooden trough where she was gutting herring, trying to make sense of what had just been said. In that split second of inattention the razor-sharp knife which she held in her right hand slipped and nicked her left forefinger, slicing through the cloth bandages that all the girls wore for protection. Evie could tell by the sting that the wound was only minor, and she paid it no mind. 'War?' she shouted back to Bill McFarlane, a retired skipper who worked with the onshore crew.

'Aye, war with Germany,' he confirmed, his voice rising, his filmy blue eyes alive with the news. 'But don't be mithering too much, they're saying it'll all be over in six weeks.'

Evie stood immobile with her knife in her hand. All the Scottish fisher girls had paused their work.

Rita McNabb, an older woman who worked shoulder to shoulder with Evie, stood frozen, her knife poised in mid-air. 'I have two sons,' she said, her voice flat.

Evie had a brother, but he was older, in his thirties, and he had children. Surely he wouldn't be expected to fight?

'We'd best get this lot packed and sent as soon as we can... I don't think Germany will be taking any pickled herring *this* season,' Bill hollered as he hauled another basket of fish into line, pushing his cap back as he straightened up, revealing a dishevelled thatch of hair as white as the salt he sprinkled on the fish.

A ripple of affirmation went through the dozen or so women who were standing around the gutting trough and their knives started to flash in the glinting sun as they began once more to slit the bellies of the 'silver darlings'. Evie heard Rita inhale deeply and then she began to sing a lively ballad. The rest of the herring girls joined in as they sliced, gutted and packed. Rona, a tall woman with short-cropped, black hair and a dour face, picked up a handful of the coarse salt that she layered with the herring as she deftly packed the fish into barrels. She threw it over her left shoulder. The round-faced young woman with plaited hair next to her, Minnie MacKay, turned and spat on the ground. All the women had been anxiously waiting for news of the war, now it had come they would employ all powers to try and keep their menfolk safe.

Evie laughed when Rita nudged her arm as Minnie McKay's out-of-tune voice rose above the rest. Singing now, as hard as she could, Evie sought to rid herself of lingering thoughts, catching the lift in mood amongst the women as more laughter bounced backwards and forwards between them, keeping time with the rhythm of their work.

Increasing her speed, Evie felt her grip tighten on the knife, and her hands were sure as she sliced and gutted and instantly graded the herring by size, deftly throwing each one to the correct basket behind. A shaft of sunlight fell across the trough, picking out the glint of fish scales, like sequins on her dark wet oilskin apron. The silver scales were also spangled through the tufts of wavy brown hair that escaped from her red-patterned scarf. With her head down again, she was completely focused, all movement and instinct – raw and pure.

As the sun sank lower in the sky so the supplies of herring began to dwindle. The steam drifters had puffed the last of their black smoke for the day and they were packed tightly together along the harbour wall, their masts bristling.

'Evie, Evie!' Bill was shouting.

She glanced up.

'See to this fella, will ya!'

For a split second she could only discern the silhouette of a man against the setting sun. And then the looming dark shape stepped forward and a young fisherman with sea-bleached hair and pale blue eyes much like her own emerged, like some spirit of the sea. He was holding a blood-soaked cloth to his right hand, and he didn't say a word, he just stood and gazed at her with otherworldly eyes. Evie felt her body prickle with sensation. Never one to be stuck for words, she could feel the sounds forming in her mouth but something about the way he was looking at her rendered her speechless.

'Go on then,' Rita cackled, giving her a nudge. 'You're the one who has the magic touch with the wounds, go to him before the poor young fella bleeds to death.'

Evie swallowed hard, wiped her knife on her apron and pushed it in her pocket and then she strode towards him, unrolling the cloth bandages from her fingers as she went and shoving them in the pocket of her old wool skirt. All the time he was looking, looking. Evie steadied her breathing and tried to settle the full beat of her heart. His face was tanned, his body lithe and the ripple of muscle on his forearm as he held out his hand for inspection was almost too much to bear.

Evie took hold of his arm. 'What have you done?' she asked, focusing all her attention on the wound.

'It was a rope.'

He winced with pain as she removed the blood-soaked cloth. A raw tear had ripped across his palm.

'It'll be sore but it's none too deep... Come on, come with me, let's find you somewhere to sit and I'll dress it for you.'

Still holding onto his arm, she led him across to a bare wooden plank propped between two barrels. 'Sit there,' she ordered, using an abrupt manner to offset the urge to settle beside him and rest her weary body against his. Plenty of the fishermen had tried to sweet-talk her, year after year. Only once had she been tempted by a dark-eyed sailor, but it had only lasted the season, and as soon as they were preparing to head back up north, she'd distanced herself from him. She wasn't ready for any commitment, despite Rita's incessant advice about finding a man. She knew what to say to placate her, give the impression that she was just waiting for the right one to come along. And now, with war coming, it would be reckless indeed to get close to a young man who was bound to be swept up in it.

But as he looked up at her and she saw his eyes creasing at the corners with pleasure, she knew already that she would have to fight hard against all her instincts to keep this one at bay... and for some reason the thought of war made her feel even more reckless.

'I'm Jamie Scott,' he said, his voice English, well-spoken, but warm like a summer's day beside the ocean.

'E—'

'Evie,' he said. 'Bill told me.'

Evie swallowed hard. 'I'll get my medical supplies.'

As she turned her back on him, she could feel him watching as she walked away towards Bill's hut.

Coming back across the cobbled quay with her medical bag slung across her shoulder and an enamel bowl of salt water in her hand, she tried to talk down her response to this fisherman. He was a newcomer, that's why he seemed interesting, he wouldn't be any different than the rest. But there it was again – that smile – and it sent a jolt of desire through her body.

'Right, Jamie Scott,' she said, adopting a businesslike tone. 'I need you to soak your hand in the bowl.' She placed it down on his knee and began removing the bloodied cloth... 'It's salt water.'

He took a sharp breath when the strong solution stung his hand. She laughed. 'Get it in there, ye big softie. I bet you didn't even feel it when you did it.'

'Yes, I did,' he said. 'I just had to pretend not to.'

Once the hand was thoroughly soaked, Evie took out some of the clean cotton swabs from her medical bag. 'Keep it in the water while I give it an extra clean.'

He sucked in air through his teeth as she deftly wiped the swab through the wound. 'We need to get all of the fish scales away, the little blighters are everywhere.'

'Yes, I know,' he breathed, reaching up his other hand to pick out a silver scale from her hair.

Evie looked up, there was a beat of silence, her breath catching as something vibrated in the air between them. She had to force herself to look away. 'That's enough, it should be clean now,' she said, hurriedly setting the bowl down on the cobbles. With a swab in her hand she stood for a moment, interrupted, needing to force herself to get on with the job. 'I'll dry the wound, and then put plenty of iodine on.' Her words felt distant, as if they were being spoken by someone else. He was smiling and nodding and as she stooped to apply a dressing, she could smell the musky saltiness of him. A warm flush spread at the base of her throat and by the time she was tying the bandage she knew that she could have easily leaned in to kiss him.

The sound of the other women clattering and calling to each other behind her, as they started to clear up for the day, roused her enough to be able to speak. 'Wear a glove over the bandage, it needs to stay in place. I'll check it and reapply the dressing tomorrow when you come off your ship.'

'Aye aye, captain,' he smiled, offering her a small salute as he stood up.

Evie could already hear the laughter and the teasing calls of the other women. 'Whoo hoo, Evie, what a handsome young man, what's his name?'

'Stop it, you lot,' she shouted, as Minnie McKay made a kissy-kissy sound.

'Your pals like to have a laugh,' he said. 'It's like being with the crew. Even though we've just been told that there's a war coming, they never let up.'

Evie sucked in a sharp breath. She'd blotted out the news of war and now it came back at her with a punch. 'They're all the same, the herring crowd, have you not worked the season before?'

He shook his head.

'Well, you'll soon get used to it,' she said. 'They have a lively humour, the fisherfolk, and they can make fun, but they'll do anything to help you. If you cross them though... woe betide you.'

'I'll remember that,' he said, lowering his voice, leaning in closer.

'So, what are the men saying about the war?' Evie said quickly, taking a step back.

He shrugged his shoulders.

'What a terrible thing, do we know what will happen now?' she gabbled, needing to fill the space between them with something.

He shook his head, smiling again.

His lack of spoken response and his seeming acceptance

that all he needed to do was gaze at her with his pale blue eyes started to rattle Evie. She was irritated with him and must have shown it because she saw his eyes widen for a split second. He cleared his throat and when he spoke his voice was solemn. 'I have no idea what will happen... We're nearly at the end of the season, so we're all going to work the herring for now and then see.'

'Will you join up straight away?' Evie breathed.

'Probably.' He bowed his head for a split second and when he looked back up at her, he smiled... 'But the lads are saying that all us fishermen should go for the Royal Navy, they're saying it might be a bit of a cushy number, and at least it will keep us at sea.'

Evie's heart clenched. 'Have you not heard about U-boats and the missiles they fire at ships?'

'Yes, but they won't catch us...' His blue eyes were burning into her. She felt a whispering shift in the air, the same feeling she had in dreams, when she could see and hear the silver herring switching and turning, sinuous in their movement beneath the sea. This time the ghostly shoal carried other sounds – faraway voices... crying out, calling for help.

'Can you hear it too?' he asked quietly, and as he spoke Evie's heart began to ache.

She looked up at him, drawing in the same breath. 'Yes,' she said, stunned.

He gave a single nod and then reached to place a gentle hand against her cheek.

'Evie Munro!' Rita shouted. 'Are you going to let us hard-working fisher girls do all of the cleaning up?'

Evie stepped back. 'I'll just put my bag away,' she called.

When her eyes met his again, it was as if she saw herself reflected back, it was uncanny. He gave a slow smile. 'I'll see you tomorrow, Evie Munro,' he said, holding up his bandaged hand in farewell.

'Yes, yes, of course,' she breathed, the ache in her chest expanding as she watched him turn and walk away, feeling that she knew him already – the salt taste of his lips, the exact feel of his body against her own and the sureness of his touch.

Later, after all the cleaning was done and the women had slipped off their oilskin aprons, Evie walked away from the harbour arm in arm with Rita and Rona, little Minnie McKay trotting backwards in front of the three of them, firing agitated questions about the war.

'None of us know anything, Minnie,' Rita said. 'We'll have to wait and see what happens... and at least the men will all be finishing the season first.'

'Aye, Minnie, you need to stop mithering. Let's talk about something else or you'll drive us all crackers,' Rona added, her face stern.

Minnie sighed and then she started to giggle as she began to tell a story about the curly-haired young fisherman she'd kissed last night.

'Don't you let 'im go any further than kissing,' warned Rita. 'That's how I ended up with my twin bairns.'

'Oh, I don't want to go further, not with him,' Minnie replied. 'I'm only practising.'

All the women cracked up laughing as Minnie turned to join the line, linking arms with Rita.

'I mean, look at me in this old gansey, a cardigan full of holes, and a knitted vest and knickers!'

'We just love our knitted knickers, don't we girls?' Rita guffawed. 'Gives us an itch in a place we can't scratch!'

Evie was laughing so much her ribs were hurting. 'Well girls, I don't know if you've noticed but I've got myself some cotton vests for this trip.'

'Ooh, very posh,' called Minnie. 'With the way that fisherman was looking at you, they might not offer enough protection.'

'Aye, well, I can handle him,' Evie growled. 'Just you watch me.'

'Come on!' shouted Rona. 'Let's get a move on, I'm starving hungry.'

With a screech the girls broke step, picked up their skirts and started to race towards their lodgings, Minnie McKay leading the way with her two plaits flying behind her. Their lively voices echoed across the harbour, reaching into the darkness that had settled over the cold deeps of the ocean; drowning out, if only for a moment, the pulse of the sea as it jostled the fishing boats and broke, wave after wave, against the harbour wall.

CHAPTER 6

The harbour was empty, the fishing boats all gone as the women walked with other groups of gutters and packers back to their work the next morning. Evie was quiet for once, listening to the low murmur of conversation and steady rhythm of leather work boots beating on the cobbled quay. Rona led the way, as she always did, despite the pronounced limp she'd had since contracting polio as a child. Evie often walked with Rona in the morning. She was always eager to get to work, but this morning her head felt dull and heavy on her shoulders. She'd had one too many glasses of whisky last night when they'd sat outside on the steps chattering and knitting.

'You should do more knitting and less supping,' Rita had said.

Each year Evie tried to follow the intricate Fair Isle knitting patterns, but she dropped stitches and tangled the wool... she'd hardly taken up her needles before the knitting was lying discarded beside her. As always, Rita had picked it up, pulled back the wool, quickly repaired Evie's work, telling her that she'd never get herself a fisherman for a husband if she couldn't knit his woollen ganseys or sea boot socks. Evie never said it out loud, but ever since she'd started work as a fisher girl aged fifteen, settling down with a man had been the furthest thing from her mind.

She'd lain awake into the small hours, tossing and turning in the bed she shared with Rita, thoughts of war buzzing through her head. Good job Rita always slept like the dead. She'd once told Evie that it was the music of the sea that sent her off, washing over her, note after note. Falling asleep at last, Evie had dreamt of Jamie, despite her best efforts to get rid of any thought of him. She told herself it was because tending his wound had been her final job of the day, no more than that. At nights during the season, she usually dreamt that she was still gutting the herring, so much so that her back and arms ached as she woke, surprised to find herself wearing a flannelette nightie and not her oilskin apron.

Bleary-eyed she walked beside Rita as Minnie McKay chattered on. Day and night she never stopped talking, so much so that she sometimes woke her bedmate, Rona, with her mutterings and gigglings in her sleep. Evie felt for the knife, relieved to find it snug against her thigh. She'd sharpened it on the whetstone last night but couldn't remember putting it in her skirt pocket. A gust of cool breeze pulled at her red-patterned headscarf and ruffled some wisps of hair; she could hear the strength of the sea as it broke against the harbour wall. A shiver went through her, it would be rough out there in the deeps, the waves would be topped with white spray. The fishing boats should be safe though; it would take much more than this for them to run into trouble.

'Penny for your thoughts, Evie Munro,' Rita chirruped.

'Nothing really, just the sea... it's choppy out there.'

'Aye, it is. But your man will be back safe, don't you worry.'

'What man?' Evie tried to furrow her brow, make out she

knew nothing of what Rita was saying, but she couldn't stop a slow smile curling at the corners of her mouth.

Rita linked her arm, pulling her close, 'You can't hide it from an old hand like me... and he's a real catch is that one, and a good man too, or so I've been told.'

'What? Don't tell me you've been asking about him.'

'Nah. I'd already heard about the good-looking fella with the sea-blue eyes who'd signed for a season on the *Embrace* with young Angus McPherson's crew. They're saying he's from Hull and he's sailed the world on cargo ships, but this is his first time on a steam drifter.'

'Oh, they are, are they?' Evie laughed, two bright pink spots of colour dotting her cheeks. 'Well, that information is of no interest to me whatsoever.'

Rita laughed, shaking her head.

Evie was restless, her thoughts scattered to the wind, as she helped prepare the gutting trough and check the tightly packed barrels of herring to make sure the pickle that formed from the melting salt and fish juice wasn't leaking onto the quay. They were ready. Rona had brewed up some hot sweet tea with a dash of whisky and the women were huddled together. Evie walked out to the harbour wall. If anything the waves were surging higher now; who knew what squalls the men would be battling out to sea. She leaned on the stone wall, breathing in the salt air till it made her heady, and her long-dead grandmother's voice echoed in her head: 'Fishing folk live and die by the sea...' Most of the herring girls had lost some member of their family at sea and the same sorrow stretched back through generations.

Years ago, Evie had had to shut out constant, haunting thoughts of the last time she'd said goodbye to her daddy. At seven years old she'd worshipped the ground he walked on, but he'd left their cottage one evening, said his usual goodbyes and had never come back from the sea. A whole crew had been lost that night during a storm that even the old salts hadn't been able to foresee. Evie had wailed and sobbed till she'd made herself sick, while her older brother and her mother sat straight-backed at the kitchen table, stunned by grief.

She pressed the tip of her index finger over a sharp piece of stone on top of the wall, needing to feel the pain of it to shut out those whispering thoughts that were best kept down below the surface. She pushed until the pain eased her, and when she looked up, she saw the first boat coming back, tossed on the waves but riding through, weighed down by fish. In the next second, Bill was shouting, and all the herring girls were scut-tling around, getting themselves ready.

Evie and Rita helped bandage each other's fingers with the strips of cotton cloth. Once the 'clooties' were in place, they secured them with twine before pulling their oilskin aprons tight. Rona and Minnie were moving the wooden buckets set to catch the graded herring, making sure they were in the exact position for the gutters to throw without a backward glance. Tubs of coarse sea salt stood waiting, ready to pack layer upon layer with the fish in a swirling rosette pattern, silver bellies uppermost, heads to the side of the barrel. Evie loved the artistry of it. She'd tried her hand as a packer, but she was a little bit too short to easily reach to the bottom of the barrel, and it slowed her up. She could have made it work but she always wanted to be the first with everything, and she knew that she was the quickest with the knife, only a fraction more than Rita, but there it was, even with the older woman's extra years of experience. She had no idea why it mattered so much, but even as a child and the youngest of the family, she'd pushed herself to be the best at whatever she chose to do. It wasn't easy, given that her brother was eight years older, but she'd grown strong just by trying, and she'd face up to anybody, even the fellas, in any dispute.

'You're a wee tiger, Evie Munro,' her grandmother had

often told her. 'I wouldn't like to be at the wrong side of those claws.'

The breeze pulled at the skirts of the herring girls as they stood waiting and as soon as Bill tipped the first basket of fish into the trough, they were working as one, consumed by the task. The herring smelt like the sea condensed. Evie felt sorry that the fishermen needed to pull so many out, but what else could they do? The herring trade was stronger now than it had ever been, and it was how they all fed their families. There was one rule though, the herring were treated with respect – caught cleanly, prepared deftly, not one fish left discarded on the quay. The fisherfolk were always grateful for the harvest from the sea.

Evie had the knife in her hand, the white bandages around her fingers still dry and clean. She was waiting for Rita to check that all the women were in position before giving the nod to begin. Evie took a deep breath, relaxed her shoulders and they were off. She was a little slow for the first few minutes, probably due to her lack of sleep, but quickly picked up the rhythm of the task, the herring flowing through her hands with a deft twist of the knife. Once she was settled, she didn't even feel the rumble of her belly when it was time for food. Her mind and body were completely in tune, no other thoughts could trouble her.

Basket after basket were tipped, sliding together into the trough, as the women continued to work, catching a short break for a sup of tea and a bite to eat only when it fitted with the herring. The day slipped by like the running of the tides, and later, when it began to rain, Bill brought them short-sleeved oilskin capes to keep the worst of the rain off. The capes helped but with water dripping down from the hood and the bulk of it around her shoulders, it always frustrated Evie that her work was hampered. But what could anybody do about the weather? The breeze had now strengthened, and it tugged at Evie's oilskin. She didn't even want to think about what the men were facing out on the waves.

When the supply of herring stopped earlier than expected, Evie caught a murmur of unease amongst the onshore crew. They were still waiting for a boat to return – it was the *Embrace* – Jamie's vessel. Anxiety clutched at Evie's heart and she glanced at Rita, trying to read her expression, but her friend's face was blank. She simply gave Evie a nod, as if to say hold fast, it will be all right.

The women huddled together, some taking the chance for a drop of whisky or a quick smoke. Evie was too impatient for either, consumed as she was by grumbling thoughts that more fishing families might be heartbroken tonight... and the promise of the young man with pale blue eyes might never be fulfilled. She wiped her knife and pushed it into her pocket, walking purposefully to the harbour wall to stand in the exact same spot she'd occupied earlier, straining her eyes through the driving rain and dull grey of the turbulent waters. Her fingers found the sharp piece of stone again and she pressed hard to make the pain ease her.

Evie stood alone until Rita came with a flask of whisky and made sure she took a good swig. 'Keep body and soul together.' She knew Rita's voice well enough to sense the forced evenness of her tone. Most of the women used it during these waiting times and Rita had lost a nephew to the sea only last year. Evie reached out and linked her arm, huddling in close, the rain whipping around them, pattering against their oilskins. Once Evie had a hold of her friend, she felt as if she were anchoring them both, especially now that the light was starting to fade into evening and the onshore crew were setting out lanterns along the harbour wall to help guide the fishing boat in.

'Even Minnie McKay's gone quiet,' Rita murmured.

Evie felt her cold face contract with a tight smile. 'This must be more serious than we thought,' she tried to quip, but her voice fell flat.

In the next second, a man's voice shouted, 'There she is!'

Evie and Rita gasped with relief, craning their necks to see through the drizzling rain. Evie wiped the water from her eyes, peering out again into the grey, restless gloom.

'Yes,' hissed Rita, pointing, and then Evie saw the shape of the small steam drifter, tossed remorselessly by the waves but bravely heading towards harbour. No one dared raise a cheer, not until the boat was safely in, but it felt like a collective held breath was exhaled as the onshore crew began to ready themselves.

Rita turned to leave.

'I'll just stay here for a while longer,' Evie said quietly.

'Aye, that's fine,' Rita smiled. 'I'll make sure we're all set.'

Evie clung to the harbour wall, watching the boat until she could see the shape of the men on board. Feeling the beat of her heart as she tried to discern which one might be Jamie. With every breath her body seemed to tingle. There was no holding back from this now, she was sure that she was going to love this man, even though she hadn't even kissed him yet. The thought made her glow with excitement.

Later, when she looked up from the trough, he was walking towards her bareheaded through the drizzling rain, and her heart raced at the sight of him. She wiped her knife and pushed it in her pocket. Seeing Rita's amused glance, the twinkle in her eye, she stuttered, 'He'll be needing the dressing on his hand changed.'

'Go on with you,' she heard Rita say, but Evie was already slipping past her, moving away from the gutting trough, running towards him. When he took her in his arms, he held her tightly against his body. Even as the rain started to come down heavier, stinging her eyes as she looked up to his smiling face, Evie pushed back her oilskin hood and reached up to kiss him, right there on the quay, with all the herring girls cheering and clapping and shouting out. He tasted of salt and fish and a trace of blood; it made her head swim with desire.

CHAPTER 7

As the *Olympic* made her return journey, stealing across the dark ocean with passengers and crew still reeling from the news of war, struggling to adjust to a new world order, Iris tried to hold firm. It was hard, given that the evening blackout served to remind all on board that something as insignificant as a lighted cigarette on deck at night might attract the attention of a German U-boat that had the potential to blow them all to smithereens. Iris needed all her powers to maintain a strong demeanour, plus she'd had to force down the misery she'd felt at not being able to go ashore in New York and meet up with Jack Rosetti.

Roisin had made one or two comments about her looking tired, asking if she was all right. Never one to confide about her most personal of issues, Iris had forced a smile and put an arm around her friend, telling her it was just the sadness of the blackouts, having to shut out the light from their beautiful ship so they could pass safely across the Atlantic.

Roisin had sighed then, tears welling in her eyes. 'Will we ever shine so brightly again?'

'Of course we will,' Iris had consoled, giving Roisin's shoulders a squeeze. She felt as unsure as the rest, but her duty as a senior member of staff was to offer support wherever she could. Avoiding the worst of the gossipmongers Iris spent her off-duty time with Roisin, Sam, or in the ship's hospitals, but it was hard to ignore the many hushed conversations among crew members about what they would do now, whether they would join the war effort. Iris had been unsure as they departed New York, but this experience on the darkened *Olympic* felt miserable. Roisin had said she would make one more trip to New York and then pursue an offer she'd had from a family in Boston to work as a nanny. Sam wanted to stick with the *Olympic* or some other big ship that would allow him to stay in service. Iris had delayed making her own decision. But on the day that she saw a liner converted to a battlecruiser and heard the passengers on the decks above and below start to cheer, she'd felt something awaken inside of her, and she'd known that she wanted to join up. This would be her final trip aboard the *Olympic;* she would apply to nurse at a military hospital.

The *Olympic* was rerouted to Liverpool, the Channel ports already deemed too dangerous for landing. As they caught sight of the port, Iris sensed the spirits of the crew lift as they always did when they were almost home, and this time there was even more laughter and light-hearted banter. Roisin was ecstatic, she had many lively family members in Liverpool and she was going to go around and see them all. As they neared land, the smell of smoke and the acrid mix of aromas from Liverpool's many factories made Iris's senses tingle. She hadn't been back to her hometown in all the years she'd worked for the White Star Line. She'd never imagined that her return would be forced, unexpected, but now she was close she was yearning for the familiar streets.

As soon as she disembarked, side by side with Sam, they were greeted by a bunch of cheery young men in khaki, already signed up. Iris heard Sam suck in a breath, no doubt thinking of his own two sons, hoping they would hold off at least for a while. Iris linked his arm and gave it a squeeze. 'It's a bit much, isn't it?' she said quietly, 'seeing the army assembling.'

He tried to smile but Iris could feel the tension in his body. 'Let's go straight to the railway station,' she said. 'No need to linger, and White Star are paying our fare back to Southampton.'

'But I thought you wanted to have a look around, see the old places?' he replied.

'There'll be time for that,' she murmured in reply. It was possible that she might decide to move back up north to a military hospital. She hadn't told Sam about any of her plans yet, she'd leave it till they were home.

Given that Iris had no idea when she would ever be back in New York, she'd decided to wear her new pale blue suit with velvet collar and eye-catching hat. Picking her way along the crowded streets of Liverpool on Sam's arm, she felt far too conspicuous as she steadfastly ignored the glances of passing sailors, factory workers and street vendors. She mustered her confidence and walked with her head held high. Sam's unruly hair and the worn blue suit stretched tight across his broad shoulders were in complete contrast to her attire, but given Sam's bulk no passer-by was going to risk making a cheeky remark, not even in Liverpool.

Less than an hour later, Iris was sitting in the ladies' waiting room on Lime Street station. She felt calm now, as she sat on a wooden bench in her wide-brimmed hat, the mesh veil covering her eyes as smoke from her cigarette gently curled into the air. A small boy stood in front of her, a lock of brown hair falling across his forehead; he seemed intrigued by her every move. Iris ignored him. She didn't mind his gaze, she'd been a very similar child – always watching, always eager for new information.

As she took another drag of her cigarette, she thought about that last evening with Miss Duchamp in her first-class cabin.

They'd smoked and drunk red wine together and it had been as if they were travelling companions rather than first-class passenger and crew member. It had felt strangely comfortable for Iris, made her feel easier about accepting the diamond necklace as a gift. Miss Duchamp had been teary-eyed as they'd said their goodbyes and she'd given Iris a piece of embossed paper inscribed with her New York address. She had invited her to stay for as long as she needed when the war was over. Iris would definitely do that; the apartment bordered Central Park, it was one of the best areas in the city. The thought of going back to New York was something to hold close, like a talisman that would sustain her through whatever was coming at them. She had a sense of heaviness, a dark shape on the horizon, and it sent a shiver down her spine. She had to believe that she would come out of this stronger, someone who would embrace the world, grasp every opportunity. Maybe when she visited Miss Duchamp in New York she would try to find Jack Rosetti... but already she felt as if he were at a distance, part of another life.

Iris took a final drag of her cigarette before stubbing it out in a plain glass ashtray. The small boy had lost interest and had moved to the door to watch the platform. A train was about to depart and had built up a head of steam that swirled around the passengers who were jumping aboard, shouting goodbyes. As a whistle blew and doors slammed, Iris couldn't help but catch the excitement, the sense of expectancy. It made her itch to be on the move, even though she still had over an hour to wait for her own train.

Rousing herself, she made her way to the lady's powder room. With a glance to the mirror, she checked that her hat was straight and the lipstick she'd applied wasn't too garish. Slipping a compact out of her travelling bag, she applied some powder to her pale cheeks. She had grey smudges beneath her eyes, she was glad now she'd chosen to wear a hat with a veil. Before she returned to the waiting room, she slipped her hand into her jacket pocket to check that the diamond necklace was still in its blue silk bag, safely wrapped in a large linen handkerchief. A spritz of her favourite French perfume was all that remained for her to feel ready to return to the waiting room.

When she emerged to meet Sam, she had to wait for a few minutes while a group of young men in khaki uniform gathered for a photograph. They huddled together, holding their pose while the photographer counted them down to the flash of the bulb. Afterwards they slapped each other on the back and laughed outrageously, moving as one towards a train crammed with men leaning out of windows, as women and children gathered on the platform, some of them crying as they waved goodbye. It felt uncanny, like a distorted carnival atmosphere... it threw her for a moment as she stood transfixed, staring at the scene, forcing down a dull ache of sorrow in her chest.

Hearing Sam's voice behind her, she moved to join him. Once they were installed in their seats on the train, Iris removed her hat and placed it with her canvas bag on the luggage rack above. Matron Beckett and Dr Mayhew were in the same compartment, sitting opposite, and it felt comfortable. Matron was pulling her knitting needles out of her large canvas bag and Sam was closing his eyes for a nap, so Iris was left with the doctor, his eyes bright and his face eager for conversation. She had only ever had work talk with Dr Mayhew and as the train started to slowly roll into action, it felt as if their communication would be just as slow and mechanical. But after a few minutes, as Iris began to relax back against the brocade seat and the train hit a steady rocking rhythm, the words flowed easily as they reflected on their various travels and experiences on board the *Olympic*. Dr Mayhew – Adam – was also joining up to serve as an army doctor, he was hoping to secure a position on a hospital ship. It piqued Iris's interest, given her own plans, not that she was ready to disclose them. She did start to wonder if a hospital ship would be the right move for her, but then the thought of being plunged back into full-time ward nursing in the pressurised environment of a voyage felt inadvisable. She needed to find her feet first, work on dry land in the best military hospital she could find.

Matron was sleeping soundly with her mouth dropped open, her knitting needles resting obediently on her lap, and Sam was gently snoring with his head against the window. Iris was starting to feel her own creep of tiredness and it seemed as though even chatty Dr Mayhew had run out of words. They made an unspoken treaty to sit in silence and Iris picked up the magazine that she had taken from her bag earlier. Her eyes started to feel heavy. As the train continued to rock on the lines, she slipped into a deep sleep, only waking to the murmur of voices and a change of rhythm as the train pulled into each station. When they came to a final halt on the first stage of their journey, steam hissing and doors starting to open, Iris was dreaming. She was in her bunk on the ship, feeling the motion of the liner, knowing that she had the luxury of dozing back into a dreamless sleep for a few more hours... Someone was shaking her arm, insisting that she wake up. Iris gasped, wrenched awake. 'Are you all right?' Sam enquired, his face creased with concern as he reached to take her hand.

'Yes, yes,' she replied, too quickly.

Her mouth was dry, and her head felt foggy, and as she tried to stand up she lurched to the side. 'Steady on,' Matron called, jumping up from the seat opposite to grab hold of her arm and then help her pull her hat and bag down from the mesh luggage rack. Iris offered a wan smile, her senses still dulled, her mind scrambling to remember where she was going, what she needed to do. That was it, they were changing trains, she was going back to her lodgings at Sam's house in Southampton.

Having said goodbye to Dr Mayhew, who lived in London, Iris, Sam and Matron Beckett endured the next stage of their journey. As Iris clambered down from the train into smoke, steam and a racket of noise, it seemed as if there were a crush of humanity on the platform – more young men in khaki, people waiting for their loved ones, stacks of luggage and children shrieking and weaving in and out through groups of passengers. The emotion of reunions going on around her made Iris's breath catch. Names were being shouted, and women paced up and down the platform looking for their men.

Iris fought her way through beside Matron, Sam bringing up the rear, shouting out to other victualling crew who were swiftly exiting the train to head to their own lodgings in Southampton. Once he caught up, they all walked together out of the station. Time seemed to have jumped forward and, knowing that she wouldn't be returning to the *Olympic*, Iris started to speak quickly to Matron... assuming that her colleague would be going back as normal on the next voyage.

'No, my dear,' Matron said with a smile. 'I'm giving notice at my lodgings and going to nurse at Netley, the Royal Victoria military hospital on Southampton Water. Soldiers will be pouring in soon, straight from France.'

'Oh... I'm thinking of working in a military hospital too,' Iris blurted out.

'You're what?' Sam interjected.

Iris took a breath. 'I'm not going back to the *Olympic,* I'm joining up.'

Sam looked put out, dumbfounded, and for a moment he didn't speak. When his voice came, he spoke quietly, 'You didn't mention it...'

She reached out a hand to him as he stood with his head bowed, 'I'm sorry, Sam, but it was only a thought half-formed until now. Of course I was going to tell you... you would have been the first person I told.'

He looked up then and gave a nod, but she could still feel the distance yawning between them.

Matron seemed oblivious to what had just passed as she

linked Iris's arm. 'I'm so pleased you are going to apply to a military hospital. Why don't you come to Netley with me?' she cried eagerly, before hastily breaking step and waving goodbye.

Once Matron Beckett had gone from view, they walked silently back through the evening light towards Sam's house, the route they'd taken together for years, usually sharing happy banter about the latest voyage. Now, they were awkward companions, each lost in their own thoughts.

'I'm sorry you had to find out about me not going back to the *Olympic* like that, Sam,' Iris said quietly as they turned together into Malmesbury Road, passing by the new red-brick terraced houses of which the residents of the street were so proud. She heard Sam take a heavy breath and then he stopped in his tracks.

'It was a bit of a shock, that's all. You're my best mate on the ship and with all the other stuff going on and worrying about my boys... it hit me harder than it should have.' He smiled then, a genuine grin. 'Of course you're doing the right thing by joining up, I feel proud that you're doing that.'

'So, everything's all right then, between us?'

'Of course it is... it's just the end of an era, that's all.'

Iris linked his arm. 'I'll try to visit Francine as often as I can, so it's likely we'll see each other when you're back home. Maybe if you get time, you could come and see me at the hospital...'

'I like a trip out to Southampton Water... but I hate hospitals, can't stand the smell of 'em, so you'll have to come to meet me. I think I might be needing a listening ear, I'll have loads to complain about, we'll be losing staff left, right and centre and we're bound to be crammed with passengers desperate to leave Europe and get back to America and Canada. It's going to be absolute bloody chaos...'

The front windows of Sam's house looked dark and empty set in their white-painted frames but the rose bushes in tubs at either side of the front door shone bright yellow in the gathering darkness. As Sam opened the door and called his wife's name, Iris heard the instant barking of Barney, the little Jack Russell terrier with a brown patch over one eye, who always went crazy when Sam returned. Having jumped up and down repeatedly to greet Sam, the dog raced past Iris and out onto the street. And then Francine was in the hallway, her black and silver hair dishevelled, eyes shining with expectation as she reached up to kiss Sam. Iris held back, she could see Sam and Francine clinging together, exchanging murmured words.

When Francine stepped back, she was trying to smile and then she was calling for the dog, using her native French as she always did when she spoke to Barney. As soon as the dog scampered back inside, Iris saw Francine knit her brows and push a stray lock of hair away from her cheek.

'I am so glad to see you, *ma chérie*,' she said, stepping forward to take Iris's hand. 'We are just a bit thrown out with this news of war and we haven't heard from the boys yet. I sent a wireless message, but they are still on turnaround in New York.'

Iris had a fleeting vision of the two boys. She hadn't seen them for a while, but they were both tall and broad-shouldered with a thatch of fair hair, just like their father. It was harrowing to think that they might be joining up as soon as they returned.

Francine beckoned for Iris to follow her into the bright kitchen with its terracotta tiled floor. As Iris started to remove her coat and hat, Sam slumped into his padded chair at the head of the table and rested back, his face lined with exhaustion, but Iris could also detect relief at being home.

Francine turned to the stove with its flickering fire visible through a small glass porthole. 'It will be good to hear all your news... Tell me how it was on the ship, hearing about the war.' She glanced back to Sam but his eyes were closed. 'My neighbour across the road, she came running over here to tell me straight away. She was shouting through the door – she seemed agitated but excited all at the same time. So strange. And then Catherine, next door but one, the young woman who lost her husband on the *Titanic*, she was in floods of tears. She is still grieving after losing him two years ago, she already knows what it will be like for so many women...'

Iris sank onto a kitchen chair, resting her elbows on the bare wood of the white-scrubbed table. Francine turned with the coffee pot and three cups, slipping into a chair opposite, and offering Iris one of her French cigarettes, flicking a silver lighter with a dolphin's head that had been Sam's gift for their twentieth wedding anniversary. Iris took her first drag gratefully as her mind and body started, at last, to relax. As Francine poured from the pot, Iris noted an ever so slight tremor of her right hand, and a droplet of coffee ran down the side of the jug and formed a tiny pool on the table. She felt the urge to wipe it away, but she resisted, not wanting to spoil this simple moment of mutual calm.

The next morning, Iris pulled the silk drawstring bag out of her jacket pocket and slipped out the diamond necklace. As she held it up, light from the bedroom window made it glint and gleam enticingly. Instantly, she recalled Miss Duchamp's promise... that she would be welcome back in New York. It made her feel hopeful. She tried not to think about Jack Rosetti, but inevitably his smiling face came to her, and she could hear the almost ghostly sound of the orchestra playing and feel his body against hers as they danced on the promenade deck.

Still holding the necklace up to the light, mesmerised by its lightning sparkle, she turned to the ornate gilt mirror above the small fireplace, holding the choker in place around her slim neck. It felt cool and heavy against her throat. It would be a perfect fit. She knew that with her hair coiffed and wearing make-up, she would look like a lady. Giving herself a firm glance in the mirror, she started to shake her head... she had no real idea of what she would be facing as a military nurse, but she would have grim work to do before she could even think about New York or wearing the necklace. She would leave it here, with Francine, for safekeeping. Something to enjoy when war was over and life could begin again.

CHAPTER 8

'Evie! Evie!' a strident voice was calling, cutting through the fog of sleep. In her dream she was home in Anstruther, in the cottage, before her mam died, before her brother left to get married. It was her daddy's funeral and a woman in black mourning dress and veil was tap-tapping at their door... Gasping, Evie woke to find Rita shaking her arm.

'Come on, sleepy head, we need to get moving... I have to find a replacement for Chrissie Jamieson at the gutting trough. She went into labour last night, two months early. I pray to God that tiny bairn is going to survive.'

Evie sat up in bed and used both hands to sweep her thick sun-bleached hair away from her face. 'Does Chrissie need any help, has she got a midwife?'

'Aye, the local woman's come. No need to worry.' Rita pushed a cup of tea into Evie's hand. 'Drink this and then get yourself dressed.'

As they walked to their work, Evie chatted incessantly, trying to dispel the lingering feeling of loss that was still hanging over her from the dream about her daddy. In her sleep, she often went back to the morning of his funeral, waking in her bed, knowing they were going to put him in the ground that day. It was strange; she had adored her mam and she'd sat with her and held her hand for all those long hours when she was dying from cancer, yet she never came back to that moment. It was always her daddy. Instinctively, she felt for the shape of the knife in her pocket; she'd be right once she got busy – no time to think about anything then.

Minnie McKay was all excited. Rita had agreed to let her have a trial at the gutting trough, she'd been training with the knife and had begged to take Chrissie's place. Evie had seen Minnie's brand-new blade, honed to perfection. She prayed that Minnie wouldn't get too distracted. All the gutters had hands scarred for life by the slip of a knife and the first week at the trough was always the most dangerous. Just thinking about it made the deep crescent scar at the base of Evie's left thumb start to pulse. She was glad now she'd grabbed an extra handful of cotton swabs from the wooden kist where she kept her medical supplies and her scant personal belongings. As she walked her mind ticked over the remaining stock – aspirin, opium drops, two bottles of iodine, one bar of carbolic soap, plenty of swabs, dressings and bandages, a needle and a length of thread, a quarter bag of dried sphagnum moss, kaolin and linseed to make poultices. Beyond the usual array of small cuts on fingers and hands, they'd only had one deep wound this season – a packer's lacerated thigh caused by the slip of a loaded barrel. The wound had been deep and turned septic, but with Evie's careful attention it had done very nicely indeed.

Today's herring catch was abundant, and towards the end of the shift the trough and wooden buckets were thickly jewelled with fish scales, more beautiful than any rich woman's sequinned evening gown. Not that Evie had ever seen one, apart from in a magazine. As they got down to the last few handfuls of fish, Evie glanced up to see Jamie, smiling as he walked towards her. It was the sabbath tomorrow, all the boats would remain in harbour until midnight on Sunday.

'Here he is...' shouted Rita, starting to laugh. 'Looking for his own silver darling.'

After all the weeks of teasing Jamie had endured, he no longer flushed bright red when the women called out. He kept his eyes fixed on Evie and walked confidently towards her.

Minnie McKay was still slow with the knife but she'd worked hard all day. Evie heard her raise her voice above the rest, calling, 'Jamie, Jamie—'

Then Minnie screamed and bright red blood gushed into the trough.

Evie threw down her knife, pulling the cotton swabs from her pocket as she ran. 'Get my medical bag from Bill's hut,' she shouted, hurrying to Minnie's side. The knife had sliced clean through the cloth bandages. They were easy to remove, and Evie was busily pressing swabs to the gaping wound at the base of her left thumb. Minnie was screaming blue murder. 'You're going to be fine,' Evie yelled above her caterwauling. 'We just need to get you sat down.' Rita already had a thick plaid blanket over a makeshift chair. 'Hush now, Minnie,' Evie soothed strongly, elevating the girl's arm to slow the bleeding, her own hands and oilskin apron slicked with blood.

Minnie was whimpering now. 'Am I going to die?'

'Don't be daft, you've just cut your hand, it's a rite of passage for us fisher girls,' Evie said as she knelt beside Minnie, with her heart hammering in her chest.

Rona arrived with the medical bag and pulled out a thick wad of cotton swabs, handing them to Evie. Evie pressed them firmly to Minnie's hand. Now that their casualty was sitting down with her arm raised, the bleeding was easing very quickly. 'This is all going to be fine,' soothed Evie, making herself smile.

Minnie was slumped, white in the face with shock. Rita had gone for a cup of sweet tea laced with whisky. Once Evie was sure that the bleeding was fully under control, she bound the swabs in place with a firm bandage.

Jamie had been there the whole time, watching silently, but Evie had been completely unaware of him. 'I'll carry her,' he said, when it was time to move back to their boarding house, bending down to scoop Minnie up as if she were no weight at all.

At last Minnie came back to life, beaming groggily at Evie over Jamie's shoulder, 'You'll have to watch out, Evie Munro,' she croaked. 'Your fella might be falling under my spell now.'

Evie blew Minnie a kiss, forcing light-heartedness as she walked along behind, but inside she was niggling with the fears that always came when one of the girls got cut – would the wound stay clean? Would it heal? Evie knew from stories passed between the experienced healers that even an incision smaller than Minnie's could turn septic, and once infection set in, a woman could die. She drew in some deep breaths, feeling the weight of the medical bag across her shoulder. She'd sutured and kept clean at least a dozen deep wounds and one or two had started to fester, but all her women had survived. She wasn't going to let anything bad happen to Minnie McKay.

Once Minnie was laid out on her bed and covered with a woollen blanket, Evie and Rita rallied together to implement their set routine, boiling up plenty of water on the kerosene stove to sterilise the needle and thread and preparing a strong salt solution for swabbing the wound. Evie didn't want to immerse the injured hand in warm water, it usually set the bleeding off again; instead she soaked some cotton squares in saline and carefully cleaned the wound.

'This is going to sting like the devil,' Rita warned, picking up the iodine bottle, propping their patient up so she could knock back a glass of whisky first.

Minnie coughed on the strong liquor and then set her mouth in a firm line.

Rita put a clean towel under Minnie's hand and poured the pungent yellow liquid straight into the gaping wound – Minnie sucked in a breath, but she didn't cry out.

Evie went straight to work once the area had been swabbed dry. The first time she'd sutured through flesh it had taken ages and her stomach had clenched so hard that she'd almost thrown up across her patient. After that, she'd practised and practised on a tightly stuffed cushion until she could do the stitches in her sleep. Minnie winced each time the needle pierced through skin. Evie could hear her gritting her teeth, but she kept her hand rock steady until the last suture was done.

'You've done well, Minnie,' Evie said, as she snipped the final thread.

Minnie nodded, a single tear escaping down her hot red cheek.

After the wound was dressed and the bandaging done, Minnie had another slug of whisky and then she turned onto her side and fell into a deep sleep. Evie and Rita exchanged a glance. 'She'll be right,' Rita said steadily. 'I'll watch over her for now, you'd best go and see your man, he's been waiting patiently outside all of this time.'

'Is Minnie going to be all right?' Jamie asked as she went out to join him, jumping up from the low wall outside the boarding house.

'Yes,' Evie replied, cutting through with certainty, not wanting to give any space for the risks that they all knew so well. 'She needed stitches but it's a clean wound and it should heal very well.'

She saw him press a hand to his own bandage, 'You know exactly what you're doing when it comes to treating wounds, don't you, Evie Munro.'

'Oh well, you have to with this work, there's always someone cutting themselves.'

'But you seem to have a real talent for it,' he insisted, 'you're like a proper healer.'

'Oh, I don't know about that,' she murmured, shaking her head. Evie knew though that there was truth in what he was saying. She often felt that the medical side of her work was a kind of calling. Her cheeks began to flush with pleasure – no one, apart from Rita, had ever commented on it before.

Jamie exhaled deeply and reached out to put an arm around her, pulling her close to the side of his body. Just the feel of his hand around her waist sent a shot of desire through her body. 'Let's go back down to the harbour,' she said. 'It will be quiet now.'

A thin paring of moon hung in the sky above the lapping sea and the stars were out in their full glory as Evie led him to the harbour wall. She leaned against him, as they both looked out to the horizon.

'It feels as if we could be on the edge of the world,' she said, her voice gently breaking the stillness.

'If that's what it is, I'm glad I'm here with you,' he murmured, his voice low, heavy.

Evie gave his arm a squeeze. 'Just the two of us... waiting for the seas to drain and the stars to fall from the sky.'

'If I could be with you forever, I'd take my chances with all of that,' he smiled, turning to face her, pulling her into his arms.

'Come on, come with me,' she urged, leading him away to the hut where she kept her medical bag. A pile of fine fishing net in the corner of the hut was all that they needed to find somewhere to lie together. As she peeled off her thick woollen cardigan, she kissed him. He tasted of fresh air and salt, and the rough wool of his clothing prickled through her cotton blouse. She helped him remove it, needing to get down through his layers until at last she could feel his skin. Her body was alive with sensation, craving his touch. They moved with the rhythm of the waves breaking on the harbour wall, she couldn't think about anything else other than satisfying the need that coursed deep inside of her. Afterwards, they lay back together, side by side, gazing up to the crescent moon framed by the window in the roof of the hut.

'Our moon is still there,' Evie murmured. 'She's gazing down at us, giving her blessing.'

Jamie smiled and pulled her close, kissing her forehead. 'You're like a story book,' he said, 'the things you come out with.'

When she woke early the next morning, Evie's body still ached with the memory of the night before. Even though it was a Sunday, and they had no work, she was up and dressed alongside Rita and checking on Minnie's dressing and bandage. Rita had told her on her way to see Chrissie Jamieson that she'd given Minnie some laudanum last night, to help settle her. When Minnie opened her eyes and gave a lopsided smile, she lifted her bandaged hand, frowning, before putting her head back down on the pillow. Evie could tell that Minnie wasn't really with it, probably still shaking off the effect of the opium.

Rita came in through the door smiling. 'By some miracle Chrissie's baby is alive, a wee boy... I've never seen one so small survive. I'm going to take her the merino wool shawl that I've been knitting, so when she's strong enough, and they head back to Shetland, she can use an extra layer to keep him warm.'

'That's such good news,' Evie said quietly, glancing back to Minnie, snuggled next to Rona in the shared bed. 'Let's hope our patient does as well.'

'We can say our prayers for her in the kirk this morning,' Rita stated, pressing her lips together in a firm line, letting Evie know there'd be no wriggling out of attendance.

. . .

For a few days all was well with Minnie's hand, she'd even started to come down to the harbour to give some one-handed help with the packing. But then, one evening, she came to Evie and told her that the wound was throbbing.

It made Evie's heart twist with fear when the bandage was unravelled and she saw the wound exposed – red and swollen, with pus starting to leak from between the stitches. Minnie's eyes were wide with fear.

Evie swallowed hard. 'We just need to soak it in a warm salt solution, Minnie, make it clean so that it can heal.'

Once the wound was bathed, it was still angry, but it looked better.

Minnie thrashed around in bed and called out during her sleep and as the night progressed Evie's heart grew heavier. Come the next morning, she laid a hand on Minnie's forehead to find that her skin was burning with fever.

'Right, Minnie,' Evie said firmly. 'We need to soak the hand again and I might need to take out one or two of the stitches so the wound can drain.'

Minnie's eyes were glazed, she tried to speak but her words were jumbled. Evie exchanged a solemn glance with Rita.

'You stay with her for as long as you need today, Evie, do whatever you can,' Rita said quietly. 'If she doesn't start to rally, we'll have to get the local doctor.'

Once the soaking was done, Evie snipped two stitches to open the wound before applying firm pressure to expel the exudate. After drying and applying a light dressing, Evie went through to the sitting room to warm a kaolin poultice to draw the suppuration. Once the wound was cleaner and oozing freely, she would pack it with sphagnum moss to promote healing. With the poultice heating on the kerosene stove, Evie sat down heavily on one of the wooden kists that also served as benches, cradling her head in her hands. She knew that Minnie's condition could go either way and the next few hours were crucial... She felt exhausted, on the verge of tears. Smelling the heated kaolin, she gritted her teeth and got up to remove the poultice with a clean towel. She sucked in a quick breath of fresh salt air from the open sash window before returning to Minnie in the bedroom.

By mid-afternoon the wound was doing as Evie had hoped and the dried sphagnum was in place, but Minnie had become delirious, and her fever was high. Evie was exasperated and increasingly fearful each time she laid a hand across her forehead.

'Get off me,' Minnie yelled, 'and take that dog out of here, I don't like dogs!'

Evie's heart was beating double time, she knew that the fever needed to break. She had to get some fluids into Minnie, flush out the badness, and maybe some aspirin would help bring her temperature down. She crushed up a tablet with her pestle and mortar, stirring it into a small amount of water. Minnie turned her face away, but Evie knew that she had to be firm, ruthless if necessary. She put an arm around her and held her tight so she couldn't move her head. 'Minnie,' she said authoritatively, 'I need you to drink this.' Minnie tried to smile but her eyes were glazed. Evie didn't wait she pushed the spout of the ceramic feeding cup into Minnie's mouth and tipped in the fluid, then held Minnie's nose to make her swallow. It worked.

Minnie was cursing now and trying to scramble out of bed. She was so strong. Evie took a cool flannel and started to sponge her face and neck with cool water. The rhythm of it started to soothe her patient and eventually Evie was able to remove Minnie's nightie and woollen vest and sponge the whole of her torso. When she fell into an exhausted sleep, Evie covered her with a sheet and sat down beside her, fighting back tears. She let herself have a moment of grief, quickly switching to anger. 'You will not die, Minnie McKay,' she muttered, feeling her jaw clench.

'I'm not going to die,' Minnie mumbled from the bed, turning over onto her side, her eyes closed and her chest rising and falling as she slept. Evie gasped, reached out a hand to feel at her forehead. The fever was breaking. Tears of relief pricked her eyes.

Later, when Minnie woke, she sat up in bed. 'What's wrong with you?' she croaked, 'Your eyes are all red.'

Evie knew that it would take a week or so of scrupulous dressings with the sphagnum moss, but she was sure that Minnie would live to tell the story.

That night, Jamie came back to the boarding house and they walked again to the harbour. The moon was full, tracing a silver trail across the sea. As they leaned against the harbour wall he rooted in his pocket and pulled out a smooth stone. 'This is for you. It's sea glass,' he said, 'You can't see in this light, but it's blue, like your eyes.'

Evie took the gift in her hand, feeling the cool beauty and the balanced weight against her palm. 'Thank you,' she said. She kissed the sea glass and slipped it into her pocket and then she reached up to put her arms around his neck. He pulled her close, enveloping her, their bodies fitting together like the completion of a puzzle – safe, familiar but also exhilarating.

CHAPTER 9

Evie grabbed the salt pot as it rolled towards the edge of the polished counter in the fish and chip shop, and placed it upright. She took a pinch of spilt salt and threw it over her left shoulder. 'So the devil doesn't get me,' she laughed to the red-faced young woman with a cheery smile who was serving.

It was a Saturday night and they were celebrating Minnie's recovery – she was back at work and much more careful with her knife now. All the herring crowd would be out on the town tonight, and it would be more raucous than ever. Most of the men would be joining up once the season ended, and who knew if they'd ever be working the herring again. It felt like they were all on borrowed time. Even as she stood in the queue, two women in front of Evie were talking about a steam drifter that'd brought up a German mine in its nets. She'd also been hearing rumours of fishermen spotting heavily armed battleships out in the North Sea. She'd questioned Jamie about it, but he'd denied all knowledge... He hadn't been able to look her in the eye though.

The vinegary smell of fish and chips in a newspaper-wrapped bundle was making her mouth water, she was so tempted to sneak open the end of the paper to take out a chip, but she'd promised the girls that she wouldn't let their fish supper go cold. They'd had a long day, the herring catches coming through were huge. She'd hardly seen Jamie, the crews were so busy. He had a routine of hopping off the drifter to come and say hello before the *Embrace* went back out, but in these last few days the turnarounds had been so quick he hadn't had time. But he'd be back tonight, and they were all off tomorrow, for the Sabbath.

'About time,' laughed Rita, standing up from the stone steps as she approached.

Evie handed over the newspaper bundles, and stifled a yawn. She'd agreed to share a bed with Minnie last night to give Rona a break, so she'd hardly had any sleep.

Rona offered a rare smile. 'I see you're feeling it, Evie – one night with miss crazy brains and you're exhausted... Don't worry, I'll swap back tonight... we're both from Aberdeen, it's my duty to deal with her.'

'Where's mine?' Minnie shouted, jumping up from the step. 'My belly thinks me throat's been cut.'

'Steady on,' Rita counselled, 'you'll have chips all over the place.'

Once the women were settled with the newspaper spread open on their laps, they all fell to eating and licking their fingers.

'Bill was telling me that we might be on track for a bumper year,' Rita said.

Rona looked up, 'Aye, well... I don't need Bill to tell me that, my back feels like it's broken in two with bending over so many barrels...'

'The more fish the merrier for me,' Evie smiled, her lips stinging with salt and vinegar.

Minnie swallowed a huge lump of battered cod. 'That may be the case for you, Evie, but I'm gutting herring in me sleep,' she said, between mouthfuls.

'That's not all you're doing, Minnie McKay,' laughed Rona. 'Will ye be singing your songs again tonight? Even though I was sleeping in a different bed, you still woke me up.'

'Sorry, Rona,' Minnie grinned. 'My mind's a whirl.'

'It's that curly-haired fisherman you're still seeing, he's giving you exotic thoughts,' Rita joked.

'Nah, me and Robert, we're not doing that kind of thing – not yet, not erotic,' Minnie said quietly.

They were all laughing now.

'Not erotic, I said *exotic*!' Rita was laughing so hard she coughed on her chips.

'Oh, you mean like this,' Minnie retorted, quick as a flash, jumping up from the step with her chips in her hand, starting to circle her hips in some version of a belly dance.

'Stop, stop,' Rita begged, starting to splutter. 'We're all going to choke to death on our food...'

Once the chip papers were scrunched and piled on the steps, Evie went in to wash and change into her going-out clothes: a pink blouse with a round lace collar and a bright blue skirt. This was the only night of the week that she let down her wavy hair, and she loved the feel of it brushing her shoulders as she walked, adding to the excitement of a night out. The other girls were still chatting and laughing on the steps.

'There's your fella,' Minnie called, and they all turned to see Jamie walking towards them.

Evie felt a starburst of joy deep in her chest when she saw him look up and give that slow smile.

'See you, later,' Evie called, skipping off to meet him, ignoring Rita's call for her to take a cardigan – 'The nights get chilly.' She linked his arm, pleased by the fresh-scrubbed, newly shaved smell of him. It always thrilled her to see the shape of his body when he wasn't muffled inside a woollen gansey and oilskins. She reached up to flatten down a clump of his thick hair and he beamed down at her, his face golden with a tan. Once they were out of sight of the other girls and heading towards the promenade, he put his arm around her and pulled her close. She could feel the roughness of his hand through the thin material of her blouse.

The Yarmouth prom was broad and bisected by a new electric tramway. Already it was busy with groups of fisherfolk, festive in the night air as they walked out to begin their Saturday-night revels.

'I think I'm finally a part of the crew, now we're coming to the end of the season,' Jamie said. 'Even had a laugh and a joke with the skipper today. He's noticed I've started talking with a bit of a Scots accent.'

'You need to practise that accent,' Evie laughed. 'But I'm finding it a bit easier to understand ye...'

A stout, red-faced landlord in a white apron emerged from a pub and stood with his hands on his hips. 'Cheap beer! Come and get your fill before you go off to fight!' he called. Evie wished that men wouldn't keep shouting about war; everybody knew what was going on, they didn't need to be bombarded with it.

'Come on, let's cross over, so we can walk by the beach,' she urged, taking Jamie's hand as they waited for a tram crowded with pub-goers to pass by. Even at this distance they could still hear shouts, laughter and raucous singing from the other side of the prom and behind them the screaming of girls on the scenic railway that swooped and rattled on a rollercoaster ride. Evie shouted hello to a group of Scots girls heading towards them, their arms linked, shrieking with laughter as a clutch of apprentice coopers ran to tease them. There was even more of an edge to the liveliness of a Saturday night, the atmosphere was electric.

'All right there, Jamie, see you when we join up,' cried a fisherman still in his woollen gansey and boots, already staggering drunkenly across their path.

'You go easy, fella,' Jamie said, patting him on the arm as they walked by.

Evie swallowed hard, she didn't comment on the fisherman's remark, not wanting to spoil what would probably be their final night out together for some time. Once they were further down, they crossed back over the tramlines. Evie knew they could get a glass of ale from a quieter pub where the same grey-haired woman stoically played the piano, tune after tune, whatever was going on around her.

Later, settled at a table, Evie looked out through the open door and saw Rita and Rona wandering by, arm in arm. No sign of Minnie – but she'd already said she'd be off with Robert tonight.

They left the pub and wandered down towards the Britannic pier. The streetlights had been switched on and the coloured bulbs of the funfair shone bright, unashamed. The sound of the sea was strengthening as the tide came in. Evie felt goosebumps on her arms. Denying she was cold, she snuggled up to Jamie as they walked.

As they headed towards the pier, the sound of the sea soothed her, drowning out the faded but still chaotic noise from the promenade. Evie glanced back over her shoulder to see the coloured lights of the town.

'Would you rather be back there, or out here with the sound of the waves?' Jamie asked quietly.

'Both,' she smiled, giving his arm a squeeze. 'And I had my share of beer and whisky last night. Minnie kept us out dancing in the street when we should have been in our beds.'

'I don't think I could do it. Not like some of the fellas on a Saturday night... They roll back onto the ship on a Sunday, still drunk, but somehow they always sober up for midnight, when we set sail. If I had that much, I'd be throwing up over the side.'

'Ye big softie,' Evie smiled, planting a kiss on his cheek.

They gazed out to sea, gently murmuring words back and forth. When they retraced their steps back along the pier and ventured down onto the beach, Jamie spread his coat across the sand and they lay there, still listening to the breaking of the waves, as they started to kiss. Evie knew that what she had with Jamie was as natural as the ebb and flow of the tide.

A sharp breeze caught the girls by surprise as they came out of their lodgings the next morning to make their way to church.

'That's a bit brisk,' Rita said, as her skirt billowed out and she swiftly planted a hand on her hat to keep it in place. Evie felt a jolt of anxiety as she held onto her own hat, instantly on the alert for the faintest sniff of a brewing storm. Glancing out to the horizon she could see dark clouds; it looked like rain. The chances were this would have strengthened when the steam drifters were heading out into open sea as soon as the Sabbath was done, at a minute after midnight. She couldn't be dwelling on every slate grey sky or bit of breeze, so, marching ahead, she called back over her shoulder, 'Come on, you lot, we'll be needing to stand outside the church again if we don't hurry up.'

'I can't go any faster,' Minnie groaned. 'My head's hurting.'

'Too many beers, Minnie McKay?' Rita teased. 'Ye need to stick to the whisky like me.'

As they squeezed together into a pew at the back, Evie saw Minnie heave. 'Don't be chucking up in here,' she warned. 'You'll be banned.'

'I'll keep it down,' Minnie whispered, swallowing hard, holding a large cotton handkerchief over her mouth.

The wheeze of the organ set Evie's teeth on edge, but once they were singing 'For Those in Peril on the Sea', she started to relax. She loved this one, even though the words brought tears to her eyes. When it came time for prayers, she squeezed her eyes tight and begged for those she loved to always be kept safe and for the war to be over soon. Minnie was nodding off next to her, so Evie put a protective arm around her, remembering how she'd been herself during that first season.

Jamie came by their lodgings for Sunday tea before he headed back to the boat. No longer daunted by the women and their teasing, he was at ease, joining in with the ribbing of the new boy – Minnie's Robert.

'Aye, Robbie, ye don't have a clue what you're takin' on with this lass, she'll run ye ragged,' Rona was saying. 'And don't ever sleep in the same bed as her, she kicks like a mule.'

Evie saw Robert's face flush bright red. He reminded her of her brother when he was wet behind the ears on his first boat – and look at him now, he could hold his own against anyone, except his wife, Sadie.

As Evie and Jamie walked through the town alone together, Evie tried to relax, but restless, unformed thoughts caught repeatedly at the edges of her mind. Even when she shoved her hand in her pocket to squeeze hard on the sea glass, she couldn't quieten it. When they kissed goodbye and Jamie turned to leave, she felt a shiver run down her spine.

'Stop it,' Evie muttered to herself as she strode away, not daring to glance back and see him leaving. Feeling again for the sea glass, she crushed it in her hand, but it wasn't sharp enough to give her the relief that she needed.

Overnight, as she lay in bed, knowing that the *Embrace* was already out on the waves, she heard a gale start to moan down the bedroom chimney. Her stomach swooped and fell as if she were out there with Jamie, riding the waves.

Waking, groggy, early for her work, she was relieved to hear the wind had dropped to a soft buffeting. She got dressed while the others still slept, and then peeled back a corner of the curtain – the sky was a mid-grey, the weather could go either way. As the day progressed with the slitting of the fish, Evie pushed herself to increase her pace, pouring all her thoughts into the work, feeling a glow of satisfaction when she saw the silver bodies piling up in the wooden buckets behind.

'You're putting me to shame today, Evie,' Rita called, 'you're like a woman possessed.'

'I've learned from the best,' Evie called back in response, as her hands continued to work unbidden. Heartened by a further quietening of the brisk wind and occasional glimpses of blue sky, Evie had begun to relax, almost laughing at herself, wondering what she'd been worrying about. It didn't stop her from picking up a clump of coarse salt between finger and thumb though, to toss over her left shoulder each time the fresh baskets of fish were emptied into the trough. As they worked through the next batch, Evie was aware of a bite of cold in the air, the intermittent sun that had peeked out from behind grey clouds was now blocked completely. When she looked up, her heart jolted – dark grey, almost black, clouds hung over the sea and the wind was pulling at her headscarf, starting to whistle and upend the empty baskets on the quay. She kept on gutting, keeping tuned in to the sounds of the onshore crew, listening for the ships as they came into harbour. When the light faded further and there was a low growl of thunder over the sea and then big spits of cold rain, Evie knew that she had every right to be worried.

Catching an anxious glance from Rita, she felt a clutch of fear. She shrugged into her oilskin cape, and looked out to sea, saying a prayer. The men were setting out lanterns on the harbour wall to guide in the remaining ships. Rita was watching the sea too and began to sing a steady ballad, full of hope, something to keep the spirits up. Evie tried to join in, but her voice failed her.

Once they were down to the last few handfuls of fish and there was still no sign of Jamie or his crew, Evie was struggling. Her knife slipped once, twice, and Rita reached out to touch her arm. 'Take some time, Evie,' she said, 'We all know what it's like.'

Evie gave a nod. 'I'm going to the pier,' she shouted through the driving rain, holding on to her oilskin hood as she walked.

The boards of the pier were slippery, and it was deserted apart from a man smoking in one doorway and a courting couple in another. As she reached the end, the wind whipped at her and she had to cling to the rail to keep her balance. The waves smashed against the legs of the pier, and Evie clung to the metal rail with rain stinging her eyes. It felt right that she was there, experiencing a small part of what the men would be going through out at sea.

She had no concept of time, unsure if she'd been there for ten minutes or an hour. Hearing a voice calling behind her, she half-turned to see a figure approaching – she knew it was Rita. Hanging onto the rail she felt her entire body tighten as she watched her friend approach, head down, fighting against the driving rain. She couldn't read her, she didn't know if she carried bad news or not. But when Evie saw her friend's stricken face and sad eyes, a heaviness settled over her.

'The boat is back,' Rita shouted, above the sound of the sea, 'the skipper said it was bad – they were standing on end one minute and slamming down on the waves the next, they had to fight hard. And... and Jamie was lost, he was washed overboard.'

Evie felt a surge of dizziness, she was clinging to the rail with all her might. It was as if she'd always known this would happen. But as she heard it said out loud, her knees gave way and she fell to the boards of the pier as if she'd been mortally wounded. She wanted to scream, but no sound would come out of her body. All she could hear was Rita's voice breaking on a ragged sob. 'I'm so sorry, Evie, I'm so sorry.'

CHAPTER 10

Evie couldn't remember anything, from standing at the end of the pier with the wind and the rain whipping around her, to when she woke up in her bed in the lodging house with just one thought in her head. *Jamie's gone.*

She'd known this pain before, as a child, when her daddy died, and then it had come in a different form when she lost her mammy to cancer. But that didn't mean she understood it, or that she was any better equipped to deal with the savagery of it. On the contrary, as she lay there groaning with a visceral pain, feeling scoured out inside, it seemed to get worse and worse each time. All that she knew was Jamie was never coming back, and it felt like the world had stopped turning.

The wind was still rumbling in the chimney and daylight was seeping in around the edges of the poorly fitted curtains at the bedroom window. *The girls must be at work.* There was a scribbled note shoved beneath a cold cup of tea and two biscuits on the scratched wood surface of the bedside cabinet. She slipped out the paper, it was Rita's spidery handwriting – *Me and you both, we're Anstruther girls. Stay strong Evie.* The paper was marked with a circle of tea, but the sentiment was there and it should have moved Evie to tears. But she could only stare at it numbly before placing it back on top of the cabinet. Heaving herself out of bed, she struggled to straighten up, but she had to start moving and she had to let some light in through the small window. The curtains always snagged on the wire, she hardly had the strength to yank them back, but when she did the pale light hurt her eyes. The sky was slate grey, she had no idea what time of day it was, and her legs could barely support her weight. There was no choice; for this one day, she had to crawl back to her bed.

When the girls came back from their work, they were all in tears, crying for Evie. Minnie was inconsolable, and Rita had to send her out to the chip shop just so they could all try to calm down.

'I'm going to work in the morning,' Evie said, feeling her flat voice echo inside her empty body.

Rita shook her head. 'You need to think about going home, back to Anstruther.'

'No.' The word came out of her mouth with force, and saying it sent a sharp jolt through her chest, as if someone was restarting her heart.

Rita was in tears, still shaking her head. 'Look at yourself, Evie, you're wrung out, you can't even get out of bed...'

Evie reached out to take Rita's hand. 'What am I going to do back home except feel out of place? You won't be back for another couple of weeks. I need to work, Rita, I need to use my knife and gut the fish, and if I do that, I will feel better.'

Rita sighed heavily. 'I know what you're saying... I would probably do the same. But if I see you fading away in front of my eyes, I'll put you over my shoulder and I'll carry you to the train station myself.'

Evie gave the ghost of a smile.

. . .

Weeks later, as the season in Yarmouth ended, Evie was starting to unravel with the thought of her all-absorbing work coming to an end. Day after day she'd pushed herself to be quick with her knife, to chat to the girls, to force food down her neck. It was what held her together. But tomorrow they would be packing up their wooden kists and taking the northbound train to Scotland. She'd always felt a tinge of sadness at leaving the season behind, but the revels that they had on the journey home, the excitement of seeing family, and the knowledge that they would be back again next year, always helped. This year she was carrying her grief and the world was at war.

And in the time since Jamie was lost, her monthly bleeding hadn't come, so there was other news that Evie would need to share.

Not yet, not today, and she would tell Rita first.

'You're what?' Rita said loudly above the rumbling of the train, as they stood in the corridor outside their compartment.

'I'm having Jamie's bairn,' Evie repeated, her hand tightly gripping the sea glass in her pocket. Not able to meet Rita's eyes, she looked back into the compartment, to Rona and Minnie, sleeping soundly with their mouths dropped open, looking as if she'd just told them as well and they were in shock.

Rita made a small groaning sound. 'Oh Evie, this is the same as happened to me, but my fella was still alive and heading home on the boat. We were married the next week.'

There was nothing Evie could say, there was nothing she could do to turn back the clock, and none of this seemed real to her. Jamie was gone and without his body being washed up along the coast, there'd been no funeral, no marking of his loss. It felt as if she might have dreamt the whole thing. He came to her at night though, tormenting the little bit of sleep she was able to get. Sometimes she was lying on the sand beside him, listening to the sound of the waves, other times she saw his white face surrounded by seaweed hair, rising up through the water, his eyes empty, his mouth dropping open in a silent scream.

Evie gasped, pressing a hand to her chest.

Rita had an arm around her shoulders now. 'I'm so sorry,' she said, consoling Evie as if someone had died. Someone had died, but Evie had new life now growing inside of her, so why did it all feel so tragic? Evie put a hand to her face, surprised to find it wet with tears. Rita was crying too. 'I'll look after you, Evie, you can come to me for your confinement... that brother of yours and his bad-tempered wife won't be much use to you. I know that already.'

As Evie and Rita strode down towards the shore amid the raucous cry of the herring gulls, they found Anstruther exactly as they'd left it – a line of regular two- or three-storey houses facing the sea, fronting a crowded, random selection of mismatched buildings – ancient, squat cottages with tiny windows; tall, narrower houses squeezed haphazardly into every available space. Some had red clay roof tiles, all were connected by a secret maze of narrow, cobbled wynds. The square harbour, with thick stone walls that defied the sea, could be so full of fishing boats in the season that a person could walk from one side to the other, just by stepping on the decks. The steepled parish church of Saint Nicholas overlooking the beach was the first thing that Evie looked for on her return. Set by the shoreline in an elevated position, the weathered headstones of the graves stood defiant against a backdrop of warm yellow sandstone that formed the walls of the ancient church.

Evie had a tiny attic room on the top floor of the white-painted, blue-doored three-storey terraced house where she'd been born, overlooking the harbour on Shore Street. She'd grown up to the sound of the sea and a view of the boats with every glance through one of the front windows. After their mammy had died, her brother Douglas had moved into the family home with his wife, Sadie, and their two boisterous, sandy-haired boys. It was beginning to feel less and less like her home, and she spent much of her time at Rita's place, further down the street beside the beach, where a lively burn carried fresh water through a channel in the sand to mingle with the sea.

Evie said a brief goodbye to Rita as a sudden gust of sea breeze pulled at her skirt, arriving back home when the children were still at school and Douglas and Sadie were busy preparing the fish and peeling the potatoes for a new wartime business enterprise – a fish and chip shop.

'Hello,' she shouted, as she came in through the door with her hand luggage and medical bag.

Douglas called out from the small kitchen at the back of the house and lumbered through with his sleeves rolled up and water dripping from his hands. Straightaway, Evie saw the lines of tiredness around his eyes and his normally ruddy cheeks appeared sunken. Even his shoulders seemed more stooped since she'd left for the season.

'Don't say anything about the war,' he murmured, glancing back to the clatter of pots and pans in the kitchen. 'Sadie hasn't taken the news well.'

Evie almost laughed out loud; she was sure that few people had been heartened by the onset of war. She started to smile, glad to see her brother share her amusement as he gave her one of his warm bear hugs. 'I'll take my bags up and then go down to the beach... See you both later.'

'Aye,' he said, 'Once we're all set for the fish suppers... things are a bit calmer here.' Sadie was still clattering in the kitchen and in the next moment she called his name. Evie gave him a glance of solidarity before running briskly up the narrow stairs. Once in her attic room, she put down her bags and went straight to the window. The few remaining boats in the harbour were gently rocking back and forth, but outside the wall, the white-foam-topped waves were coming in more strongly now. As always, the weather had changed in an instant. Evie didn't even remove her coat, she ran straight back down the stairs and out through the door onto the cobbled street. Anxious now to be on the yellow sand littered with clumps of dark-brown bladderwrack and bright green sea lettuce fresh from the sea, so she could reclaim the beach as the tide withdrew. She was also grateful for some respite before she would have to share the news about the baby.

As the months in Anstruther went by Evie's belly grew, and even as the baby started to kick, she still didn't know how she felt. There was a barrier between her and this accidental child left behind by Jamie. With no man to marry, all except Sadie, her sister-in-law, were wary of what they said. Sadie had suggested she marry the village bachelor, Herbert Murray, twenty years Evie's senior – ugly as sin and with a temper to match. At least fighting her corner and squaring up to her sister-in-law had made the blood start to pulse through Evie's body again and, for the first time, she'd run her hand over her belly and whispered to her child, 'Don't you worry, I'll take care of us.'

Working in the curing shed, helping the fishermen clean the boats and repair their nets, all the work that she'd always done outside of the herring season continued as normal. Through the autumn and winter she was working, even as her belly grew so big she could hardly bend down. Any spare time she got she spent walking the shore, no matter what the weather; in fact if a gale was blowing and the sea was rough, she was right there, letting it push against her body, strip her hair back from her face. She could feel Jamie then, in the wind that blew over the waves, in the cold water that she waded in knee deep, in the sharpness of the stones and the shells beneath her bare feet. That's where he was, where he would always be.

By late spring, when they should have been preparing again to leave for the herring season, the village was emptied of young men and many of the steam drifters stood idle. Anstruther was distracted by the interruption of its natural rhythm, and already at least three women wore black mourning dress. It took the sting out of Evie's predicament – none of the younger women had their men home and a good few were pregnant. Evie prayed every day that her bairn would come; she needed to move on to the next stage of existence and start to earn a living again. Some of the girls from the village had left for the Highlands to help gather the sphagnum moss which would be dried and sent to France to be used in dressings for the injured men. Evie was itching to do something; she hated having to live off her brother and his wife.

The room in Rita's cottage had been ready for weeks and Morag, the local woman who served as a midwife, would be there for her when the time came. Evie could tell that her sister-in-law felt put out that she wasn't planning her confinement in the family home, but her attic room was tiny and she couldn't bear the thought of having to suffer Sadie's heavy-handed ministrations.

In those last few weeks of her pregnancy, as the spring sun shone between scurrying clouds and intermittent showers of rain, Evie walked the shore constantly, feeling her bairn move and kick inside the waters of her womb. She knew it was a boy and she talked to him now, when they were on their walks, telling him about his father, describing the herring and the fishing boats, the sea and the sky.

When she said something special or sang him a song, she was sure he responded with a single kick. Sometimes she could feel the rounded heel of his foot, it was smooth like the sea glass she still carried in her pocket.

'Not long now,' she whispered as the waves broke, 'not long now.'

The first pain came when she was wading in the sea, a tight squeeze that she thought at first was like those she'd been having for some weeks now... getting ready. When the next one came ten minutes later, it made her pause, she felt her heart beat stronger in response. Giving herself more time, she continued to wade in the sea with her skirt gathered in one hand. With the next pain she felt a flush of warm wetness between her legs as her waters broke, fluid running down her legs and into the sea. She washed herself with salt water and then made her way out, shoving her damp feet into her leather sandals.

Rita smiled when she opened the door of her cottage. Evie was leaning against the stone door jamb for half a minute as another pain hit her.

'Everything is ready, exactly as we left it, with the crib by the bed. When you're settled, I'll go and get Morag. She was over the other side of the harbour with Mrs Henderson earlier, but I've heard that she's already given birth to a baby boy.'

Evie paced the wooden floor and looked out of the window of the second-storey bedroom for hours, leaning on the sill and gazing out to sea when the pains came. They were stronger now, much stronger, she had to take deep breaths to manage them. Morag had asked her to lie on the bed, so she could examine her.

'Your baby is lying with its back to your back, if it stays that way, it will be a stargazer, face up, when it comes out.'

'Is that all right?' Evie asked, sensing a slight frown, a tinge of anxiety in Morag's voice.

'Yes, yes, of course,' she said, straightening her apron. 'It just means that the labour might take a bit longer, that's all.'

Evie nodded, starting to breathe through another contraction.

The hours went by, more pains, more pacing, and now she was pouring with sweat. The midwife had been called away but Rita was there with her, rubbing her back, mopping her brow, urging her to take frequent sips of water. When Morag returned, she asked Evie to lie back on the bed so that she could feel the lie of the baby and press her ear against the curve of Evie's belly to listen to the baby's heart.

This time she couldn't hide the worry that showed in the furrow between her brows. 'It's hard to hear the bairn's pulse with the way that it's lying,' she said.

Evie's breath caught. 'Is the baby still all right?' she said, feeling her own heart flutter with fear.

'Yes, yes, it should all be fine. Just stay on your feet, keep moving so we can get the head to come right down.'

With her legs starting to feel weak, Evie continued her ritual of pacing and breathing. Rita was now feeding her sugar water for energy, and she'd snuck a shot of whisky in there as well.

'I was in labour a full day with the twins,' she'd said, and it had comforted Evie.

But as the day wore on and the light faded, Evie gazed out at the moon, shining bright and clear over the harbour, leaving a silvery trail across the water. She was gasping with the pain now, it felt like one pain coming on top of another.

'Do ye feel like ye want to bear down?' Morag kept asking, and the answer was always no. But when the urge came on her, it seemed to take over her whole body and she wanted to push and push with all her might. And now the midwife was saying, 'No, not yet.' Evie ground her teeth in exasperation but then a moment came when she felt something move and there was a gush of warm fluid. 'Get on the bed quick now, Evie,' cried the midwife, 'baby's on the way.'

Evie's body knew how to do this part, worn out as she was from pain upon pain, she was relieved that she could connect with the urges of her body. She pushed and pushed, but still the midwife was looking down between her legs. Evie could sense the tension in the air, she was so glad of Rita there, by the head of the bed, holding tightly to her hand.

'Keep pushing, Evie, push as hard as you can.'

With a ripping, tearing sensation deep inside her, Evie felt something moving at last.

'Come on now!' urged Morag. 'I can see the baby's head.'

Evie kept bearing down but something felt stuck. It didn't seem right. Then a pain seared from the opening between her legs, right up through her body, and with one more push the baby was delivered.

'Mother of God!' Evie heard the panic in Morag's voice. She was scrabbling with forceps and scissors and cutting the baby free. Evie propped herself up on one elbow. She could see the midwife wiping out the baby's mouth and nose and then frantically rubbing his back, and then she turned him over and rubbed his front. *He's not breathing, he's not breathing.* Feeling Rita place a hand on her shoulder Evie glanced up to see tears welling in her friend's eyes.

Morag was blowing on the baby's face now, tickling his nose with the corner of a towel. Still he lay lifeless as a dead fish, no breath in his body, the cord that had been wrapped tightly, twice around his neck, cut away and lying forlornly at the side.

'Give him to me,' Evie ordered.

'There's nothing more we can do,' Morag said quietly.

'He's gone now,' Rita said gently, in a way that brought Evie close to tears.

Evie swallowed hard, her throat dry. 'Give him to me,' she repeated.

Morag wrapped the baby's limp body in a clean white towel and handed him up the bed. He lay slick and motionless, blue-lipped, silent in her arms, just like Evie imagined the poor drowned body of his father to be. She clutched him tighter, willing him to breathe, wanting a way to trade her life for his. She gazed at his tiny face, his tufts of hair slicked back. Bending her head she kissed his cheek – he tasted of salt.

'Let me take him, Evie,' Rita said quietly.

But she wouldn't give him up, she held onto him as Morag delivered the afterbirth. 'You've a very bad tear,' she said. 'I'll need to put some stitches in.'

Evie didn't react, she just lay back, still holding onto the baby, wanting to feel the sharp pain stabbing inside of her, reaching up through her empty womb and into her useless body. If the women hadn't been there, she'd have gone down to the shore and waded into the water with her dead baby in her arms. Melting away into the ocean, together with Jamie at last.

Only when Morag had finished could Evie hear other sounds above what felt like a pounding of blood in her head.

'Can I take the baby, now. I was thinking that maybe we could get him baptised?' Rita asked gently.

'No,' she snapped, clutching him closer. Evie couldn't really make sense of what she was saying. Her poor baby boy hadn't even drawn his first breath and she was asking about baptising him.

Rita put her arm around her then, held onto her. 'Your little angel is already in heaven, Evie. We can't bring him back, but wouldn't it be nice if you get him baptised?'

Angel. Heaven.

Visceral fear clutched at Evie's heart, squeezing so hard she could barely catch her breath. Then she started to gasp and sob, emitting a deep guttural wail that came from the very core of her. Still she clung to the baby, rocking back and forth as the sound that came out of her spiralled through the crack of the partially open window, echoing across the harbour, reaching up to the moon and the stars.

Rita must have taken the baby from her, because when she opened her eyes she thought she saw him there in the crib beside the bed. She groaned and turned in bed, exhausted from sobbing. Finally lapsing into sleep, she dreamt of Jamie's white face and seaweed hair rising from the sea... She gasped awake. Blackness was coming for her; she could feel it settling at the edges of her mind.

At the funeral, a small wooden coffin carried by Evie's brother was gently laid into the tiny hole in the graveyard of the parish church, overlooking the beach and the harbour. Evie felt dead inside as she clung to Rita on that bitingly cold May morning. She'd even been grateful to take Sadie's arm when Rita broke down as the freshly dug soil began to fall on the coffin lid.

Afterwards, Evie was ordered back to her bed for more rest. It felt like punishment and for a few days she took it, because she thought she deserved it. Then, hearing Rita downstairs moving the furniture around, scouring and cleaning, Evie got up out of bed. Feeling constricted, not able to breathe, she tore away the cotton bindings from around her chest, the broad strips of cloth that Morag had insisted she wear to flatten her breasts and stop the milk from coming. She made herself walk, even though she felt as if the stitches were pulling her insides out. The next day when the midwife came to remove them, Evie soaked up the pain, it made her feel clean and whole again.

'It looks like the wound is festering a little, down there,' Morag said, advising some salt water or iodine.

Evie lay back and let her paint some iodine on, the more it stung the better, she didn't care. Nothing else made sense, other than she needed to get away from Anstruther. But with no herring season this year, she was stuck. Rita had already told her that she needed to stay put.

'You can't leave, you're still recovering from the birth, it'll be too much for you,' she kept saying.

But it was the only thing that Evie knew would start to make her feel alive again. Rita gave up, in the end. She had no choice; Evie was proving herself fit by walking every day and helping around the house.

One morning, Evie was up at dawn, down on the shoreline, watching the sun trace warm yellow across the silken water. The sea was so calm, she could barely hear the breaking of the waves, and even the cry of the herring gulls seemed muted. Shoving her hand into her skirt pocket, her fingers touched the sea glass. She grasped it firmly and pulled it out – admiring the blueness of it, tracing its smooth surface with her fingertip. Gazing out across the water, she stood for a few moments, feeling the shape of it in her palm. She stood weighing it in her hand, thinking about him, feeling the touch of his hand on her body. Then she raised the sea glass to her lips and kissed it gently. It felt right to return it to where it belonged, to where Jamie lay. Walking across the beach to the lively freshwater burn that flowed against the wall that formed the boundary between the beach and the graveyard where her son was buried, she gazed over to the small headstone that marked the grave. Kissing the sea glass once more she dropped it down into the rapidly flowing water, knowing that the current would take it straight out into the sea. Hearing the soft sound of it breaking the water, she murmured Jamie's name softly, saying goodbye.

Walking away from the sea she looked again across to the graveyard. Yesterday she'd been there to place some yellow tulips on her son's grave. Even as she'd laid the flowers, the bright petals had already started to wilt on the mound of fresh soil. It had brought tears to her eyes, and she'd slumped to her knees and wept. In the end, Archie Ross, the gravedigger, had come to her, with his shovel across his shoulder. He'd leaned down to place his calloused hand gently on her shoulder. When she looked up, she'd seen his rheumy eyes shining with tears. It was well known in the village that Archie had lost all his three children to measles many years ago.

'I'm sorry,' she'd mumbled, making to get up from the ground.

'Stay and cry for as long as you need,' he'd said softly, 'grief needs to be worked through...'

Evie had nodded, wiping her face with her sleeve. She'd tried to offer a smile but he'd been walking away, raising a hand in farewell.

Gazing back to the small wooden cross that bore her son's name – Martin Munro – the same as her father, who lay in the next grave with her mother, she'd felt a connectedness that could only be found in the place where a person had been born and raised. This would always be her home, she knew that. But, before the day when it would be time for her to take her own rest, there was so much that she wanted to explore. Picking up one of the wilted tulips, still a vibrant yellow but soon to fade, she'd gazed at it for a few moments before placing the flower gently back with the others on top of the grave.

Evie was still looking over to the church, wondering if she should go back again to her son's grave, when she heard a sound behind her. She turned, and it was Duncan McBride, an Anstruther lad who'd recently come back from France to recover from a shell blast that had taken his left arm. His head was down, and he was walking quickly, the bandage on his stump starting to unravel. Evie could hear him muttering to himself and then he started to sob. The raw sound of it caught at her heart and she began walking towards him, gently calling his name. Duncan looked up, his face terrified, and in the next second, he was frantically wading into the sea.

Evie ran after him – he was already up to his thighs in

water. Her skirt held her back but she used all her strength to catch him as he tried to throw himself headlong into the sea. Grabbing him with both arms she held on tightly to his thin body.

'Let me go!' he screamed. 'I'm no use to anyone now!'

'You are of use, you are Duncan McBride, you're still your mother's son... Come on, come with me!'

He was still fighting against her, sobbing uncontrollably.

She stood firm even though her feet were slipping on the shingle. 'Duncan,' she shouted. 'It's me, Evie Munro... we were in the same class at school... remember? We got the strap off Miss Forsyth on the same day for eating treacle toffee.'

He glanced at her. His eyes were wild, but he stopped struggling and seemed to quieten.

'Evie...' he said, frowning.

'Yes, Evie Munro... I'm a friend of your sister, Anne.'

His teeth were starting to chatter now but he was looking at her again.

'Come on, Duncan... let's go and get you a hot cup of tea, hey.'

Evie almost cried with relief when she felt him start to yield and, as she took a step, so did he. Once they were out of the water and onto the beach, gently she urged him to sit so that she could reapply the loops of bandage that covered the remains of his poor arm. As she removed the bandage, she saw the vicious bright red scar and puckered skin. She'd never seen an amputation before. 'It's healed very well,' she soothed. He nodded then and held still while she bandaged the stump.

'It's good that you still have the use of your elbow,' she added. 'It will make a big difference to what you are able to do with the arm.'

He didn't seem to connect properly with what she was saying but at least he was paying some attention and he'd started to flex his arm at the elbow.

'Come on, let's get you back home. Your mam will be going spare wondering where you've got to.'

Meekly, Duncan allowed Evie to pull him up from the sand and they walked together back towards the McBrides' cottage. As she led him home, she began to feel a glow of satisfaction at what she'd just achieved. It made her recall something that Rita had mentioned to her only last week. The war required an ever-increasing number of nurses, and with Evie's experience of treating wounds, maybe she should think about volunteering. In fact, Rita had heard that the War Office were looking for women with the right experience to join up as special military nurse probationers. Evie had barely taken notice until now but helping Duncan had caused something to reignite... she would ask Rita for more details of the training, this was what she could do and she could do it well. Already, her mind was going over what supplies she would need to replenish her medical bag and what kind of uniform she would be wearing when she was an army nurse.

PART TWO

I love the touch of the clean salt spray on my hands and hair and face,

I love to feel the long ship leap, when she feels the sea's embrace,

While down below is the straining hull, o'erhead the gulls and clouds,

And the clean wind comes 'cross the vast sea space, and sings its song in the shrouds.

But now in my dreams, besides the sounds one always hears at sea,

I hear the mutter of distant guns, which call and call to me...

From 'Guns at Sea', by Imtarfa (pseudonym) – thought to be a naval officer in a military hospital on Malta during the First World War

CHAPTER 11

HMHS BRITANNIC, 23 DECEMBER 1915

What in heaven's name is that girl doing? Iris couldn't believe what she was seeing. They'd only been on board for a few hours and all the nurses were laughing uproariously as their one and only probationer cavorted around, lifting her uniform above her knees, showing her shapely legs and black wool stockings for all the world to see.

In her many years of nursing, Iris had never seen such a display by someone on duty. She'd worked hard to achieve her own status as a trained nurse, she'd had to revise all areas to convince the army selection panel that she was cut out to be a Queen Alexandra's Imperial Military Nurse. She was proud of the grey uniform with its bronze medal pinned to a scarlet-trimmed cape and impressive handkerchief cap. And now, after a full year of service at Netley military hospital in Southampton, she had gained a red stripe on the sleeve of her uniform. Sister Phelps had given special mention to this girl, she'd said she was sharp as a tack and had been a top candidate on the special military training programme for war nurses, plus she'd worked as a fisher girl, so, like Iris, the sea was in her blood. But if she wanted to fulfil her potential on board a hospital ship, the girl would have to apply herself far more seriously than this.

'Stop that at once,' Iris bellowed, as the tousle-haired nurse pulled her uniform even higher, exposing her knicker legs.

'Sorry,' the nurse shouted down the ward, immediately dropping her skirt so it fell crumpled to regulation ankle length. 'I was just showing the other lasses how to dance a cancan.'

'This is a hospital ship, and even though we do not yet have any patients, you are on a ward!' Iris motioned for the girl to walk down to her, as the other three young women, all newly qualified Voluntary Aid Detachment nurses, stood wide-eyed and silent in their brand-new starched aprons with scarlet crossed bibs.

Iris pressed her mouth into a firm line. 'What is your name?' she asked, as soon as the girl stood before her. She was smaller than Iris, but her lithe body and strong shoulders served to accentuate the slim waist from which her apron was hanging unravelled at the ties.

'I'm Evie Munro,' she said, meeting Iris with a level gaze.

Iris felt a flush rise from beneath her broad starched collar. She knew that her supervisory role rested heavily on this, her first day on the ward, but when Sister was off duty, she was in charge, and there had to be discipline and some level of decorum amongst the nurses.

'I know you are a probationer, but you've already had some basic training, so you should know better,' Iris said, trying to muster authority.

'I'm sorry,' the girl repeated with a smile, her Scottish accent lively and, to Iris's ears, mildly teasing. 'It's a good job I didn't get to the part with the cartwheel.'

Iris heard one of the other nurses giggle. She had noticed this Nurse Munro at the centre of things during lifeboat training earlier in the day, making the others laugh. It seemed that she was popular with the group. In which case it was even more important to make sure that she behaved appropriately.

'Do not let it happen again,' Iris said, trying to put an edge to her voice. 'If you need to dance, do it off duty... and tie up your apron. Maintaining a smart uniform is essential.'

'Yes, Nurse Purefoy,' Nurse Munro nodded, her full mouth on the edge of a smile. Despite a fleeting trace of sadness, the young woman's blue eyes were full of life and with her heart-shaped face and wavy hair springing out from beneath a crisp nurse's cap, she was a natural beauty. Even in the stiff uniform – or maybe more so because of it – there was a wildness about her that was captivating, irresistible.

'Right, nurses,' Iris called, striding up the ward with Nurse Munro trotting behind her, tying her apron and straightening her cap as she went. 'As you know we are sailing to the port of Moudros on the Greek island of Lemnos in the Aegean Sea. This is our first mission and we will be collecting over three thousand wounded men. We are an acute surgical ward, which means we will be receiving the most severely injured soldiers. That's why we are next to the operating theatre. In order to achieve the required standard, we need to be fully prepared and get very used to working together as a team. All stores will have to be checked, all procedures worked through so that we are ready and able to offer the best possible standard of care. You have all spent at least some time on the wards of a military hospital, so you know how demanding the work will be. We need to pull together... Those of you who have never been on a ship before may suffer some seasickness. Sister Phelps has already started to feel a little queasy. The sickness will pass in a few days, and then you will have your sea legs...' Iris clapped her hands. 'Now, we have work to do, nurses. Let's get on!'

. . .

Nurse Munro might not have made a favourable first impression, but my word did she work hard that first afternoon. Iris had never seen a nurse so unrelenting. She could shift huge boxes of supplies that were only usually managed by male porters on the military ward where Iris had previously worked. All with a smile and an unreserved sense of humour – which would, Iris thought, need to be tempered once they had patients on board. She had an authority about her as well, not in an over-bearing way, it seemed that she was the one with all the ideas and the rest were happy to follow. Iris had fallen lucky.

The three VADs – Nurse Franklin, Nurse Kipling and Nurse Dooley – were also making a good start. Miriam Dooley, a sturdy young woman with a direct gaze and pale red hair pinned back savagely, as if to display the full force of her integrity, had worked as a stewardess so she already had her sea legs. Nurse Franklin and Nurse Kipling were increasingly pale-faced against the blue of their uniforms. Iris called to them from behind the table where she was sorting dressings. 'You both need to take some rest. I'll measure out a dose of peppermint water and spirit of chloroform... go to your cabins and stay there for as long as you need.'

'I'll check on them later, we share the same cabin,' Nurse Munro called as she strode down the ward, her arms stacked with a huge pile of white cotton sheets, ready to make up the iron-framed hospital beds that lined what would have been the first-class dining room, if the *Britannic* hadn't been requisitioned for war even before she'd been fitted out. Iris still hadn't quite adjusted to the incongruity of being on board a vessel, equivalent in stature and identical in layout to the *Olympic* but with most of the luxurious fittings and fixtures removed. The first shock had been seeing the giant ship in dock without any trace of White Star livery; instead her hull was painted white with large red crosses and a horizontal green stripe. At night the ship was illuminated with a string of green lights so there could be no doubt that she was carrying wounded men and therefore, according to the Geneva convention, should be free from enemy attack.

That first day on board, before they'd set sail, it had felt strange being back on a ship after almost a year spent on dry land at Netley. Having trained at the Liverpool Royal Infirmary, the Southampton hospital had seemed huge, daunting at first. And with the daily influx of many injured soldiers, some still in their dusty bloodstained uniforms, brought by ships crossing directly from France, the emptiness of the outward-bound vessel had seemed quiet, too quiet. Inevitably, as she'd lain on her bunk in a single berth which would have been a second-class cabin on a cruise liner, she'd missed Roisin. There'd been a flurry of letters from her cabin mate early on, when she'd started her work as a nanny in Boston, but nothing for ages. She was probably just busy, they all were. Miss Duchamp had written, telling her about life in New York and repeating the invitation to visit 'after all this is over'. But there hadn't been one word from her stowaway. It felt like Jack Rosetti had disappeared into thin air. Inevitably, however, his smiling face often danced into her dreams. It was utterly infuriating.

Gazing down the length of the ward, seeing it take shape, Iris was feeling more and more fired up. She'd been quickly inspired by the sense of purpose and the buzz of activity around her; even seeing what would have been the ballroom fitted out with operating stations and the pantries that would have stored fine foods being stacked with medical supplies... it felt positive, a good use of the giant ship.

Later, Sister Phelps made an appearance, still pale from her seasickness but able to walk the length of the long ward with her eyes narrowed, checking every single detail. Iris hovered in the background, directing her nurses but aware of Sister's broad shoulders and straight back as she walked stiffly in her QAIMN's uniform. Sister had had a fearsome reputation at Netley, but Iris had only brushed past her in the corridor. Now, the formidable woman was very present, and Iris was trying not to be daunted by her. When she reached the end of the ward, Sister turned on her heel and stood surveying the lines of beds and the activity of the nurses, her chest rose as she drew in a slow breath and then she offered Iris a single nod.

'So, it looks like we've done all right then,' Nurse Munro chirruped, not quite far enough under her breath.

Iris turned to give her probationer a firm glance, but all she got in return was a cheeky smile that was impossible to resist. 'Yes, we are definitely doing a good job,' she said quietly, gesturing for Nurse Munro to get on with her tasks as Sister marched back down the ward.

Evie was sure Sister Phelps had to be a close relative of her Anstruther school teacher, Miss Forsyth; the same greying mousy hair, corseted frame and stern expression. She prayed that Sister didn't have the same mean streak. Every summer, Miss Forsyth had brought strawberries into class, to sit and eat while the pupils were slaving over their sums – never sharing one, not even with Susie McDonald, the class swot. That was until she made the mistake of sending freckle-faced Gilbert Anderson to stand in the corner close to where she'd rested her basket. The glee on his face when he'd started to eat those strawberries, the juice running down his chin. It made Evie smile every time she thought about it. He'd got the stick so hard for it, but even as the teacher thrashed him, he'd been laughing. Gilbert had been one of the first to join up, Evie had seen him back in the village, proudly wearing his Royal Highlanders uniform... never imagining that he'd be shot and killed even before the end of that first year. She swallowed hard, keeping back the tears as she thought of the other boys from her class who'd also been lost and of course, young Duncan McBride, whose life had been changed forever by his injury.

She hadn't told the army people at the interview that she could suture a wound and she was a dab hand with a knife, not wanting them to think that she had ideas above her station, but she'd brought her medical bag and her instruments onto the ship, just in case. When she'd seen the operating tables illuminated by electric light and the metal trolleys and equipment that had been set up in the ballroom, it had sent a pulse of excitement through her body. She'd already overheard two keen young surgeons discussing incisions and amputations. Maybe she would get the chance to be part of a surgical team. She wouldn't be able to approach Sister Phelps, but she was hoping that Nurse Purefoy would be willing to let her explore all aspects of nursing, including theatre work. Evie was fascinated by Nurse Purefoy – her strict words and disciplined demeanour were regularly undercut by the sparkle of her sympathetic blue-green eyes. Evie knew that she could have come down on her much harder when she'd seen her doing that dance, but she hadn't, she'd been fair. She also sensed, though, that she wouldn't be able to mess with her; below that sharp, professional surface there was iron will and passion waiting to burst out.

When her shift was over and she'd dined in the vast mess room with Miriam Dooley, they returned to the grand cabin they shared with Lucy Kipling and Charlotte Franklin. It had been converted into a dormitory from one of the most luxurious state-rooms, and a section of carved panelling, a posh-looking side table and a bevelled mirror still remained. Charlotte had travelled first class on the *Olympic* with her maiden aunt when they'd done a tour of the continent, so she was familiar with how the cabin might have been laid out. Evie breathed it all in, wanting to enjoy every tiny detail. She'd never met a rich person before, never mind one with such distinctive features – a full mouth accentuated off duty by bright red lipstick, and a shock of jet-black, wavy hair. Once she'd listened to enough of Charlotte's stories of travels and balls and eligible young men, she'd adjusted to her way of speaking, and thought she seemed like a girl who'd muck in with the rest of them. Lucy Kipling was a pale-skinned, quiet young woman from London, a headmaster's daughter whose grey-eyed gaze would have been impossible to read if it hadn't been for the ever-changing set of her mouth. Lucy had listened thoughtfully to Charlotte's story of the grand tour and, even though Evie hadn't quite worked her out yet, she'd seen her suppressing a giggle when Charlotte told them about her Aunt Dolores getting them lost in the streets of Venice and having to accept assistance from a cheeky gondolier who took them a very long way round to the hotel and flirted outrageously with Charlotte the whole time.

Lucy and Charlotte were sleeping off their seasickness – what Charlotte called a touch of 'mal de mer', and Miriam had flopped down on her bed to read a magazine. But, as ever, Evie was restless and needing to be on the move. Pulling the pins out of her hair, she sighed as she ran her hands through it. Crouching down to root under her bed, she pulled her red checked headscarf from the well-stocked medical bag that she'd stashed next to her cork life jacket. Tying the scarf in place, she called out to the others,

'I'm going to nip up top, for my own grand tour.' Miriam glanced up from her reading and started to giggle.

As she made her way up the stairs towards the promenade deck, she began to feel desperate for the sea breeze on her face. It felt glorious to be riding so high above the water, and to be out on the ocean and not confined to the shore. The fisher girls never got the chance to go out on the boats – there was an ancient superstition that women were bad luck and Evie had never known any women allowed on the steam drifters apart from two new brides who had married in Yarmouth and travelled back to Scotland with their husbands. But her daddy had taken her out as a girl; he'd even started to teach her about navigation and he'd let her have a go at the wheel, telling her that one day, maybe she could be the first ever woman to fish the herring.

Evie leaned on the rail at the side of the ship, watching the spray, letting her mind roam... Tomorrow would be Christmas Eve, the first she'd spent away from the village. She was glad. It always ended in a row between her and Sadie and then she'd go off to Rita's to drown her sorrows and stagger back home worse for wear. It was time for a fresh start – not that she would have wished for a war just so that she could have the opportunity to see a bit of the world. Feeling restless again, she set herself the task of walking around the vast deck, getting to know the full layout of the huge vessel, claiming her territory.

Seeing the shape of someone enjoying a smoke, leaning on the rail of the boat deck, she was about to slip by quietly when she realised it was Nurse Purefoy. She looked relaxed, at ease with herself, and Evie did wonder if she should simply pass by, leave her to her solitude. But something stopped her from doing that, she was intrigued by this woman and wanted to know more about her.

'Hello there,' she called softly, not wishing to startle her.

Nurse Purefoy shot up, instantly chucking her cigarette over the rail.

'Sorry,' Evie said, coming up beside her. 'It's only me, I didn't mean for you to waste your smoke.'

She could see that Nurse Purefoy was rattled, desperately trying to assemble the on-duty demeanour that she'd worn all day. Evie tried a smile but that didn't seem to work so she thrust a hand in her pocket and pulled out the silver whisky flask that she always carried. 'Fancy a swig of this?'

Nurse Purefoy looked a little startled and then she narrowed her eyes for a second when she saw Evie's red headscarf. 'I knew you were trouble right from the start, Nurse Munro, and now I find out you've been secreting a flask of liquor...'

For a moment Evie couldn't read her expression, but then she saw the corners of her mouth begin to curl in a slow smile – and Nurse Purefoy was fishing in her own pocket now, pulling out a slim flask with an engraved pattern.

'And besides, I have my own supply... thank you very much.' She was already unscrewing the cap and offering a 'cheers'. 'Don't you dare tell a living soul that you found me out here smoking and drinking.'

Evie giggled as she unscrewed her own flask and clinked it against Nurse Purefoy's. 'Your secret's safe with me... And don't you tell Sister Phelps about my flask... or she'll be after confiscating it, so she can drink it herself!'

'Oi!' Nurse Purefoy warned. 'I can't get involved with any chit-chat about Sister... but you can stay here with me for a while if you want. Tell me a bit about yourself – I hear you've been a fisher girl...'

Evie was happy to lean shoulder to shoulder with Nurse Purefoy to tell stories of the herring season. She could sense that her colleague was listening intently, taking it all in, and she seemed to have a similar fascination with the sea. And when Evie asked her about her own background, she was thrilled to hear that she'd worked as a first-class stewardess on the *Olympic*, sister ship to the *Britannic* and, of course, the infamous *Titanic*. Evie couldn't get enough description of the luxury liner and the staff and all those posh passengers. She could have listened all night... She was begging for more when

Nurse Purefoy gave a yawn and threw her final cigarette stub over the rail.

'Come on, Nurse Munro, time for our beds...'

Evie's head was buzzing, she knew that she wouldn't be able to get to sleep for ages. 'I'll probably just walk a bit more around the deck... But can we meet up again tomorrow night in the same spot?'

'Yes, that would be nice,' Nurse Purefoy said, her voice edging once more towards a more formal tone. 'Goodnight, Nurse Munro.'

Evie reached out a hand. 'Please call me Evie, when we're off duty.'

She saw Nurse Purefoy take a breath, pause for a moment, then she said, 'Yes, I think that would be all right... and you can call me Iris, but only while we're out here, like this. You must keep it quiet though; Sister's put me in charge of you and all the brand-new VADs, so we have to be professional when we're on the ward... and you need to know that I will be just as strict with you at work. Understood?'

'Understood,' Evie grinned, as Iris took hold of her outstretched hand and gave it a firm shake.

CHAPTER 12

Once Iris was back in her cabin, she began to feel exhausted. She'd been grateful for the lively chat with Nurse Munro, it had taken her away from the haunting thoughts of Sam King that had dogged her while she'd been out at the side of the ship. It had always been her routine to have a smoke and then go off to see him at the bar. Sam had been killed just over seven months ago when the *Lusitania* had been torpedoed off the coast of Ireland, tantalisingly close to home. How ironic that she'd felt relieved when he'd written to tell her that he'd switched from the *Olympic* after it had been converted to a troop ship and joined the *Lusitania* to fill the stewarding gaps left by the young men who'd joined up – including his own two sons, Louis and Phillipe. Working on the horrendously busy military wards at Netley, she'd only once managed to meet up with him when she'd been off duty. He'd been his usual self, grumbling and laughing about the other old codgers who made up the team on the *Lusitania,* but Iris could tell that he was having a much better time in his natural environment – behind the bar on an ocean liner. Now, it seemed madness for the passenger ships to have continued back and forth to New York... but who would have thought that a German U-boat would have attacked an unarmed vessel?

Iris sighed and started to shrug off her uniform. At least it had been quick... the ship had sunk in eighteen minutes. She shuddered, taken back to the day of the sinking when she'd heard a ripple of consternation on the surgical ward and a small cry from a VAD who'd had a brother on board. Iris had finished her bandaging and walked briskly down the ward to make sure the nurse was all right, never imagining, until she'd been given the name of the ship that had been hit, that Sam might be involved. The orderly who'd told her the detail of the tragedy had said that the whole of Liverpool had been heartbroken – so many of the crew had been born and bred in the city and a crowd had been gathered on the dock to greet their loved ones off the ship. Iris knew exactly where they'd have been waiting; she'd imagined Sam coming ashore so many times, heading straight to the railway station, anxious to get home to Francine.

She'd spoken to her ward sister and managed to get a half day's leave to go and see Francine the next day. Walking alone from the train in her borrowed mourning dress – a black coat and veiled hat – the sadness almost overwhelmed her. As soon as she'd turned into Malmesbury Road, she'd seen the black bow tied to Francine's door. The street had been silent, bar one small child, a boy of about four walking with his young blonde-haired mother. With a jolt, Iris had recognised Francine's neighbour, Catherine, one of the *Titanic* widows on the street. She'd met her a few times at Francine's, so she'd raised a hand in greeting. The small wave and sad glance in return had made Iris's heart twist.

Iris had paused outside the house, her chest heaving as she'd tried to catch her breath, struggling to compose herself. 'It's all right, Sam, I'm not going to chicken out,' she'd murmured. She could almost see him then, leading the way. It had given her the push that she needed to knock on the door. She'd heard the dog barking excitedly, and it had made her ache with sadness to know that she would never see Sam greet Barney again. When the door opened, the dog had shot out expectantly, racing past Iris and onto the street. Francine had appeared at the door, her black and silver hair dishevelled, her eyes dulled by grief, the skirt of her mourning dress stained with some spill.

'Yes?' she'd breathed, looking past Iris, not recognising her.

'Francine,' Iris had said gently, lifting her mesh veil.

'Oh, Iris,' she'd croaked, suddenly unsteady on her feet.

Iris had grabbed hold of her, pulling her close, feeling her body convulse with grief. 'I am so sorry,' Iris had said, her voice breaking on a sob.

'Me too,' Francine had gasped, her voice almost a whisper. 'I got a wireless message saying, *Much regret, Samuel King not saved.* That is all Cunard sent. And they haven't found him, Iris, they have not found his body yet...' She'd looked up, her eyes dry but her chest heaving with sobs. Iris had held her, keeping her steady. When Francine had stepped back, she'd composed herself and then she'd called for the dog. As soon as Barney had scampered back inside, Francine had run a hand through her hair and straightened her skirt. 'I am so glad to see you, *ma chérie.*'

Walking into the hallway, Iris had been sure she'd felt a shift in the air and heard the murmur of Sam's voice. Thinking of it even now made the tiny hairs at the back of her neck prickle with sensation. Even though her rational mind still told her that it was nonsense, she was sure that she'd felt Sam's presence there still, in the house.

Francine had murmured, 'You can feel it too, hey...'

Iris had had no choice but to nod.

'It's nothing to worry about, *chérie*. The ones who have gone, they are still holding onto us... they don't go till we do.' Francine's matter-of-fact tone had required no reply.

Iris stood in her petticoat, staring at her reflection, her mind still with Sam and Francine. Seeing a photograph pinned next to the mirror... her own smiling face next to Roisin's, both in their stewardesses' uniforms, gazing confidently into the camera, she began to find her way back to the present. The picture had been snapped by one of the photographers who regularly visited the *Olympic*. He'd seen them chatting and laughing over some funny story that Michael had told them and had asked if he could take a picture. Iris hadn't thought they'd ever see it, but he'd developed it and brought a copy back for each of them on their next trip to New York. Seeing that happy moment from what felt like another lifetime made Iris smile. It was the only personal item she'd brought, apart from a gold velvet cushion with a tasselled trim that Francine had made for her cabin. She'd decided to travel light in her new role as an army nurse, so the rest of her belongings had been left for safe-keeping with Francine. She'd had the photograph pinned where she could see it since that first day at Netley hospital when she'd returned to the nurses' quarters after a gruelling shift on the surgical ward. Seeing the horrors of war seared onto the faces and the bodies of those injured soldiers had been life-changing. She'd known then that she would have to draw on every ounce of her nursing experience and all her memories of happier times past, to stick to the path she had chosen.

Sam had been the first to use the phrase... *the path chosen*... when he'd questioned her about whether she truly knew what she'd be letting herself in for. She'd made out that she did, of course she did, and he'd offered a grim smile. She wondered what he'd think now, of her going back to sea after what had happened to him. He would have tried to dissuade her, she was sure of that, but once she'd stood firm, she knew he would have understood because he'd been the same. He couldn't bear to be confined to dry land for too long – he needed to feel the sea breeze and be on the move. He would have been pleased though, that she still had her base back in Southampton with Francine – a true friend who felt like family, and a cupboard full of belongings ready to reclaim when war was done. She'd shown Francine the diamond necklace before she'd left to join the *Britannic,* and her friend had been thrilled, making Iris try it on there and then. Miss Duchamp had been right, the choker fitted perfectly and it really suited her. Thinking of the diamonds sparkling in the light made Iris feel a glow of pleasure that helped to calm her even more. If anything happened to her on the ship, she'd told Francine to keep the necklace, sell it to raise some money for anything that she needed.

Turning from the mirror, Iris reached for her high-necked white cotton nightie, slipped it over her head and then took up her tortoiseshell brush to go through her hair, one section at a time. The thrum of the ship's engine deep in the heart of the ship had already started to soothe her towards sleep, as it always did.

Iris made sure that the continuing preparation for the reception of casualties proceeded smoothly the next day. Nurse Franklin and Nurse Kipling were still a little under the weather, but they had both returned to work, and it was good to see them chatting and laughing together as they worked. Iris had a few niggles about Charlotte Franklin; she was thin and seemed erratic in her mood at times. She prayed that she wouldn't be one of those nurses who swooned and fainted at the first sight of blood. Nurse Munro was bright-eyed and full of energy as always as she worked side by side with Miriam Dooley. All in all, Iris had a good team and she was determined to get the best out of them.

By afternoon the ward was spotless, organised and ready to receive a visit from some of the doctors who formed part of the *Britannic*'s sizeable surgical team. Iris had her nurses lined up and waiting as the white-coated surgeons approached. She was confident that they would make a very good impression.

'Iris?' called a familiar voice.

'Dr Mayhew,' she gasped, quickly reining in a too enthusiastic greeting of the smiling young doctor when she saw Sister Phelps glance back over her shoulder with narrowed eyes.

'Fancy seeing you here, so good to have you on board...' he whispered conspiratorially.

Iris spoke quietly to him as he hung back for a few moments while the rest of the doctors walked steadily down the ward, trying to keep pace with Sister Phelps as she forged ahead.

Iris spoke rapidly, aware of her junior nurses eavesdropping on every word. 'I know we're not meant to mingle on the decks and Matron has even suggested roping off some areas to try and stop fraternisation between the nurses and male crew... but I'll look out for you in the dining room, see if we can make arrangements for a catch-up.'

He gave a nod and trotted after the group, glancing back with a cheeky grin once he'd regained the ground he'd lost. Iris stood with a spot of bright pink on each cheek, not daring to glance at any of her nurses. She murmured for them to listen to what the senior surgeon, Dr J.C. Hobbs, was saying about the advantages of using a Thomas splint to stabilise fractured femurs... Many lives had been saved by the simple metal device which reduced complications from a traumatic injury where much internal blood loss occurred. Iris had nursed patients with the revolutionary splint many times at Netley. It was a shame that it took a war to drive ahead such important advancements in medical technique.

Later, after the tour of the ward and operating theatre had been deemed satisfactory by Sister Phelps, the staff were given some free time. Iris smiled as she saw her nurses link arms and start to chat animatedly. Nurse Munro dominated the group, as always, but Iris could see that she now had lively competition from Nurse Franklin... Nurse Kipling and Nurse Dooley started to giggle as they all filed past on their way off the ward. Once the sound of their voices had faded, Iris slowly exhaled, glancing around the deserted ward.

It wasn't until the *Britannic* reached Naples to take on coal that Iris was able to snatch a brief chat with Dr Mayhew. The whole crew had been up on deck, thrilled to experience coming into harbour. As the four huge buff-coloured funnels of the ship gleamed against the backdrop of a cloud-topped Vesuvius, Iris breathed in the atmosphere, wishing that she could go ashore, see some of the sights.

That evening during her secret liaison with Evie, as they stood at the side listening to the sounds of Naples settling for the night, Evie started to laugh at the wavering voice of a Neapolitan man singing. Iris was desperately trying to dissuade her friend from singing a Scottish ballad in reply, when they both became aware of a man's voice calling softly through the gloomy, greenish light of the ship.

'Somebody's calling your name,' Evie giggled. 'It's a man.'

'I know who it is, I told him to look out for us tonight,' Iris replied, stubbing out her cigarette and tossing it into the dark waters of the harbour.

'Come on, come with me,' she whispered, taking Evie's hand.

'Why are we whispering?' Evie whispered, starting to giggle again.

'Dr Mayhew,' Iris called softly. 'Where are you?'

'I'm here,' he said, stepping out of a shadow.

Evie drew in a sharp breath. 'Jesus, you scared the living

daylights... Oh, I know who you are, you're one of the surgeons who came to look around the ward.'

'Yes, I am,' he smiled, reaching out to shake Evie's hand. 'Adam Mayhew... And you are?'

'Evie... ha! Just had a thought, Adam and Evie.'

'Except this isn't the Garden of Eden,' Iris added firmly.

Evie started to chuckle and at the sound of footsteps and other whispered conversation further down the deck, Iris shushed her.

'Look, don't worry,' Adam said. 'I know Sister Phelps and the other senior nurses have their views on keeping the nurses separate from doctors and ship's crew, but it is so old-fashioned... in less than a week we're going to be thrown together in an operating theatre, fighting to save patients' lives. If we get reported, I'll tell them that we were discussing medical cases and surgical techniques.'

'Can we do that anyway?' Evie piped up.

Adam laughed. 'You have a very keen probationer here, Iris... Exactly what we need for fighting a war.'

'She's one of the best I've ever worked with,' Iris smiled, 'and if you two want to discuss surgical techniques... who am I to stand in your way.'

Iris could see Evie brimming with pleasure at her words. 'Well, that's even better, isn't it,' Evie declared. 'How can Sister object to us furthering our knowledge... we could have nightly seminars or something.'

Adam nodded and Evie started to grin.

'But...' Iris said, 'Nurse Munro here will have to wait until we've had a little chat first... maybe she could take a turn around the deck.'

While Evie went for a walk, Iris and Adam reminisced about their time on the *Olympic*. She was surprised to learn that Dr O'Malley had stayed on to serve as ship's doctor on the liner.

'It's now a troop ship – I hope none of those soldiers need an appendix removing,' Adam smiled grimly.

Iris sucked in a breath. 'That was some night, wasn't it... even before the ship started to rock with that storm.'

'One of many storms, from what I remember,' Adam continued. Then, as they revisited the glamour of the transatlantic liners, he described evenings in the first-class restaurant with the orchestra playing and then later in the smoking room, with glasses of brandy and cigars. And Iris thought of the Atlantic breeze, the promise of New York and that one night she'd danced on the promenade deck.

'Happy days, hey,' Adam sighed, a tinge of sadness in his voice.

'As they say, you don't know what you've got till it's gone.'

They stood together in companiable silence, both lost in their own thoughts for a few moments until Iris started to giggle at the sound of Evie returning. She was singing 'The Bonnie Banks o' Loch Lomond' and the Neapolitan man had now increased his volume so much that a dog somewhere on dry land had started to howl.

'I told that girl not to be singing any Scottish ballads,' she laughed. 'We'll have Sister Phelps awake and then there'll be hell to pay.'

Adam was laughing now, as Evie came into view.

'For goodness' sake, Dr Mayhew, talk to her about surgery will you?' Iris begged as the howling dog set off others, which immediately resulted in shouting voices from the decks below and from dry land.

The next morning, Iris stood with pride at the top of the ward surveying the equally spaced beds made up with pristine white linen. All pillowcases facing the same way and hospital corners sharp. Nurse Munro and Nurse Franklin were swabbing the floor with a strong disinfectant solution. Evie gently teased Charlotte, who had never held a mop in her life and was complaining about it chafing her hands. The clean tang of the mop water was pleasing and made Iris pull back her shoulders and give a satisfied smile. She'd just come from the adjoining theatres – nothing could look shinier or more ready. Even Sister Phelps had no more suggestions other than to say that perhaps the nurses could have some well-earned leisure time. Nothing wrong with taking exercise out on deck, breathing the sea air, enjoying the views of the Mediterranean Islands. And Sister had even announced that the swimming pool would be open for use if any of the nurses wanted to swim. Bathing dresses would be provided and, of course, it would be strictly women only.

Iris had once tried out the pool on board the *Olympic*. Roisin had been a good swimmer and she'd dared Iris to join her for a secret dip when they'd been delayed at Southampton. It had been an exhilarating experience, the thrill of sneaking in there, and Iris had waded into the shallow end of the pool up to her waist. She'd never had the opportunity to learn to swim and, having worked with old hands like Sam, she'd always been told that it was best for crew members not to learn, so that if they went in the water they'd cling to the wreckage and wait to be rescued. Wear the life jacket and float till you get picked up, was what Sam always said. But when she'd seen Roisin gliding through the water, she'd asked to be shown the basics. She didn't necessarily want to try and swim, but she was interested to know how it was done. Roisin had managed to get her lying in the water and she'd held her hands while she'd practised kicking with her legs. By that time, Iris had started to feel shivery, and when they'd heard a door opening in the changing room, they'd both leapt out and wrapped themselves in towels, not daring to go back for fear they'd get caught.

She didn't feel like having another go, but Evie had been

keen and she'd been full of it when she came back up on deck that evening.

'I can swim like a fish, even though the fish is missing a fin,' she'd laughed. 'But I'll keep practising, so when I go back to Anstruther, I'll be able to swim out into the sea and back again, feel my body in the water.'

Evie's voice sounded light-hearted, but Iris detected a note of melancholy. There was something Evie wasn't telling her, Iris was sure of it, but she already knew enough of her friend to not push for information. She would have to wait for whatever it was to emerge.

Instead, she linked Evie's arm as they watched a glorious gold, pink and purple sunset. Iris wondered what it would be like to be on a leisure trip aboard a cruise liner in this part of the world, enjoying the warmth of the sun and passing beautiful landmarks – the distinctive red coast of Portugal, the grey Rock of Gibraltar that towered above the ship, the narrow Straits of Messina guarded by Mount Etna, and so many golden islands. By day the sea was a sapphire blue, but at night as the glowing white, green-lighted hospital ship steadily made her way across, the waters were mysterious. Iris knew that the vessel would look strange from the shore, lit up as she was when all other wartime vessels were darkened. She wondered if the hospital ship looked unreal, like a floating ghost on the water.

CHAPTER 13

At last they were approaching the Aegean island of Lemnos and sailing into the deep harbour of Moudros – the gathering point for all casualties from the battles of Gallipoli, Greek Macedonia, and Mesopotamia. Last night, Evie had snuck into the operating theatres and seen the glint of steel instruments and the operating tables ready and waiting. She hadn't known if she felt terrified or excited. Dr Mayhew had promised that he would make sure she got some experience in theatre and the thought sent a thrill through her body.

As they sailed into harbour, she stood close to Iris at the side of the ship, feeling the thump of her heart against her ribs as they listened to a barrage of shelling and gunfire. When a big one fell, they felt the ship vibrate. Iris shot a glance at Evie and reached out to take her hand. The *Britannic* was lively in the choppy water and the sky an ominous grey; they would have to wait till darkness for the lighters to be able to make their way across the bay with casualties, then the stretchers would be hoisted by derricks up onto the ship. Evie felt as if an electric current were running up and down her spine, she shivered with it.

The Allied armies were under constant bombardment from Turkish guns, the air laden with the smell of cordite and something earthier, more primal. Evie tried to imagine what it must feel like to be a soldier lying wounded on a beach, listening to the harsh cacophony of war against a background of the sound of the waves. She'd heard stories from an experienced VAD who'd been on another hospital ship during the early Gallipoli campaign, in the blazing August heat. The nurse had told of men arriving on board badly injured but also suffering terribly with heat stroke, maggoty wounds and infestations of lice. The nurses already knew from their preparatory talks given by the senior surgeon, Dr Hobbs, that more men were being evacuated due to fevers, dysentery, colic, pleurisy and tonsillitis than gunshot wounds. He'd said it was exactly the situation that the British and French armies had faced during the Crimean War, sixty years ago, when they'd fought the Russians. Turkey had been a loyal ally then, apparently. It made Evie's head spin to think about the absurdity of war. Dr Hobbs hadn't mentioned the work of Florence Nightingale in the Crimea, but Iris had filled her in later about the contribution Miss Nightingale had made at Scutari hospital to enforce hygiene standards, fight infection and save so many soldiers' lives. Evie loved to have the electric light on the *Britannic* but if she ever did get the chance to carry a lantern and mop a soldier's brow, she would do it, even though Iris seemed pretty sure all the stuff about their esteemed founder of modern nursing being a gentle soul carrying a lamp was probably made up by the newspapers. No nurse worth her salt could fail to understand the tough approach and at times physical strength required to nurse patients, especially severely injured casualties of war.

Although the *Britannic* was out of range of shelling, Matron had given instruction that the nurses must not linger at the rail once the ship dropped anchor. Evie had enjoyed seeing the ever-changing landscape as they'd sailed around the coast of

Britain and then through the Mediterranean. Having never travelled further than the east coast during the herring season, the experience had been magical. She'd always wanted to go out on the ships and now, with this first voyage, Iris was already telling her that she'd caught the 'travel bug'. When this was all over, she was determined to sail the Atlantic, see the Statue of Liberty and explore New York City. By that time she would have her nursing qualification... maybe she could find work as a nurse stewardess, like Iris.

Iris pulled her away from the rail. It was time to go back to the ward for a final run-through and then all the nurses had been ordered to rest. The casualties couldn't be moved during daylight, they needed the cover of darkness. The hospital ship was out of range but for those men lying on stretchers waiting to be evacuated, there was a risk of being hit by enemy fire. No matter how hard Evie tried to imagine what was coming, she couldn't quite grasp the reality.

'You'll just get on with it,' Iris said with a tight smile.

Evie prayed her friend was right, as with a final glance to the darkening sea and grey sky, she heard the staccato rattle of gunfire ricochet from the shore.

'Nurse Munro!' Iris screamed, 'This man is haemorrhaging, I need more swabs now!'

Evie swallowed hard, her throat dry as she hurtled along the deck. Grabbing the white cotton squares she ran to the side of a stretcher dripping fresh blood. The soldier's face was ashen; he appeared unresponsive as Iris pressed the fresh swabs hard against a welling hole in his exposed abdomen. Her hands and apron were bright red now, as the young man's life blood continued to flow relentlessly onto the deck.

She snatched an extra breath to try and stop herself from

feeling woozy. Further down the deck a soldier was screaming and trying to struggle up from his stretcher. She saw Miriam grappling with him and then Charlotte, pale-faced, and frozen to the spot, tried to make a move to help, but she needed to support herself against the ship's rail. The next moment Lucy sprinted past to help... Even in her heightened state Evie couldn't help but feel surprised by the tenacity of her quietly spoken colleague.

'This is a fresh wound, he must have been hit by enemy fire as he left the beach,' Iris shouted, grabbing more swabs.

Evie's head was spinning, her chest felt tight, she could hardly breathe. She looked more closely at the tousle-haired soldier... He was no more than a boy, nineteen at most, his face was slack, his pupils dilated, no rise and fall of his chest.

'He isn't breathing,' she said firmly, as Iris glanced agitatedly in her direction. Then she saw her feel at the young soldier's neck with two fingers. Iris nodded and straightened up from the stretcher, picking up the blood-smeared label that was pinned to his tunic and reading aloud, 'Private Simon Jenkinson, Lancashire Fusiliers, broken ankle... His initial injury was relatively minor,' she muttered.

Evie stood gazing down at the dead boy, his pale brown hair dusted with sand, like a child who'd been playing out on the beach. Iris murmured a quick prayer. Evie swallowed hard and then reached for the rough wool blanket that lay askew at the bottom of the stretcher. She pulled it gently up over his lifeless body and then covered his poor, blanched face. There was no more time for last offices; hopefully the ship's chaplain would be able to attend the young man later.

At a shout from an orderly as he helped pull another stretcher over the side of the ship, Evie ran after Iris to the next man, her feet slipping in blood as she went. The turbaned soldier on the stretcher was groaning in pain, his right leg twisted out of shape and his neck covered by a grimy gauze dressing pad. Evie picked up the label attached to his dusty uniform and called out the detail... 'Sergeant Sandeep Singh, 14th Sikhs, compound fracture of the femur and neck wound.'

Iris seemed steadier now, her mouth was set. 'This man needs to go straight to theatre... I'll give him a shot of morphia first, to ease the pain.'

Evie reached for the man's hand as Iris produced a syringe from her pocket and removed the plug of cork from the needle. She stuck the injection through the man's uniform into his thigh.

'That should ease you, Sergeant Singh,' Iris said. 'We're sending you to theatre to get your leg fixed... go with him, Nurse Munro, go with him!'

Evie ran by the side of the stretcher as the orderlies moved rapidly along the alleyways. Already the patient seemed more relaxed as the morphia worked its magic.

'Over here,' a voice shouted as they entered the operating theatre. Evie paused momentarily, taking in the stark reality of the scene when she saw Sister Phelps in a white gown, ready to proceed. Thankfully, Dr Mayhew was instantly by her side, picking up the label pinned to the man's uniform. He read quickly as Evie added the extra information, 'Nurse Purefoy has just given him another dose of morphia and it seems to be taking effect.'

'That's useful to know,' Dr Mayhew said, already directing the orderlies to transfer the soldier to the wooden theatre table. In the adjoining space an injured man was screaming out in agony, his arm dangling loose by the side of the stretcher. Evie nipped across quickly and moved the arm back across his body as a young doctor held a chloroform mask over the poor soldier's face.

Evie's breath was coming quick, she was ready to act, all fired up but not sure what to do next.

'Nurse Munro has a special interest in theatre work, she will be able to assist,' Dr Mayhew called, and Evie saw Sister Phelps give a decisive nod and gesture to the handwashing sink. 'You know the routine,' she shouted.

Something clicked into place then as the ordered set of procedures that Nurse Purefoy had insisted they rehearse, time and time again, came back to her. She scrubbed her hands vigorously with carbolic soap, grabbed a white cotton theatre gown and expertly slipped her hands, one at a time, into the surgical rubber gloves. In moments she was beside the table, ready to do whatever was required.

'The fractured femur has to be the first job,' Dr Mayhew explained. Sister was already cutting through the bandage with a large pair of scissors. At the sight of white bone poking through the man's flesh, Evie sucked in a quick breath. She felt her stomach start to heave but she squeezed it back down, concentrating on the task in hand. She had never fainted in her life and she wasn't going to start now. 'We need to reduce the fracture and fit Sergeant Singh with a Thomas splint,' Mayhew said.

'I'll get the splint,' Evie called, already halfway to the equipment store where the distinctive metal and leather devices rested in a row against the wall. Evie ran through the procedure in her head. The leather ring would be fitted against the patient's groin and traction would be applied to the leg, which would be fastened securely to the bottom of the splint. In her head this had been an easy procedure, effortless almost, but as she heaved on the leg alongside Sister Phelps, she realised why surgeons developed such strong muscles.

'Well done, Nurse Munro,' Sister Phelps called across the table once the patient's leg was secure. 'We need to irrigate the open wound now – plenty of carbolic acid solution and then apply iodine.'

This was familiar territory for Evie, she had the bowls and

the liquids ready, and the job done in next to no time. Thankfully the traction had reduced the fracture so that the bone was no longer protruding. Even though they were under pressure, and she knew that a horde of other needy patients were waiting for theatre, Evie made sure to clean the wound meticulously. She knew too well the disaster that might ensue if the wound began to suppurate. As Dr Mayhew sutured, Evie prepared to remove the dressing that swaddled the man's neck... Sister had already moved along to the next operating station to help secure a many-tailed bandage around the freshly sutured abdomen of an Irish soldier who was so tall and broad, his shoulders and feet overhung the table.

As Evie peeled away the gauze pad, a dusting of sand scattered onto the operating table. She sucked in a breath: the whole side of the man's neck had been sloughed off and the wound looked nasty with clear signs of suppuration. The expanse of raw flesh must have been left without a dressing change for days. It was difficult to see where they could suture... Some stitches had been put in to close one end of the wound, but it looked raw. Awful. Evie forced herself to look again, think through logically. The stitches were secure; if they cleansed the wound thoroughly and doused with iodine, then maybe, given time, nature would do its work and the whole area would heal from the bottom layers up. It would leave a terrible scar but at least the man's life might be saved. Sphagnum moss would be useful if the suppuration increased; she'd already made sure that the ship's supply was clean and dry and stored correctly, it would work well on an excoriated wound like this.

Dr Mayhew had finished suturing the leg and he was beside her now, staring nonplussed at the neck wound. Their patient moaned and moved his head from side to side. 'He'll need some more pain relief soon... and I've no real idea what we can do with this area on his neck.'

Evie spoke up, succinctly outlining her plan.

Mayhew gave a quick smile. 'Do it; there is nothing else I can offer... He might deteriorate anyway with the open fracture of his femur... Who knows.'

In that split second, Sergeant Singh groaned and opened his eyes. Evie reached for his hand and spoke gently. 'I know you are in pain,' she said firmly, 'but the doctor will give you another injection of morphia in a moment. We've stabilised your broken leg and we're going to treat this nasty neck wound.'

The man on the table squeezed her hand and then he started to cry, big tears rolling down his cheeks and into his dark beard. Evie spoke gently again. 'Hold fast, soldier, we are doing all that we can to help you. After I've cleaned the wound and applied a dressing, we'll move you to a bed on the ward. We will look after you, Sergeant Singh.'

'Thank you, nurse... You are an angel to me, an angel,' the man croaked.

By the time they had their casualty settled, removed to the ward, and Evie had the theatre table washed down and sprayed with carbolic acid, the next patient was being transferred. 'We don't have enough gowns to keep changing,' Mayhew said, 'but scrub your hands and get yourself some fresh gloves.'

As she stood at the sink, Evie felt the deck of the ship start to gently roll beneath her feet. She gritted her teeth; it was all part of working on a hospital ship, but it wasn't going to make things any easier.

Back at the table she needed to grab hold of a young soldier who was starting to scream and writhe in agony as he clung to the remains of his right arm. 'Don't take it, don't take it,' he was shouting. She saw a flash of pain cross Mayhew's face and by the smell emanating from the arm and the black, withered flesh, she knew that the arm was beyond saving, this was an advanced case of gangrene. There was no choice but to amputate.

Evie turned her head to quickly confirm with Mayhew, before trying to soothe the young man, but Corporal Harry Walker had now broken down completely and was sobbing his heart out, still begging for them to save his arm.

'I am so sorry...' she said gently, 'but your arm is already dead, it is no use to you... there is nothing we can do to save it.'

His body contorted and he clutched at her angrily with his good arm.

'I'm sorry,' she repeated, as in the background the surgical instruments clinked into place as Mayhew placed them side by side on a sterile cloth and then quietly prepared the chloroform mask.

Corporal Walker started to thrash from side to side. 'You can't, you can't do this to me!'

'We have no choice,' she said firmly. 'If we don't amputate, the arm will get much worse and the infection will spread to the rest of your body.'

He looked her in the eye then.

'It is the only way to save your life...'

Her heart twisted as his chin became to tremble and tears welled in his big blue eyes, as if he were a frightened child. 'What's my mam goin' to say when I come home with me arm missing?'

'Trust me, she'll just be glad that you're alive.'

He took a deep breath before his face contorted. 'Do what you need to do, just do it... but please give me something for this bloody awful pain.'

Dr Mayhew was already there at the head of the table with the chloroform mask. 'Breathe this in – that's it – and when you wake up, it will all be over.'

Unfortunately, the arm had gone too far to save anything below the elbow. Mayhew cut it back high, to give enough healthy flesh for Corporal Walker to have the best chance of survival. Evie kept her nerve all the way through, the deck continuing to sway, holding fast to the arm while Mayhew used the surgical saw to cut through bone. Once they were on to the suturing, Evie felt the tight knot inside her chest start to relax as she stood steadfastly beside the table, passing swabs to Mayhew as the pitching of the ship began to calm.

'You have the makings of an excellent theatre nurse,' Mayhew murmured as he drew the black silk sutures through the flesh to bring the edges of the wound tightly together. He glanced up for a moment to fix her with his sharp hazel eyes. 'You have a talent for this.'

Evie didn't think it would be appropriate to be seen grinning from ear to ear in an emergency operating theatre, but for a few moments, until she needed to dress the wound and apply a stump bandage, she felt the glow of his remark as a warm ache in her chest. And later, after four more cases that took them through into the early hours of the morning and then the intense cleaning that was required to prepare the theatre for the next round of surgeries tomorrow, she felt exhausted but also calm, fulfilled. As she walked through onto the ward, only then did she realise the magnitude of the task the medical team had performed. The pristine rows of beds were crammed with soldiers, clean white bandages bright against their khaki uniforms dusty with sand from the beach where they'd lain waiting for evacuation, their military caps beside their pillows or at the bottom of beds, each displaying a regimental badge. The smell of the wounds, old and new, and the unwashed stink of their bodies met her in the same instant as the groans of pain, the sobs and the shouting and chatter of the less severely injured as they called to each other, looking for their mates or simply striking up soldierly conversation. Evie walked the length of the ward, taking in all the detail, proud of what they'd done this night and of the meticulous preparations that were now showing their worth.

Spotting Sergeant Singh and Corporal Walker, she went

along to check their dressings and make sure they were comfort-able. Both were sleeping, oblivious to the noise of the ward. She placed the back of her hand against Sergeant Singh's cheek; there was no sign of a fever and the dressing on his neck was secure. A bed cradle held a sheet tent-like above his fractured leg, she lifted the edge of the cover to check the splint, praying that the wound on his thigh would heal.

In the next bed, Corporal Walker seemed to be burning up. She lifted the chart at the bottom of his bed. His temperature was elevated. Hopefully, now that the necrotic arm had been removed, he would fight off the infection. The young man's head rested peacefully against the smooth white pillow, his pale brown hair had been combed and as he slept off the chloroform, his face was unlined, smiling almost. The stark bandaged stump was a cruel reminder of what the young soldier had been through. Evie checked for any seepage from the wound and then adjusted the bed sheet over him, like a mother tucking in her child at night.

Seeing Iris at the top of the ward, pulling out a clean basket of dressing pads and bandages, she went to her and offered to help.

'You need to take your rest now, Nurse Munro, you've been working very intensely.'

'No more than you, and you're still on the ward.'

Iris sighed and offered a tired smile, 'I can't argue with that, can I, you always have an answer for every—'

'Help, I need help here!' a shrill voice shouted from three beds down. Evie moved swiftly to aid Charlotte as she fought to keep a broad-shouldered patient with a ruddy face in bed.

'What's up, soldier?' Evie asked, matter of fact.

'I need a piss, that's all,' he shouted, his broad accent distinctly northern. This big fella was another Lancashire Fuselier.

'Oh, I see,' Charlotte gasped, wiping a hand across her grimy face. 'This gentleman needs a urinal.'

'What's your name?' Evie asked, easing the man back into bed as Charlotte headed down the ward to the sluice.

'Sergeant James Todd, but you can call me Jimmy,' he grinned, gasping in pain the next second and clutching a hand to the large dressing pad on his chest. 'Buggers went and shot me when I was carrying a stretcher with me mate on... He didn't make it.'

'Take it easy, steady your breathing,' Evie advised, taking slow breaths herself as the soldier started to ease into a more comfortable state.

'Thanks, miss,' Jimmy gasped, as the pain and the sorrow started to ease.

'Can I get you some morphia?' Evie asked gently.

'Nah, I don't want the drugs if I can 'elp it, but if there's a bottle o' beer on the go...'

'I'm afraid not, Jimmy.' Evie smiled, patting his shoulder as Charlotte appeared by the bed with a glass urinal in her hand. 'Sorry, they all seem to be in use, it took me an age to find one.'

'That's fine, yer doin' a grand job,' coughed Jimmy, grabbing the urinal out of Charlotte's hand.

'Call me if you need anything else,' Evie offered, moving swiftly to assist Miriam and Lucy, who were struggling to change the heavily bloodstained sheets of the huge Irish soldier Evie had seen in theatre, a giant of a man with a flat boxer's nose and a stubbly red beard who was still sleeping off the chloroform.

'Captain Riley is too large for this bed,' Lucy gasped, bracing her slight frame against him to stop him from rolling off the side as Evie helped Miriam pull out the soiled sheet and replace it with clean. He had a large abdominal dressing with a rubber drainage tube. 'Dr Hobbs removed half of his liver,'

Miriam said quietly, her eyes round with wonder... 'I didn't know a surgeon could even do that.'

'Let's prop him over on his side, while he's still sleeping,' Lucy offered. 'It will give his back a rest, stop him risking a bed sore.'

'Good thinking,' whispered Evie, walking briskly down the ward for two extra pillows – one for his back and one to support his uppermost leg.

The nurses' work continued intuitively as the male orderlies went about their duties making sure the patients who were conscious had food and drink. Evie had never imagined that the whole ward could come together so completely, but as the deck started to sway once more in the choppy waters of the bay, the nurses moved from one bed to the next, settling their patients. When the pale early morning light began to glimmer through the portholes, only then did the nurses start to feel their exhaustion and none raised any objection when Sister Phelps appeared at the top of the ward and ordered them to their beds. A contingent of nurses had already taken their rest, so now it was their turn.

Evie walked off the ward, leaving Iris in deep conversation, giving her handover to Sister Phelps.

Walking quietly with her three friends back to their cabin, she linked arms with Charlotte at one side and Lucy at the other as Miriam led the way, marching steadfastly ahead. None of them spoke, but Evie could feel an increased intimacy, one that could only come from the shared work they had performed. It had been sink or swim, and now that they were surfacing from their first shift, it felt as if they were clinging together.

As two orderlies passed with a shrouded stretcher, Miriam turned with a sad but resigned expression. They couldn't save them all, they could only do their best. Evie felt the first wave of sheer exhaustion begin to hit her. She didn't even know if all the hospital beds had yet been filled, but once they were, the ship would weigh anchor and trace her route back to England. They needed to pace themselves; the voyage would be gruelling and the work would be non-stop. She was ready for it though; once she had taken her rest, she knew that she would be able to go back to the ward and give it her all, soaking up as much experience as she could.

As the days of the return voyage slipped by with the routines of bed baths, dressing changes, bandaging and observations, Evie continued to assist Dr Mayhew in theatre. The process of debriding wounds and amputating limbs that could no longer be saved went on, so there was plenty of experience to be had.

Corporal Walker was making a good recovery from his surgery and Evie now had him crying less, sleeping better and able to perform small tasks one-handed. It felt like a privilege to carry on the work that she'd started with him in theatre. He still remembered the words that she'd said to him; he'd told her they would stay with him for the rest of his life. Evie couldn't remember exactly what she'd said, she was just glad that she'd been able to persuade him, and they hadn't had to force the situation.

Unfortunately, Sergeant Singh wasn't faring anywhere near as well. He'd spiked a fever that was now raging through his body. The suppuration from the wound on his neck was active and Evie had started to use sphagnum moss packs, but the condition of the thigh wound was deteriorating. The skin was bright red and raised up. Dr Mayhew thought there was little they could do apart from apply kaolin poultices to draw the wound and pray that the man would beat the sepsis. Evie knew that time might be short for the softly spoken Indian soldier who she had tended so carefully. He was incoherent now and delirious. In the days where they'd had proper conversation, she'd found him polite, intelligent, such a lovely man. She knew that she couldn't stand by and let him drift off to the next world without a fight, and she regularly spoke to Iris, who was equally troubled by their patient's deterioration, about what else they could do.

'We have to try something different,' Evie insisted after she'd taken Sergeant Singh's temperature and found it rising higher.

As soon as Dr Mayhew entered the ward, she was there, speaking forcefully. 'I have a plan... We need to open the thigh wound and let the pus out. I can clean out the cavity with carbolic solution and then pack it with sphagnum... just like I did with one of the fisher girls who developed sepsis.'

Mayhew frowned, not quite understanding the reference to fishing, but he instantly agreed that they had nothing to lose – the man's condition was worsening rapidly.

Evie wasted no time preparing her trolley and Iris was there to assist. It felt like a grim task, removing the sutures to release the pus, but Evie felt satisfied seeing the amount of green exudate that came from the wound. She swabbed and cleaned and then poured in iodine before applying the sphagnum and covering it with a dressing, saying a silent healing prayer as she pulled up the single sheet that covered Sandeep Singh's fevered body. Alongside many others, he was already on the list for tepid sponging to try to bring down his fever and Evie made sure to push as many sips of fluid into him as she could.

Leaving Sergeant Singh after a full day on the ward, there was still no reduction of his fever, but Evie wasn't ready to give up hope yet.

As she stood with Iris at the side of the ship that evening, they had a rule of not speaking about their patients, so instead

Evie asked Iris to tell her what she remembered about India from when she lived there as a child. Iris said that Sergeant Singh was from the Punjab region in the north-west of the country, far different from her own birthplace of Madras, but as she spoke of the colours and the heat of the midday sun, Evie absorbed it all, hoping that the whispers of India would somehow help Sergeant Singh towards a recovery.

They were only two days away from Southampton now, almost home, and the tally of those who were recovering, those who were still critical and those who had died was already being made. Still, Sandeep Singh clung to life and during the last twenty-four hours Evie noted with relief that his temperature had come down a notch. Evie could tell that Iris and Dr Mayhew held out little hope, but she would not give up, and now every time she performed her nursing duties she spoke to him, willing him to live.

On the final morning, Evie was on the ward early, anxious to check on all the patients, but especially Sergeant Singh. Walking down the row of beds, she thought she heard him groan, and then he was calling out – calling her name.

'Nurse Munro, where are you?'

'I'm here,' Evie replied, catching her breath as she arrived at the side of his bed.

'Nurse Munro,' he croaked, 'I just need to tell you...' He paused for breath. 'I heard your voice... and I haven't given up, I will never give up.'

Evie gasped, she knelt by his bed. 'I am so glad,' she said, placing a gentle hand on his arm. 'I thought you were a goner for a while there.'

He gave a hoarse laugh and when he spoke again his voice was measured. 'When I return to India, I will tell my wife and my two boys all about the stubborn nurse who wouldn't let me die. You will never be forgotten, Nurse Munro.'

Evie felt tears prick her eyes and she swallowed hard to

keep them at bay. 'And I will never forget you, Sergeant Singh,' she said, patting his arm and offering a smile before she went to the next bed where Captain Riley had started to rear up and was in danger of falling. 'Nurse Franklin, Nurse Dooley,' she called to her friends down the ward, 'I need some assistance here, please.'

None of the new recruits were prepared for the loss they would feel when they docked in Southampton and their patients were stretchered off to be transferred to military hospitals on dry land. Evie said a tearful goodbye to Sergeant Singh and Corporal Walker. Once the last patient had been taken, the ward stood silent and empty. Evie looked at Iris to see her sniffing and swallowing hard alongside Miriam and Lucy. Even Charlotte, who had claimed vehemently any number of times that she would never allow herself to get too close to any of the patients, was in tears.

Evie saw Iris scanning the rows of dishevelled beds at each side of the ward: sheets and blankets lay askew, discarded dressings, grubby remnants of food and slops of tea were evident. Clearing her throat, Iris raised her voice to give them direction. 'Our patients have gone but we still have a great deal of work to do... Nurse Munro and Nurse Franklin, you strip and wash the beds down this side. Nurse Kipling and Nurse Dooley, I want you to work your way along the opposite side. Come on, girls, get the linen baskets, I don't want to see any sheets and pillowcases on the floor.'

As soon as the nurses were actively engaged with their tasks, the conversation quickly turned to what they might be doing with their onshore leave. They would have about ten days before the *Britannic* departed for the next tour of duty.

Evie would be catching the train home to Anstruther – back to see her family, spend time with Rita and visit her son's tiny grave beside the sea. She knew that they would never find out what became of the soldiers they'd got close to, but the memory of her very first theatre cases would stay with her forever.

And then, as soon as they loaded up the ship again in Moudros harbour with more injured soldiers, new crises would be dealt with, new bonds would be formed, and their work would continue.

CHAPTER 14

HMHS BRITANNIC, NOVEMBER 1916

Apart from Sister Phelps, with whom Iris still had a formal, but now much easier working relationship, she hadn't yet managed to become particularly close to any of the other Queen Alexandra trained nurses. Maybe it was because she'd been a wartime recruit and not someone who'd trained fully with the army... She wasn't sure and it didn't really matter, given that she'd always been an independent, self-contained sort who could manage with or without companionship. *Bit of a misfit,* that's what Aunt Edith Purefoy had said when Iris had insisted that she didn't want to invite friends home from the strict all-girls school in Liverpool that she'd attended. In fact, she didn't seem to need any other company than a book to read or some music playing on the wind-up gramophone.

Iris hadn't questioned her late aunt's stark assessment of her personality while she'd been living in the austere Victorian brick-built house in Birkenhead, always cold even in summer and mostly smelling of mildew. She'd been grateful that her middle-aged unmarried aunt had rallied to the cause when the child of her only brother had been deposited in the tiled hallway of her home like some package delivered from India. But what her nursing and stewardessing had taught her was that she was good at making friends, and the relationship she now had with her junior colleague was joyful and important to her.

On this, the first evening of their sixth trip, Evie was still full of their joint stay with Francine in Southampton – she'd loved the French food and the fresh coffee, and she'd been thrilled to try on Miss Duchamp's diamond necklace. It had looked stunning against her lightly tanned skin and the jewelled flashes had brought out the blue of her eyes. Iris knew that hers was a pale elegance in comparison to Evie's vibrant beauty; the necklace still looked good on her, but it was nowhere near as dramatic as on her friend, almost as if the jewellery picked up on Evie's vivacious personality.

Iris leaned on the ship's rail, quietly smoking a cigarette and occasionally nodding her head, as Evie enthused about their stay in Southampton.

'It's a shame you never got to meet Sam, you two would have got on like a house on fire,' Iris said, after she'd taken her final drag on the cigarette.

She heard Evie suck in a sharp breath. She'd noticed the same reaction when Francine had talked about Sam's drowning, during the many conversations they'd had while staying at the house. Iris reached out a hand, thinking her friend must be triggered back to the death of her father, who'd been lost at sea when she was a little girl. But somehow this felt sharper, more recent and Iris couldn't help but wonder if there was something else there as well, something still raw.

Even as Iris was still pondering, Evie raced ahead with her conversation – she'd heard that there might be the chance of a trip ashore when they reached Naples this time. Nurse Franklin – Charlotte – had been trying to arrange for them all to go on a rapid sightseeing tour while the ship was taking on coal. Iris knew already that she wouldn't be able to accompany them, she'd remained resolute on her decision to keep her off-duty friendship with Evie completely separate from their work on the ward, so as not to compromise the authority she had over her junior staff. She wasn't sure that Sister Phelps or Matron would give permission for the nurses to go ashore anyway, but she hoped that it would work. Evie had become obsessed with Naples and Mount Vesuvius; every voyage she'd been so excited as they approached Italy, saying she was a Neapolitan at heart.

'When all this is over, you should apply to work on the passenger liners,' Iris said once more. They'd had many discussions about what they'd do once the war was over. 'You could work the Mediterranean route or see Australia and New Zealand... It would suit you.'

'Yes, I'm definitely going to do that,' Evie breathed, her eyes glinting with excitement as she leaned out over the rail until the curls poking out from beneath her red-patterned headscarf were caught by the breeze.

Iris stood peacefully, drawing in the smell of the salt air and feeling the rhythm of the huge vessel as it moved through the water. Lost for a few moments in her own memories, she was back on the *Olympic* with the sound of the orchestra playing, the clunk of ice against the side of a cocktail glass and the tinkling laughter of one of her first-class passengers, Mrs Fontaine. Reaching for the flask of whisky in her uniform pocket she unscrewed the silver stopper and took a swig, needing to catch herself before she moved on to the next phase of her daydream that always involved dancing on deck with her stowaway. The two identical promenade decks on the *Britannic* had been covered over to serve as wards for the officers. On the return journey last time around, Iris had been promoted to take charge of one of them. It had felt strange to be up there, in a space that was so instantly memorable, tending to injured men in hospital beds. She still couldn't quite believe the juxtaposition of her two lives.

The next morning, bright and early, after a breakfast of porridge served in the dining hall, Iris supervised her nurses as they undertook the outbound journey tasks. The nurses were in full flow, in perfect synchrony now that the work was so well-practised. Almost a year had passed since that first voyage when she'd had to tell Evie off for dancing a cancan. She'd been right about the other three nurses – Franklin, Dooley and Kipling had all turned out to be first-class VADs. Nurse Franklin could still be a little hot-headed at times, and she'd once seen her storm off the ward after a disagreement with an orderly, but Iris admired her spirit, and for a young woman of her class, buckling down to do the work that was required, she had proved herself time and time again.

The distinctive tap of leather soles on the deck boards signalled the approach of Sister Phelps.

'We have a new orderly to replace the man who went off sick with pneumonia on our last voyage,' she announced, as soon as she gained her prominent position in the centre of the ward. Iris saw the corseted bodice of her grey uniform rise as she took another breath. 'I appointed him myself, and he should be on the ward in ten minutes with the freshly laundered bed sheets... Nurse Purefoy, please let me know if the young man is tardy.'

'Yes, Sister,' Iris replied, glancing up from her rolling of bandages.

Twenty minutes later, Iris heard the rumble of trolley wheels and a man's voice shouted, 'Sheets for Sister Phelps!'

Iris felt as if an arrow had pierced her heart, and she reeled with the shock.

Turning, she saw the new orderly already unpacking the

trolley. When he looked up from his work, she saw his mouth drop open and he plonked the sheets back down, askew, on top of the trolley.

Iris stood rooted to the spot with her hand pressed to her breastbone as Jack Rosetti strode towards her, a grin slowly spreading across his face.

'Iris Purefoy,' he murmured.

He was two strides away, Iris couldn't speak, but when she saw him open his arms and prepare to embrace her, she gasped and stepped back.

His face fell and he stopped short, as if stung.

Iris shook her head, stuttering, 'Not here...' She was aware of the junior staff within earshot, imagining them all paused in their activity and about to witness their nurse in charge taken into the arms of the new orderly.

He furrowed his brow, opened his mouth to speak but then Evie's voice called down the ward. 'New orderly, we need some sheets up here, quick sharp.'

He backed away and Iris could only stand and watch as he turned and called up the ward, a smile spreading across his face as he received a twinkling response from Evie.

'You look Italian,' she heard Evie say. 'Are you from Naples?'

'No, I'm from New York,' he replied confidently, 'but you're almost right about the Italian, my father was born in Sicily.'

Iris's head was swimming, and she took a deep breath to try and steady herself. It felt like all her imaginings and memories of this man over the past two years had been immediately swept away. She could see exactly what he was now: no more than a superficial philanderer who could shift his attentions to any other woman on a whim. Her chest was tight, and she felt like she could burst as a hot flush spread from beneath the starched collar of her uniform, not with shame but with pure anger. She swallowed hard and clenched her jaw, unable to block out the sound of Jack Rosetti's mindless chat and Evie's rippling laughter. She forced herself to take up the next bandage and she rolled it tight, much tighter than any of the other bandages she'd ever rolled in the whole of her nursing career.

Mercifully, Jack had a busy schedule and many other deliveries to make to the other wards on the ship. As he scooted down with his trolley, she felt her skin prickle. She held her breath as he passed on his way off the ward, keeping her head down and her eyes firmly fixed on the bandages, but she knew the exact moment when he cast a glance in her direction. It was as if she could feel everything that he did. Once he was gone, she exhaled heavily and leaned with both hands on the table to steady herself. What had just happened was unimaginable. How could he have found his way onto her ship? America wasn't even in the war yet!

'He's nice, isn't he... our new orderly,' Evie called in passing as she made her way down the ward with her arms full of his freshly delivered sheets, to start making up the beds.

Iris ground her teeth and didn't reply until she could see Evie glancing at her with concern. 'What? Sorry... oh, I was busy counting these bandages... I think we need more stock.'

Evie sauntered closer. 'I was only saying that he's nice, our new orderly. Handsome too.'

'I didn't really notice,' Iris said distractedly. It was clear that Jack hadn't given away any hint that he knew the nurse in charge. She wanted to keep it that way, she was determined to stand firm and completely ignore the man. How dare he assume that he could walk back into her life and pick up where they'd left off? He hadn't even written as he'd promised. No, that was it, she would not tolerate any further overtures from such an unreliable, insincere, lying... Her mind continued to whirr over all the known and potential faults of Jack Rosetti.

. . .

That evening, as she stood at the side of the ship, Iris was almost oblivious to the glorious copper-red sunset on display. Sighing heavily, she took another big swig of whisky from her flask and then lit up her third cigarette. Despite her every effort to simply push Jack out of her head, the thought of him was overwhelming, nagging away. The effects of the whisky had started to take the edge off but as soon as she heard Evie calling to her, the hairs at the back of her neck prickled. She tried to suppress her anger. *It's not Evie's fault, she doesn't know what happened on the* Olympic... *it's not her fault.* Iris repeated this mantra as Evie marched jauntily towards her, then propped her arms on the rail, shoulder to shoulder with Iris as always.

Despite knowing that her friend was an innocent party in all of this, Iris felt uneasy in such close proximity, and she was tempted to gently edge away. Instead, she clung tightly to the rail with one hand and took a deep drag of her cigarette with the other. Evie was chatting on about some story Charlotte Franklin had been telling them about her time on board one of the cruise ships when she'd stayed out all night and then had to sneak back to her cabin before her maiden aunt, who was her chaperone, woke up. Iris was only half-listening, but the detail she caught made her recall the young woman in the silk sequinned evening gown she'd seen on the *Olympic*, the same morning she'd heard that war had been declared. Another jolt of memory that linked her to Jack. At least with the war intervening it now felt like decades ago. So long in fact that it made her feel older than her years, as if her existence now would be forever at war. Suddenly weary, she gave another heavy sigh and had to fight to hold back tears.

Sensing her discomfort, Evie rounded off her story and linked Iris's arm. 'You look tired tonight, are you all right?'

Iris straightened up, squared her shoulders. 'Yes, of course. It's just this war... it goes on and on, doesn't it?'

'It does,' Evie breathed, 'and in a few days we'll be receiving more casualties. We'll be patching them up, sewing them back together and the physical scars will heal... but having seen the state those men are in, it's not what's happened to their bodies that will hold them back, it's what's up here.' Evie tapped her forehead with her free hand.

Grim as their conversation was, at least it put the whole Jack Rosetti issue into perspective for Iris. After all, what was it they'd had all that time ago? A brief encounter on board a cruise liner. If it hadn't been for the war, she would probably have met someone else by now and it would all have been lost in the ether.

Iris tried desperately to hold on to that sentiment during the next few days as Jack Rosetti made repeat trips to the ward with supplies. Sometimes he even called by with just an empty trolley. Each visit followed the same pattern – she heard the rumble of the trolley approaching the ward, she steeled herself. He called out a greeting when he entered the ward which she steadfastly ignored and then Evie or Charlotte came down to chat to him briefly. She'd also seen him in the dining hall, sitting across the way with the other orderlies and the junior medical staff. He seemed very chatty with Dr Mayhew, of all people. It had started to feel as if he had come on board to steal all the people she had become close to. Evie was now very friendly with him, and she'd even seen her linking his arm as he'd made to leave the ward. When she'd caught a sharp glance from Iris, the probationer had swiftly withdrawn, but the rules were clear, and Evie would do well to remember them. Nurses should not be seen fraternising with male staff on the ward and if Sister Phelps had been on duty, Evie would have been in real trouble.

On the morning before they reached Naples for coaling, Iris felt her skin prickle as Jack came onto the ward. This time he brought his trolley over to her desk and stood waiting for her to glance up from her paperwork.

'I just want you to know that I am really glad to see you again, Iris,' he said quietly.

She felt her cheeks flush instantly.

'That may be,' she replied sharply, 'but we are both here to get on with the work and it is best if you remain silent about our previous acquaintance.' She saw his eyes flash with what could have been mock sorrow, but she couldn't tell – she didn't even know this man anymore. 'How on earth did you end up on here, anyway?' she hissed.

He took a step back, his eyes wide, I went back to Galway to see my family again and most of the young men, including my two cousins, had joined up. There were women in mourning, it was awful. I felt like I needed to do something to help the war effort. I couldn't join the army and head straight to the trenches, I couldn't do that to my mom. But a buddy of mine was home on leave from the Royal Army Medical Corps and he'd heard that they were looking for crew for hospital ships. So I hopped on a ferry and went straight to Southampton... I love being at sea on these giant vessels... as you know.'

Iris pursed her lips. 'That was in a different lifetime,' she muttered, 'and I can see that Nurse Munro is trying to attract your attention, so I suggest you get on with your work.'

'Yes, Nurse Purefoy,' he said, his tone ambiguous. With a small salute, he trundled away from the desk with his trolley, leaving Iris with an ache in her chest and an iron determination not to let it get the better of her.

Standing out at the side of the ship that evening, Iris was glad of a turn in the weather that brought a brisk wind, driving rain and choppy seas. As she clung to the rail with the ship pitching beneath her, a rumble of thunder in the distance seemed entirely appropriate to her mood. And there were only three more days to go now, before they would be busy with their patients and the return journey would fly by. Then, if Jack was going to stay on board as a permanent feature, she might well consider applying to another hospital ship, couch the move in terms of wanting to vary her experience. She would sorely miss her nurses though, especially Evie Munro. But the closeness developing between her friend and Jack Rosetti was already setting a distance between them.

CHAPTER 15

On the approach to Naples, during the afternoon when the nurses had their leisure time and some took tea or went for a swim, the ship's siren sounded an alert. One of the crew was sure he'd seen a U-boat within striking distance.

Iris made certain that all her nurses followed the drill, and until the 'all clear' was given they wore their cork life jackets. It had happened many times and as voyage after voyage proceeded without incident, she was concerned that the crew and medical staff were becoming complacent. They had been reassured over and over by the captain that the sturdy *Britannic* with her reinforced hull could not only withstand a torpedo, she could outrun any U-boat. In addition, they were protected by the Geneva convention that forbade attacks on hospital ships.

'That's all well and good,' Sister Phelps had confided to Iris, 'but I have it on reliable authority – a cousin of mine in the Admiralty – that mines have been laid by German submarines in the Mediterranean. So even a vessel such as ours, clearly marked with a red cross, is still at risk.'

Sister had made it clear that Iris shouldn't make the detail of their conversation known to any of the junior staff, but she implored her to be on her guard. Iris was much closer to the staff; she knew that most of them understood the risk. Evie had talked on day one about mines being brought up in the nets of fishing boats off Yarmouth. Mostly, the nurses pushed down their fears, and Iris had become an expert at doing just that. But now, with this turn in the weather persisting as they sailed into Naples, she began to feel a heaviness in the air, a heightened threat that seemed to come from the sky above as well as sea below. Maybe it was exhaustion getting the better of her, she didn't really know, but as she stood out on deck in the shelter of a covered walkway, watching the grey, driving rain, it felt like a foreboding. For once Evie didn't join her out on deck... Iris remained there alone until she stubbed out her final cigarette and retreated to her cabin.

Evie was disappointed that her trip into Naples had been cancelled due to 'inclement weather', as Charlotte had called it.

'We'll go next time,' her friend had said with a sigh and a smile that tried to be cheery.

Evie had been frustrated; she would have gone ashore what-ever the weather, she would have revelled in it. What would have happened if the fisher girls had said they weren't standing out in the wind and the rain to gut and pack herring? She'd grown to like Charlotte, despite the gulf of social class that yawned between them, but at moments like this she couldn't help but wish these posh women had more backbone. Even as she thought it, her mind flashed back to Charlotte on the ward full of casualties, working every bit as hard as anyone else over a twelve-hour shift, her apron covered in grime and blood. She knew that she was being unfair, but she had to vent her feelings somewhere, especially since her off-duty hours with Iris had become more and more strained during this trip.

It had started on that first day when they'd been unpacking

stores... She'd seen Iris glancing up the ward with that stern, matronly look in her eye when she'd been chatting with the new orderly, Jack Rosetti. And then every time he'd been on the ward, she'd sensed her looking, judging. It hadn't stopped her having a laugh with him though. It was a breath of fresh air to be able to chat to a young American fella with a twinkle in his eye. Most of the orderlies were older men, worn down by years of service, but Jack was different; he seemed fresh and new, and for the first time since Jamie died, she'd started to feel the power of attraction. Charlotte, the more forward of the group, had also tried to chat to him, but Jack was out of her league... because on this ship the social ladder was all topsy-turvy. Jack was good company, but he always kept that little bit of distance and one eye on the ward door. Every time she'd suggested they meet up in an evening, he was playing cards with the other orderlies or the boiler men – there was always some excuse. Evie hadn't pushed it, she enjoyed the banter, but deep down the thought of being touched by another man brought back the tight sorrow of Jamie's loss that she'd fought so hard to subdue.

With the driving rain outside and the jangled thoughts in her head, for the first time Evie hadn't wanted to go up on deck. She didn't know how Iris would react; maybe she would be more standoffish tomorrow. But it was warm and bright in the cabin and Charlotte had produced two bottles of French wine from her trunk that she'd been 'saving for a rainy day'. She even had a corkscrew and a proper wine glass – just the one – that they all passed around. Evie had never tasted wine before; it was delicious and it took away all thoughts of the bad weather, Iris waiting on deck, her poor drowned lover and the other loss... her stillborn son, which she had pushed so deep she couldn't even go to the place where it was buried.

.   .   .

Iris knew that she should have spoken to Evie about Jack Rosetti; she'd seen the quizzical glances her friend had sent down the ward when Iris had been watching them chat. She hadn't meant to be disapproving – after all, she'd made the decision not to pursue contact with Jack – but she knew that it must have shown on her face.

Standing in front of her mirror, brushing her still damp hair, she groaned with frustration. Why couldn't life run along simple lines? Why couldn't she have spotted Jack as they were embarking, and then been prepared for him showing up on the ward. It had all gone wrong. She glanced at the photo beside the mirror – her smiling face next to Roisin's, what an uncomplicated time. Would she ever be able to feel simple happiness again?

She knew this wasn't all about Jack, it was the work that she'd been doing, the horrors that she'd seen first at Netley and now here on the ship. She had regular nightmares – dripping blood, gaping wounds, burning bodies and the silent screaming faces of young men. She wasn't sure if she'd ever sleep properly again.

As always when these raw thoughts came at her, she reminded herself that her lot was nothing compared to what the men were going through on the battlefields. She stared hard into the mirror. 'You can do this,' she growled at her reflection, raking the tortoiseshell brush too hard and painfully snagging a section of hair.

The weather worsened as they approached Naples and they were forced to remain at anchor in the harbour for two full days as the storm battered the ship. Their daily shifts continued on the wards, but they were shorter hours and Iris consciously slowed up the pace of the nurses' work. It was important to try

and keep up morale when the sky was slate grey, the wind
howled and tossed the ship from side to side at her moorings.

There were no more visits to the ward from Jack Rosetti,
she didn't even see him in the dining room. Perversely, Iris
found herself starting to miss the sight of him. It wasn't until the
weather had cleared and they were heading out into open sea
that she spotted him at the side of the ship. The curve of his
back, the set of his shoulders as he stood, gazing out to sea, triggered her back to the *Olympic*. When he turned with a flash of
excitement in his eye, he offered a grin which she fought against
returning, raising a hand in greeting instead. She saw him
moving in her direction, but she wasn't ready for conversation
yet, so she turned on her heel and walked away. The sky had
lightened, the ship was underway and with every step Iris
couldn't help but smile more and more.

They hit more rough weather in the Bay of Naples and the
Britannic had to fight her way through. All medical staff were
ordered to sit tight in their cabins, but Iris and Evie still met up
at the side of the ship, neither of them mentioning the one
evening Evie had stayed away, and both laughing hysterically as
they clung to the rail with the rain coming down hard and the
ship pitching. It was exhilarating, and even though they didn't
stay out long, Iris went back to her cabin feeling as if something
had healed between the two of them.

The next day in the Straits of Messina, the ship broke through
into clear skies and calm blue waters. Iris always enjoyed
moving through this narrow passage with land so close on either
side that she could smell the earth. She breathed in the air,
filling her lungs, enjoying a moment of peace. With the sun on
her face she felt reborn, and when she saw Jack again, leaning

out at the side of the ship, waving to Sicily and blowing kisses as they passed by, it felt right to walk towards him.

'So, you have family there,' she said, settling close enough to strike up conversation.

She saw him startle and his eyes were wide when he turned, surprised by her presence. 'How did you know that?' he asked, making every effort to stop himself from smiling.

'Evie told me.'

He seemed guarded. 'You know, you've got the wrong idea, there, about her...'

Iris felt irritated; she'd come to speak to him, see if they could make amends and now he was going on about Evie. She felt something twist inside of her. Clearly this wasn't the right time to start any chat, maybe that time would never come. She shook her head and turned away, ignoring him as he called after her. She had no time for this; in two days they would be hauling aboard more injured soldiers and their hard and gruesome work would begin again, whatever was going on with Jack could wait.

She did glance back though before she descended to a lower deck and he was still watching after her, running a hand through his hair till it stuck up on end. *Let him wait,* she thought, *we have plenty of time.*

That night the ship's company gathered in the mess hall for a church service, Iris knelt beside Evie and she reached out to hold Iris's hand. They both knew what was coming tomorrow; they would need to work together. As they sang the familiar hymns, Evie cried during 'For Those in Peril on the Sea' and Iris cried at 'There Is a Green Hill Far Away'.

The next morning dawned as perfect a day as November in the Mediterranean could be. Iris emerged from her cabin early, smiling as she leaned on the rail to witness the sunrise tracing a magical path across the calm sea. She turned her face to the sky, feeling the warmth and the gentle movement as the ship sailed across the azure waters. Seeing light catch the windmills and the whitewashed, blue-shuttered houses of a closely packed Greek village built high up the steep side of one of the islands, she enjoyed a moment of pure calm as she drew in the play of light and colour.

Arriving a little later than usual for breakfast, she'd missed Evie, who always wolfed down her food and then, restless as ever, was gone. Dr Mayhew was there with the other young surgeons. He raised a hand in greeting, and she smiled in return. In the next moment she saw Jack sitting with the other orderlies. He was grinning in her direction – he must have thought the smile was for him. Her cheeks flushed and she ducked her head down before sliding into a seat beside Nurse Kipling and Nurse Dooley, opposite Nurse Franklin who was swirling her porridge with a spoon while chatting merrily to the staff nurse beside her. Sneaking a glance back to Jack, she could see that he had an amused glint in his eye. She returned his gaze but couldn't offer any further reciprocation as Sister Phelps was already at the head of the table with her eagle eye tuned into every nuance of the nursing staff who sat before her. Sister didn't expect her nurses to be quiet at breakfast, they were allowed to laugh and chat amidst what was invariably a pleasant, lively atmosphere in the mess hall. As always, on the day they were due to arrive at Moudros, the joking and friendly banter were animated.

As Iris scattered sugar on her porridge and took the first spoonful, Nurse Kipling was telling her about the latest chapter in the book she was reading. *Far From the Madding Crowd* was one of Iris's favourites and she enjoyed their daily discussions. Suddenly, a loud boom sounded deep inside the ship and then a dull, deafening roar shook the breakfast pots. In the next second, the whole ship shuddered violently, and crockery smashed to the floor.

Nurse Kipling gasped, Nurse Franklin emitted a single scream and Sister shot up from her seat.

Iris exchanged a frightened glance with Miriam Dooley. Having worked as stewardesses, they both knew immediately that the ship was in deep trouble. Iris lay down her spoon and gripped the table.

The dining room was unnaturally silent. Iris looked up and held Jack's wide-eyed gaze across the room. In moments the warning siren sounded and as one the room rose from their seats and began evacuating without a word; seamen, orderlies and surgeons leaping over tables and benches as Sister Phelps held up a hand to steady her nurses so that they could file out swiftly but decorously. 'We need to move quickly, nurses,' she said determinedly. 'Go straight to your cabins, put on your life jackets, collect your valuables and then make your way to the boat deck. I am in no doubt whatsoever that we will be proceeding to the lifeboats.'

Nurse Kipling emitted a small mournful sound. Iris took her hand, trying to soothe her. 'We will be fine, we've all practised the lifeboat drill and there will be seats for everyone... I'm just glad we have no patients aboard.'

'Thank the lord for that...' Sister added, moving swiftly ahead, leading the way.

'This is so exciting,' Nurse Franklin almost squealed. 'Like the *Titanic*.'

'Hopefully *not*,' Iris responded brusquely. 'We are aiming to get all crew off this ship alive.'

Duly chastened, Nurse Franklin put her head down and proceeded in a purposeful manner.

Breaking away from the group, Iris went to the trained staff quarters. Doors stood open as nurses hurriedly collected whatever they could think of to take with them. There was a buzz of conversation as staff emerged from their cabins, some still wearing their pyjamas with items of uniform hastily added over the top. All were wearing their life jackets – the sight of it sent a shiver through Iris's body.

In the cabin, Iris took the photograph from beside the mirror and stuffed it in her pocket. The velvet cushion was too bulky, she couldn't take that, but she fished in a drawer and pulled out her leather purse. The rest of her possessions were insignificant. Then she got down on her knees and dragged her life jacket from under her bed, hastily pulling it over her head, fumbling with the ties.

The alleyways were deserted as she made her way to the boat deck. Crew were assembled in an orderly fashion, awaiting evacuation. She scanned the group, looking for Evie or Jack. Nurses Franklin, Kipling and Dooley were already installed in a lifeboat with Sister Phelps, but there was no sign of her friend, and she didn't appear to be part of the group waiting. Iris felt conflicted; she knew that she should obey Sister's order to the letter, but she would never forgive herself if Evie or Jack, for whatever reason, were left behind.

The ship was listing slightly but appeared stable, so she turned and started to run towards the stateroom that Evie shared with the other nurses. The door stood ajar and Iris scooted in – no sign. Rising panic was in her chest now, as she wondered where her friend could be. Acting on instinct she threw herself down on her knees to peer under the bunks – all four life jackets had gone, so at least there was that. She ran back out into the alleyway; she could hear the lifeboats still active, surely she had time to check the ward. Running in through the door, she saw that some of the beds had started to slide together and the sound of breaking glass came from the sluice area. With the deck sloping markedly now, she ran into the operating theatre, where steel instruments and trays were crashing to the floor.

Her heart was pounding against her ribs. She had to get out before it was too late and hope to God that Evie was safe.

She tried to increase her pace, but her feet were sliding on the sloping deck as, despite everything, the *Britannic* continued to steam ahead. It felt surreal – all of this had happened so quickly. Gaining the side of the ship, she clung to the rail for a few seconds, feeling calmer in the warmth and the brightness of the sun. Observing a lifeboat wavering in the air, stuck in position with men calling for help, she realised that any attempt to leave the ship now, as time had gone by, would be precarious. A feeling of dread clutched her heart as she watched the lifeboat hit the water. It appeared to have been safely launched, but almost immediately it started to drift towards the churning propellers. The crew were inexperienced oarsmen and unable to control the lifeboat's direction. Iris let out a scream and shot a hand to her mouth as she saw the boat caught and then mashed to pieces by the huge iron propellers. Screaming men were thrown out into the sea. The water was streaked with blood and full of debris. Another boat was left hanging, with men dangling from it, ready to throw themselves to the mercy of the sea rather than suffer the same fate.

Iris swallowed down a huge sob. She had to move *now*, or she would never get off the ship alive. Running as fast as she could towards the deserted dining hall, she heard a crescendo of noise as the last of the crockery smashed off sloping surfaces. Her feet skidded on the wooden deck boards as the ship continued to tilt into the sea. An untethered wheelchair hurtled towards her and she leapt out of the way, grabbing hold of a deck bench to stop herself from falling. The ship heaved and slanted even further. Panting, she reached up with one hand to rip off her starched cap which had slipped forward, obscuring her vision. She felt something shift beneath her and somewhere, deep inside the vessel, came a loud crack that sounded like an explosion. The hospital ship was breaking apart.

Seeing an injured young man, a crew member clinging to the ship's rail, she threw herself forward. 'Hold fast, I'm coming to help,' she yelled, sliding helplessly towards him. By sheer luck she landed heavily against the rail right beside him. He turned his head in her direction, but his eyes were wide with terror, unseeing. One arm hung useless at his side – it was badly broken. Gripping the metal rail with both hands she looked over and could see the water rushing up to meet them. 'We need to jump!' she screamed but he was shaking his head. Her heart clenched. Whatever she did now would be crucial. He was in shock, she would have to drag him with her. 'Come on!' she shouted, grabbing his good arm. In the moment he loosened his one-handed grip a wave washed over and swept him out of her grasp. His mouth opened in a scream as she lunged forward, almost touching his hand. But she was a second too slow, and she saw the look of horror on his face as another wave heaved him over the side.

Still clutching the rail, drenched to the bone, she felt as if someone had punched her in the gut. Sucking in a deep breath, she tried to straighten up, spurred on by the terrified screams from injured men in the water who desperately needed help – crew members who hadn't made it to a lifeboat, some of them thrashing around, some slumped in their lifejackets. The water was rising faster now – she needed to act. She felt a hollow dread that started in her stomach and rose to her throat; for a moment she was paralysed. Then a bloodcurdling cry from the sea made her gasp. Loosening her vice-like grip on the rail, she scrambled over the side and plunged into the waves.

Water rushed in her ears and salt burned her nose, her lungs felt like they were bursting – she was in so much pain it made her angry, angry to think that this might be how she would die. *No. Never.* Kicking as hard as she could, once, twice, she started to move. Something sharp scraped against her leg but she felt no pain. With one more effort her head broke the surface and she was bobbing in the water, sucking in air. Her sodden uniform was heavy, dragging her down, and dread clutched at her heart. She used all the power in her limbs, but she was hardly able to swim. Her chest seared with pain as she kicked with her legs, and at last she was able to make some progress. Frantically she glanced around, her vision was blurred, but then she saw the injured men and the sea stained red with their blood. She tried to move towards them but still her uniform impeded her. There was no other choice but to lie back in the debris-strewn ocean with her arms spread wide and try to stay afloat.

If the sea took her, it was meant to be – there was no more that she could do now. The pale face of the young crew member who she'd tried to rescue flashed against her eyelids; she felt hollowed out, struggling to grasp the enormity of what had happened to the ship from the moment of the explosion – whether it was a mine, or a missile fired from a U-boat. She glanced from side to side, looking for other members of the nursing crew... Most had got away in lifeboats.

If she hadn't stayed to search for Evie, she would have been with them.

She drew in a ragged breath, feeling the air stinging her throat and down into her lungs. The injured men who'd been caught by the blades of the ship's propeller were still shouting, they were in terrible pain... If only she could reach them. In a split second she felt her legs sinking. She lay further back and forced her body to relax, exhaling a deep sigh of relief as she levelled up in the water. *Stay alive. Just Stay alive.* She closed her eyes, aware of the gentle rocking motion of the sea. The warm Aegean sun caressed her upturned face as she lay floating, her unravelled hair fanning out like a halo around her head.

Iris squeezed her eyes tighter at the violent, deafening roar as the beautiful *Britannic* sank to the bottom of the sea. She felt the wash from it and took some deep breaths to stop herself from panicking and upsetting her balance in the water.

After that, there seemed no concept of time as she drifted in the water with her eyes closed to avoid seeing the hacked and mangled bodies slumped in their life jackets, aimlessly floating. She could feel her face stinging in the sun, so she knew she must have been there a while. She tried not to dwell on the fact that she hadn't spotted Evie or Jack in the lifeboats. She didn't even know if she would come out of this alive herself. She thought of Sam and his advice to cling to the wreckage if you ever ran into trouble. Neither of them had fared too well with that, but at least she was still breathing. Feeling her leg brush against something solid, she briefly opened her eyes, unsurprised to see another dead body floating peacefully by.

CHAPTER 16

More time passed, and Iris didn't know if she were awake or dreaming but a voice was shouting in a language that she didn't understand. She blinked open her gritty eyes and carefully turned her head to the side, trying to adjust to the glare. Sinking a little, she started to cough on sea water, then she was aware of a small fishing boat with a dazzling white hull pulling alongside her, and a Greek fisherman with a weather-beaten face leaning down to the water and holding out both arms for her to grasp. Still unsure whether this was a dream, she sensed she had no choice but to grab the fisherman with all her remaining strength and cling to him as she was hauled aboard.

'Thank you,' she gasped, breathless, sodden, and lying like a caught fish in the bottom of the boat. The fisherman smiled and nodded, and another kindly Greek was helping her up, when a Northern Irish voice shouted from close proximity, 'You all right there, nurse!' Squinting in the sun, Iris could make out the face of a *Britannic* crew member; by the remains of his uniform he looked like a ship's cook. He was sitting on a bench, his tunic ripped and one arm dangling at his side. When she raised herself further, she could see that the limb was fully dislocated and severed through the bone; it must have been sliced by a propellor blade.

'What's your name, sailor?' she said, keeping her voice steady.

'I'm Eddie Heaney,' he grinned, still chatting as if they were on a jolly outing. Clearly, the man was in shock; Iris knew that she would need to apply a tourniquet to his arm or he might bleed to death. Struggling up from the deck, she heaved herself beside him. She still had her surgical scissors attached to her pocket by a chain and she was about to cut a strip of cloth from her apron when she saw that the man's arm already bore a thin rope, securely applied. One of the fishermen pointed to the makeshift tourniquet and nodded.

'Good work,' Iris said, offering a thumbs up. She did however tear a strip from her apron so that she could construct a sling to give some support for Mr Heaney's arm.

The next moment the fishermen were shouting and then hauling another body out of the water. A young blond sailor who reminded Iris very strongly of the soldier who had been her first casualty on that initial voyage. This poor boy had a huge abdominal wound, a slice that had cut through his uniform and into the flesh. She saw his chest rise and fall, just the once, and then his head fell to the side. The fishermen who'd rescued him shook their heads, their eyes sorrowful and then, so they would have space to pick up more survivors, they carefully slipped the sailor back into the water and he drifted away.

Iris felt incredibly sad to be leaving the boy behind – he looked so alone. Pressing both hands to her eyes she held back tears. This was no time for grief. She shifted her attention to Mr Heaney. He was quiet now, his face a greenish white.

'You need to lie flat,' she said firmly, easing him down onto the bench and supporting his mangled arm.

They could hear their next casualty from afar, he was shouting loud and strong. When they got to him, Iris recognised the senior ship's surgeon, Dr J.C. Hobbs. As he was hauled aboard, Iris realised that the man was still wearing his pyjamas. He appeared unscathed and greeted her as if she were waiting to do a ward round. He moved straight to the side of the injured man, examining the wound. Satisfied that all appropriate action had been taken, he slipped a flask of brandy from inside his life jacket, took a swig and offered it to Iris and the fishermen, who all declined. Then he rested back with a heavy sigh and closed his eyes.

In due course, a boiler man was hauled aboard, a big soot-stained fella, his life jacket barely reaching around his broad chest. Even before he was laid out on the deck, Iris could see that it was too late for the poor man. Dr Hobbs checked him over, just in case, but then shook his head. The fishermen stood with their heads bowed for a few moments and then they reverently lifted the body over the side of the boat, letting it float back out to sea.

Iris swallowed hard, it was impossible not to think of Sam – his body had never been found. It made it harder, especially for Francine and his boys, not to have a grave, not to know what became of his mortal remains. Iris knew that Francine planned to visit Queenstown when the war was over; over a hundred bodies from the sinking had been buried there in a mass grave. Iris had said she would go with her... lay some flowers, maybe take a flask of his favourite whisky so they could raise a toast.

Iris wasn't prepared to lose any more friends. She made herself face the horror and she scanned all the floating bodies within range. There were no nurses, and although she spotted one poor soul with a split skull in an orderly's uniform, he didn't have Jack's dark curly hair... She held onto that, held it close to her heart, prayed that he would be safe.

The fishing boat was moving purposefully now towards the shore. Iris could see a rocky island and a cluster of white houses with red-tiled roofs growing ever closer. She sat quietly as the fishermen steered their craft across the calm water. The sun was still shining, the sky was clear and the waters of the Mediterranean were lapping gently against the side of the boat. It seemed impossible that a huge liner had sunk so rapidly and completely vanished from view. She felt strangely dislocated in this idyllic setting, knowing that the *Britannic* now lay at the bottom of the sea while she was in a small boat with two fishermen, a badly injured ship's cook and a senior surgeon wearing navy-blue pinstriped pyjamas.

'I think we are about to land on the island of Kea,' Dr Hobbs offered as the golden beach of a Greek village came into view.

The shallow-bottomed boat landed almost on the shore and, even though her right leg was now stinging furiously, it was easy for Iris to walk through the shallow water with her uniform gathered up in both hands. The fishermen carried Eddie Heaney, who had now lapsed into a semi-conscious state, and Dr Hobbs pulled up his pyjama legs and waded resolutely through the sea.

'Follow me,' Iris shouted, gesturing for the fishermen to keep walking towards a frantic group of survivors assisting bloodied casualties laid out on sheets and wooden beds that had been dragged to the beach. With a surge of relief she spotted Dr Mayhew, and then two nurses in uniform – aprons stained with blood and caps askew.

'Evie!' Iris shouted, recognising her friend kneeling by the side of a casualty. Nurse Franklin was at the other side, holding the patient down. Evie was fully engaged with what she was doing, she had a needle in her hand and she was suturing a wound.

Dr Mayhew came running to greet Iris, and, once he could see that she was uninjured, he directed the fishermen to place their casualty beside the man that Evie was working on. 'It's a good job your friend can suture like a first-class surgeon,' Mayhew called. 'I've been the only doctor till now.'

Dr Hobbs was already re-examining Mr Heaney's wound. Iris could see that he seemed unresponsive. The surgeon's voice was gruff: 'I think the best we can do for now is to cut through the skin and sever this arm completely and then bandage up the stump until we can take him to theatre... Mayhew, do you have a scalpel?'

'No scalpel, but Nurse Munro brought a medical bag into the lifeboat and she has a very sharp knife that has been extremely useful so far.' Mayhew held the knife by the handle in a pot of water that was boiling over an open fire. After a few minutes he brought it over to Dr Hobbs. 'Apparently, it's a fisher girl's knife, used for gutting herring, but it's razor sharp and as good as any surgical knife I've ever used.'

Dr Hobbs nodded approvingly and set to work at once to fully amputate the arm.

'Iris!' Evie shouted, as soon as her suturing was finished, dodging around the patient and running to grab her in an embrace. 'I was so worried about you... I thought you were a goner.' Iris could see tears in her friend's eyes and she held her close, gave her an extra squeeze.

When Iris spoke her voice was thick with emotion. 'I'm not going anywhere, not for a long while yet... Now, where are we up to with these patients?'

'Mostly sorted, there's just that man there, the orderly, his legs gone at the thigh,' Nurse Franklin said, pointing to a thin-faced older man groaning in pain and holding his right leg. A sudden gush of blood spurted onto the sand.

'Quick, give me your life jacket,' Evie ordered Iris, already undoing the ties. 'I had some dressings and bandages in my medical bag but we soon went through them, we're cutting up the life jackets now.'

Iris rapidly slipped off the cork life jacket and handed it over, then she went to the side of the casualty, kneeling on the sand, pressing her hand over the wound in his leg. 'You hold fast,' she said firmly. 'We're just getting a bandage for your leg, we'll soon have you sorted.'

He groaned softly and opened his eyes. Iris could see that he had almost given up. 'Stay with me,' she implored, squeezing his hand.

'He's lost a lot of blood,' Evie said quietly, as she applied a field dressing to his thigh. 'Are you all right to stay with him?'

Iris nodded.

The casualty gave a long sighing breath, as if he was letting go. 'I think I'm dying,' he murmured, his voice weak, his face slackening.

'No, you're not dying,' Iris asserted, squeezing his hand. 'Look at me,' she ordered.

He opened his eyes and smiled, 'It's too late now... and I've had a good life.'

She brushed his thin hair back from his face, hoping by her attentions to keep him hovering on the brink of life rather than accepting death.

'What do we have here, nurse?' Dr Hobbs' voice had an authoritative edge.

The man's eyes opened and he whispered, 'Is that you, Dr Hobbs?'

'It is indeed,' replied the senior surgeon. 'And you are one of my most trusted orderlies, Tommy Anderson.'

Iris saw the orderly take a deep breath and then he tried to raise himself on an elbow.

'Lie back down, my man, you've lost a lot of blood so you'll feel very light-headed, but it's all under control now.'

'Thank you,' Tommy said, his voice sounding stronger. 'Fancy me getting the top brass to sort me out.'

From that moment, as Iris held his hand and Dr Hobbs expertly used Evie's knife to tidy up the wound and then suture, the man began to rally.

A naval destroyer had arrived while they were working,

pulling in at the small quay to collect the casualties, who were all being transferred to stretchers. Only then did Iris start to feel the throbbing pain in her right lower leg. Pulling up her skirt, she saw her black wool stocking shredded and matted with blood from a deep gash.

Iris struggled over to Evie, who was sitting on the step of a small, whitewashed house that belonged to one of the islanders. She was repacking her medical bag and looked up with a smile as Iris approached, before frowning. 'You're limping,' she said. 'Sit down here, let me take a look at your leg.'

Iris meekly complied as Evie deftly cut away the remains of the stocking. 'It looks deep, but I don't think it'll need stitching,' she murmured.

Iris's head was feeling swimmy, and she knew that she needed to lie down.

'Whoa, whoa,' Evie called, a tiny note of panic in her voice. 'Lie back here, that's it.'

Iris felt something soft beneath her head, then she must have blacked out because the next thing she knew Evie was propping her up and holding a drink to her lips.

'You've already had some water, so this is some milk sweetened with honey that Mrs Haralambos has kindly provided.' Evie smiled and indicated an elderly Greek woman who was gazing in their direction. 'We haven't had anything to eat since breakfast, have we, and it was only a bit of porridge.'

Iris thought back to that one spoonful she'd had before the explosion... Was that this morning, was it even this day? Obediently, she sipped the honeyed drink and with every mouthful she felt less dizzy.

'I cleaned your wound and treated it with iodine while you were out for the count,' Evie laughed. 'Thought it was best that you didn't feel the sting.'

Iris glanced down to see a dressing pad and tidy bandage. 'Good job,' she croaked.

'The ship that collected the injured men gave me some new dressings and bandages, so at least you didn't end up with a length of apron or a piece of life jacket.'

'I did well,' Iris smiled. It must have been a bit of strange smile because she saw the fleeting concern in Evie's clear blue eyes.

'What happened to you, Iris? I was worried sick.'

Iris felt her voice return much stronger as she told her story.

Evie's eyes grew wider and wider. 'You've had quite the experience,' she said at last. 'I had an easy time in comparison: I went to get my life jacket and medical bag, then rattled around the theatre to get some more dressings and suture thread. And I was lucky, I managed to get away in the last lifeboat before it all started to go wrong.'

Iris reached for her hand, 'I was looking for you, and for Jack...'

'Jack? You mean Jack Rosetti, the orderly?'

'Yes,' she said, and she gave her friend a bashful smile. 'I should have told you... but it all felt mixed up. I met him on my last trip on the *Olympic* – he was a passenger. We got close in a short space of time and when he came on board as an orderly, I was shocked... I was thrilled to see him, but I was on the ward, so I couldn't show it... then, he went to chat to you, and you were getting on so well, it seemed as if he'd shifted his attention. As easily as that.'

'What? To me?'

Iris nodded.

'Well, he's a handsome man and I can't deny I do like him, but apart from the banter, Jack kept himself to himself. Even if I suggested we meet up on deck, he was always playing cards or busy with something else... But now I can see why – the poor man only had eyes for you.'

Iris shook her head. 'No, I don't think—'

'Yes, Iris, I know it now, any fool can see it.'

'Any fool except me,' Iris said with a weary smile, resting back against Evie's shoulder. When she spoke again, her voice was shaky. 'Do you think he's all right, though... have you heard how many souls were lost?'

'They're saying it's about thirty all told – none of the nurses, we're all safe... Mostly crew who worked in the stokehold, the ones who piled into the lifeboat that was swept into the propeller...'

'I know, I saw it.' Iris's voice was stark, sombre.

'It was terrible,' Evie swallowed, 'I don't think any of us will ever forget it...' Then, forcing her voice to be steady, 'But Jack will be fine, just you wait and see. I can feel it in my bones.'

They stayed close, Evie supporting Iris, and the warmth of the sun started to relax them. As they gazed to the turquoise sea lapping the golden beach, pieces of debris started to wash up and a deck bench appeared – all that was left of the hospital ship.

'Thank God we weren't drowned...' murmured Iris.

Evie didn't reply and Iris felt her body tense up. She shifted her position and looked up at her friend.

'Are you all right, Evie?'

'Yes, I'm fine,' she replied, but she couldn't disguise the sadness in her voice.

CHAPTER 17

HMHS VALDIVIA, EN ROUTE TO
SOUTHAMPTON, DECEMBER 1916

Iris grabbed at the ship's rail, feeling the hard metal dig into the palms of her hands. The sea air buffeted her as she stood at the bow, looking down to the white spray against the hull as the *Valdivia* cut through the ocean. So much smaller than the *Britannic*, the two-funnelled hospital ship felt cramped and stifling with its portholes kept firmly closed below decks.

After spending time on the island of Malta, enjoying the space around her while they awaited transport home, Iris was feeling agitated already. She was glad to be on the move again though. Rest and recuperation had been enforced for the *Britannic* nurses, and Iris had become increasingly frustrated, especially after they'd spent time in Athens where they'd visited the Parthenon and even been invited for afternoon tea at a very swanky hotel. All of this would have been wonderful if the world hadn't still been at war.

After the second day onshore, Iris had been itching to be back to work so that she could quell the nagging anxiety about what had happened to Jack. Although all the nurses had stuck together, the other crew members had been picked up and transported on many different battleships. She had asked around, but it had been impossible to establish exactly what had happened to him. Even though she'd been reassured many times that his name wasn't on the list of fatalities, Iris needed specifics. On top of that, she was hardly sleeping. Night after night the awfulness of her experience, the horrific scenes she'd witnessed, came flooding back. Her work was the only way she knew to stave off the trauma and the anxiety. She gripped the rail harder just thinking about the frustration of it all.

She'd sensed the same restlessness in Evie too, though it was true her friend had revelled in visiting the artefacts of Ancient Greece, drawing in every morsel of the experience. As always, Iris was in awe of Evie's natural curiosity and her facility for learning. Sometimes, she felt like a tired old maid beside her vivacious colleague. There was still something that nagged Iris about Evie though. She would brush away any questions about her past life – though she could tell stories of the other fisher girls and the herring season for hours on end. It felt odd and it made Iris sure that there was something her friend was hiding. She hoped that one day it would all come out, for Evie's sake.

Iris tightened her grip as the ship rolled in the water. Exhilarating as it was to be so close to the sea and really feel the movement of the deck beneath her feet, Iris had got used to the steadiness of the giant liners. Sister Phelps, Nurse Franklin and Nurse Kipling had been struck with seasickness again and even Evie was a bit queasy. Iris spent hours at the bow, looking ahead, imagining sailing into Southampton harbour and then walking the short distance to Francine's. It was almost Christmas again; her life seemed to be flying by with this war. It had been over two years already and there no sign of an end to the conflict. What was it that Sam had said, that morning on the *Olympic* when he'd told her that war had been declared? *None of them even know what war means, it's outside of their experience.* He'd been right; so many young men had scampered off to war as if it was some glorious excursion, but how many had lost their lives already? How many widows and fatherless children had been left behind? The reality was there to see with every shipload of maimed, shell-shocked soldiers that were sent home.

At moments like these, Iris felt overwhelmed by grief and frustration. How could it be right to keep throwing young men's lives away? The war was like an insatiable monster that they were all servicing – it seemed grotesque. She took a few deep breaths, in and out, and felt someone place a gentle hand on her back.

'Iris?' It was Evie, her face creased with concern.

'Sorry,' Iris sniffed, swiping away tears.

'No need to apologise, we all need a good cry every now and then.'

Iris nodded.

Evie put an arm around her. 'We'll soon be back, and then we can find ourselves some useful work to do... What do you think, back to sea or a military hospital on dry land?'

Iris pulled out her handkerchief and wiped her wet cheeks. 'I think I might need a bit of time on dry land after this one. What about you?'

'Oh, I'm happy to go where you go... I'll need to head up to Anstruther for a bit first though – even my sister-in-law, Sadie, has been fretting about me. But I'll be back.'

Iris shoved the hankie into her pocket and pulled out a cigarette, turning away from the breeze to light up. Leaning against the rail, next to Evie, her mind began to whir. She needed the busiest place, the most demanding work to still her demons. In the next moment she had it, 'I want to go back to Netley hospital in Southampton... They take soldiers straight off the boats, it's the biggest military hospital in the country.'

'That will do very nicely,' Evie grinned.

. . .

Evie rested quietly at the rail, mulling over the idea of following Iris to Netley. It would work well for her. Once she'd seen Rita and had spent some time with Douglas and the boys, she'd be ready to be on the move again. It was time again, also, for her to visit that tiny grave in the churchyard by the sea. It came to her often enough in dreams – seeing Douglas place the appallingly small coffin in the grave and hearing the soil as the first shovel was cast down. She still saw Jamie's poor drowned face rising from the water. It felt as if he would never leave her. She'd long accepted his death, but it would always feel unfair given that she'd only known him for a matter of weeks. On other nights, he came to her as a living, breathing man with a warm body and sweet breath and they lay on the sand and listened to the sound of the sea. How she loved those nights, she wanted them to go on forever. Even now, standing at the bow of the ship, she felt her belly ache with longing. What she would give to spend just one more night with her man.

She'd always believed in destiny and that some good often came from a bad experience, but she was struggling to even imagine what could possibly come from the trauma that she'd endured. Why take both – her man and her son? Even touching on the surface of it now made her feel as if she'd stepped out into the cold and dark from a warm room full of happy memories. She raised a hand to her lips, imagining that it was the kiss of her lover, letting her mind circle and drift until she was back in the present, aware of the cold ship's rail beneath her hands and Iris's warm arm against her shoulder.

Evie shivered. The Mediterranean breeze wasn't cold, it was only the weight of the past that made her feel drained. She took some deep breaths, filling her lungs with the salt smell, starting to reinvigorate as she imagined each breath as balm for the soul. She wished she could stand at the bow of the ship and watch every single, now familiar, landmark go by – Sicily, Gibraltar, Portugal and onwards, heading north, back home to

Southampton. The thrill of travel and seeing these places was something that she savoured; she could never have imagined that last herring season, as she stood out on the east coast, braving the icy wind and rain off the North Sea, that she would one day be sailing the Mediterranean, seeing new lands. She missed the herring lasses though – she would never have laughs like she'd had with Rita and Rona and Minnie McKay. But she was a different person then – an innocent – she hadn't truly known what it meant to be alive in the world and suffer pleasure and pain, side by side.

After a long journey home in trains packed with soldiers and fractious children, Evie arrived back in Anstruther. Even though she'd been home regularly during the long turnarounds between trips to Moudros, it felt like an age since she'd been home. She'd missed Christmas but was arriving in time for Hogmanay. Not that there'd be much of a celebration – last year she'd been on her first trip aboard the *Britannic* and the year before she couldn't even remember where she'd been and what she'd been doing. She'd have to try her best though this year, not to argue with Sadie, not to disagree with Rita. She wanted this to be a perfect homecoming, something she could treasure.

Approaching the door to the family cottage, she could hear the shouting voices from the street.

'You've done what?' Sadie was screaming. 'You've joined up! A man of your age with two young boys and a wife to support!'

Evie held her breath, poised at the door with her suitcase in her hand. She could hear the timbre of her brother's voice; he sounded upset, but she couldn't make out the words. Sadie was weeping now, and Evie felt like crying along with her at the thought of her only brother offering himself up on a plate, freely risking his life. She turned on her heel as Sadie raised her voice again, swallowing hard as she made her way briskly through the warren of cobbled streets to Rita's place.

Seeing a black bow on the door of a cottage in Rita's street, Evie's heart clutched with fear. Her friend's twin boys had joined the Highlanders in the second wave. But no, it wasn't Rita's house, it was next door. Heaving a sigh of relief, instantly she felt angry with herself – the black bow meant that Mrs McCleod, Rita's gently spoken neighbour, had probably lost her only son, Peter. Evie still remembered him as a runny-nosed boy with a cheeky grin. Tears welled in her eyes as she stood and knocked at Rita's.

'Evie!' Rita called as she opened the door and grabbed her for an embrace, laughing and crying all at the same time. 'Look at you,' she was saying. 'In your fine blue coat, it is so good to see you...' Then she looked at the suitcase in Evie's hand. 'Have you not been to Douglas and Sadie yet?'

'There's a hell of a row going on, Rita. It sounds like Douglas has gone and joined up without telling her.'

'I'll get the whisky bottle,' Rita said. 'Get your coat off, you probably need to leave your brother and his wife to sort themselves out, it might be better if you stay here for the night.'

Evie nodded, she knew already that by the time she'd had one too many glasses of whisky it wouldn't be wise to engage with Douglas or Sadie.

Waking mussy-headed in the room that Rita's sons shared, she groaned and rolled over, watching the pale winter light seep in through the window. She didn't remember coming up to bed, and Rita must have undressed her because she was in her petticoat, her top clothes, coat and suitcase resting neatly on the twin bed at the opposite side of the room. Rita always knew to keep Evie in the boys' room; she'd never once set foot in that second-floor bedroom since the tragic night of the stillbirth.

Slowly, she got up from the bed and walked to the window. When she pulled back the curtain the stark light hurt her eyes, but once her eyes adjusted she could see the harbour and the fishing boats and it made her feel sad, to see how few boats were there now. She couldn't work out if it was the homecoming, or her ongoing grief, or trauma at what she'd been through on the Britannic, but she had tears welling in her eyes. She swayed a little as she stood in the light, knowing that she needed to get dressed and go down to the beach. And then, when she was ready, she would go to her baby's grave.

Rita was still in bed as Evie snuck out through the door. Her flat-heeled leather boots beat a rhythm that echoed in the empty street as she made her way down to the shore. There were sounds of activity from the harbour – fishermen were always up early. She shouted a greeting, raised a hand here and there, but she didn't stop till she reached the beach. The breeze had got up and it was cold, whipping at the plaid wool scarf that she had around her neck. Pushing her hands deep inside her pockets, she walked to the water's edge. It was almost unbearable to be back here. Even though Jamie had never been to Anstruther she'd brought him back from Yarmouth as surely as if he'd sat beside her on the train. And in these waters she'd walked carrying their son, she'd talked to him, taken him to her heart. She gave an involuntary sob, too stubborn to let it take her. Unthinking, she clenched her hand in the pocket of her new wool coat, forgetting for a second that she'd dropped the sea glass into the freshwater burn that day she'd rescued Duncan McBride from the sea. It frustrated her now that she'd thrown it away, but at the same time it annoyed her that she still felt the need to cling to something that connected her to Jamie.

She cried out in anguish, watching the gulls take off in fright as she shouted to the sea.

Walking towards the graveyard, she regained some control. She wanted to compose herself before she encountered her child. How old would he have been now? Two? Three? Her mind was too stymied to work it out, and she'd lost track of time since she'd left the village.

A single dried-up stalk remained of the flowers she'd last brought to the grave. She stooped to pick it up and toss it to the wind – she wanted nothing dead to be lying on the final resting place of her son. She didn't know what she'd find this time to lay on the small mound of earth – maybe a sprig of holly, or, better still, she could collect some shells from the beach and make a pattern out of them, press them into the soil so they'd stay put and never wilt.

Squatting down beside the grave she reached out to trace the name on the stone – Martin Munro. She wished she'd known him in one breath but in the next she was glad that she hadn't. What if she'd lost him later when her attachment had grown – at two, three? She didn't know whether it was easier having this yearning for a little boy that she'd never known. Sometimes, especially when the weather was warm and children were playing out, she had a strong sense of him; how his laugh would have sounded, how his hair would have stuck up at one side, just like his father's.

She exhaled heavily, trying to clear her thoughts. She would come back here each day and then, on the final morning, she would leave her token on the grave.

Walking to Rita's to collect her suitcase, her legs felt heavy. She didn't know if she had the strength to face what was going on with Douglas and Sadie, but when Rita's ashen-faced neighbour emerged from her cottage dressed all in black, Evie knew that she had to stay strong. There were so many people suffering in this war, why did she have the right to even think about giving up?

Clutching the imaginary sea glass one more time, she stopped to offer her condolences and tell Mrs McCleod that she was sorry for her loss. Before they parted, Evie took the thin

woman in her arms and held her rigid body against her own. 'I'll
see you again later, before I leave,' she said in parting. Mrs
McCleod nodded and went on her way, towards the beach.

Rita was up and about and brewing tea in the kitchen. Evie
sat at the well-worn table to share a cup with her friend and talk
about this and that.

'Have you heard anything of the Aberdeen girls?' Evie
asked, after Rita had given a full account of the dire state of
work for the older men, including her husband Gordon, who
struggled to manage the fishing with their bad backs and their
creaking knees.

'Aye, Rona writes regularly,' Rita replied. 'They're desperately missing the herring season, like the rest of us, and struggling to make ends meet. But Rona's steady and she's working in
the curing and the smoking sheds along with the old fellas... Oh,
and there's news on Minnie McKay, she's taken a leaf out of
your book and she's nursing now at the Aberdeen Royal Infirmary – I hope to God she's not talking those poor patients to
death.'

Evie laughed out loud. 'She knows how to chat, she does for
sure... but she's a lovely girl and she's bright and bubbly, she'll
be a real asset to any ward.'

Rita twisted her mouth in a wry smile. 'Not sure about
that... Do you remember that belly dance she once did for us
with a bag of chips in her hand?'

'Ha! Yes, I do.'

It made Evie smile to reminisce, but there was always the
sadness lurking. She couldn't ever imagine being able to go back
to those happy, innocent times and feel the same joy.

After drinking the dregs of her tea, Evie left Rita's and
made her way back through the streets to the cottage where
she'd been born. The house was quiet as she stood and knocked
at the door. It was never locked, so she went straight in, calling
out to anyone within range that she was home. Two excited

nephews ran from the kitchen still in their pyjamas, they threw themselves at her and she collapsed onto the small settee with one at either side. Ruffling their identical sandy hair each in turn.

'Mammy's been cryin',' said Neil, the eldest, looking expectantly at Evie, perhaps hoping for some explanation.

'And Dadda was shouting last night,' the little one said, his eyes brimming with tears.

Evie pulled him onto her lap. 'Now then, Alan,' she soothed. 'You know what grown-ups are like: they do shout and make a fuss, but they'll be right as rain again soon, just you wait and see.'

'I'm not sure about that,' Douglas's voice rang out from the kitchen. 'I've gone and done it proper this time,' he said as he walked through, his face lined with exhaustion.

Evie offered him a sympathetic glance, not wanting to dislodge her clingy youngest nephew to give the customary hug.

'Is Sadie all right?' she asked. Then, seeing the frown on his face, she said, 'I came to the door last night, I overheard enough to know what was going on. Didn't want to disturb you.'

He drew in a heavy breath. 'I'm not sure that she'll ever be all right.'

'She'll come round,' Evie offered gently.

He heaved a sigh. 'I really don't know if she will, but in the end I had no choice... I couldn't sit here peeling potatoes for the fish and chips while all the other eligible men go off to fight... I just couldn't...'

At the start of the war, Evie would have told him it was right for him to go off and do his bit. But that was before she'd seen the pages and pages of lives lost in the newspapers – stark names in black and white of the thousands of young men who would never return home. And she had spent time on the hospital wards, bearing witness to the destruction of the bodies and souls of the survivors. It was impossible to encourage him to take this step, even though she fully understood why he was doing it.

'Are you going to war?' Neil's eyes were round with excitement.

Douglas frowned. 'I am, yes, son. I am.'

'Well, that's good, because now I can tell Marty McDonald at school, that my dadda is brave after all.'

She saw tears welling in Douglas's eyes and he turned away, his shoulders square and rigid as if he were holding his breath.

Evie breathed for him and made sure to come up with a response. 'But your dadda's always been brave and strong... he had to deal with me when he was younger, and I was like a spitting tiger!' Evie emitted a pretend roar and started to tickle Alan on her knee. The little boy squealed with laughter.

'I'll go and tell Sadie that you're here,' Douglas muttered over his shoulder.

The two boys gazed after him as he left the room.

'Where've you been all this time, Auntie Evie?' the little one asked.

'I've sailed the seas and seen many lands and all of their treasures,' she announced dramatically, widening her eyes for effect. 'The Parthenon in Greece, Mount Vesuvius – a huge volcano in Italy, so high that it wears a crown of cloud – and the towering Rock of Gibraltar.'

The boys were avid listeners, so Evie continued: 'Did you know that the Mediterranean Sea is so blue and clear, you can gaze down through the waters and see brightly coloured fish swimming...'

Both boys snuggled closer, and Evie was grateful for the warmth of their young bodies and the smell of their newly washed hair.

When Sadie appeared with red-rimmed eyes, her voice was quiet but otherwise she seemed to be herself. 'So, Douglas has told you then... about joining up.'

Evie nodded, feeling for her sister-in-law. They'd had many spats over the years, they were both iron-willed women, but she knew how much Sadie loved Douglas. Evie still felt the weight of Douglas's news, and she knew her brother well enough to be sure that he wouldn't change his mind, so there was nothing to be gained by laying bare her own fears. She cleared her throat. 'It would only have been a matter of time before he was called up anyway,' she offered, knowing this to be true. 'I've met plenty of older men who've been serving.'

'You mean the ones on your ship who have already been blown to bits,' Sadie snapped, pressing her mouth in a firm line.

'I'd like to lie to you and say no, they were having an easy time of it... but I can't do that... I'm sorry, Sadie, if I could do anything to stop this, I would. I'd lay down my own life to stop more men joining up.'

Sadie sighed and lowered herself onto the sofa and Evie put an arm around her as the boys slipped to the floor to play on the rug with the wooden trucks that Douglas had made for them last Christmas.

'I don't want him to go either...' Evie said. 'But like I said, he will be called up anyway and if he doesn't go, he'll feel like he's a lesser man. It will drag him down to rock bottom, and that won't be good for you or the boys.'

For the first time ever, in all the time that Evie had known her, Sadie said, 'Yes, you're right.'

Evie gave her shoulders a squeeze.

Sadie turned to her with a wan smile. 'It seems we have no choice. And if he has to go, it's better that he volunteers.'

A heavy weight settled inside Evie as she sat with her arm around Sadie for as long as it took for her sister-in-law to start breathing more easily. When she began to straighten up and issue orders for the boys to get ready for school, Evie began to relax a little. It was good to feel the reinstatement of ordinary daily rituals, the things that Sadie would have to cling to while Douglas was away.

When the time came for her to leave for Southampton, Evie went back to the graveyard with the bag of shells she'd collected and crouched down to press them into the icy soil. As she performed her task, the hem of her blue coat brushed away a circle of frost from the side of the grave, leaving a transient mark of her presence. Her fingers were freezing cold, but she pressed the shells firmly into a pattern that she'd already practised on Rita's kitchen table. Once she was completely satisfied with the combination of colour and shape, she leaned over to kiss her baby's headstone, holding back the tears, as she always did at this stage in her leaving.

After calling by Rita's to say goodbye, she went to the family cottage to collect her suitcase. This time she kissed and hugged Douglas and the boys more times than she had ever done before, and she even held Sadie in a tight embrace. Patting Douglas on the shoulder, telling him to keep his head down in the trenches and if he was going to get shot, make sure it was in the foot. It was hard to keep her voice light, after all she'd seen on the wards, she had to swallow hard to hold back the tears that wouldn't have helped anybody, herself included.

As the train puffed out of the station and headed south, Evie felt the familiar lightening instantly followed by a stab of guilt that she always had when leaving Fife. She pressed her forehead to the glass of the window and made herself watch the landscape slipping by, almost lost in billows of steam.

'You'll be back soon enough,' her mother's voice sounded in her head.

'Yes, I will,' she murmured in reply, reaching into her

pocket for the letter that had been delivered to her Anstruther address only that morning. She'd already scanned through it many times – it was from Iris, she'd been up to Netley, and through Sister Phelps, who had also decided to return to the military hospital, she'd managed to secure a position on the surgical ward for both of them. And, given that Sister had supervised Evie's practice for almost a year, she would automatically become a qualified nurse.

Evie drew in a satisfied breath and gazed out of the window at the clean, white-frosted landscape. The bright sun reflected light dazzled through the train window, and Evie drew in the warmth as she rested her head back against the seat, relaxing her body to the rhythm of the train, feeling the buzz of the journey singing through her body, as it always used to back in the days when she was setting out for the herring season.

PART THREE

Keep the Home Fires Burning,
　　While your hearts are yearning.
　　Though your lads are far away
　　They dream of home.

Ivor Novello 1914

CHAPTER 18

The grand facade of Netley hospital stretched away into the distance, the February sun reflecting off the many windows and the frontage of the building sharply defined against the perfectly clear sky.

It took Evie's breath away. Iris had told her that the hospital was huge, but she hadn't conveyed any real idea of how vast the brick structure with its impressive pillars and arched windows actually was. Evie stood in her blue wool coat and red plaid scarf, rooted to the spot, her medical bag slung across her shoulder and a suitcase in her hand. Her eyes picked out the symmetrical lines of the architecture. Set as it was amid a vast parkland of grass and trees, the place looked more like an elegant stately home than a military hospital.

Evie couldn't wait to see the wards, and the operating theatre and the brand-new X-ray facilities that were situated in a wartime hutted extension to the rear. It seemed unreal but the hospital also had its own gasworks, a saltwater swimming pool fed from the sea, a grand officer's mess complete with ballroom, and a pier that extended into Southampton Water.

She glanced at her watch. Iris was coming up today from

Francine's and they were meeting at the entrance in another twenty minutes. She had time for a short walk in the grounds. She'd see if she could find the pier – Iris had said it was opposite the domed hospital chapel that stood midway along the frontage. As she walked towards glimmering Southampton Water, she breathed in the salt smell and heard the cry of gulls overhead. Evie thought it was a shame that the hospital ships couldn't sail straight up from the English Channel and unload their casualties at the pier, but Iris had told her that the water was too shallow. Instead, the patients were loaded directly onto trains and the line had been extended recently to run right up to the hospital – it was where she had alighted.

Evie knew already from her time on the *Britannic* what condition the injured men would be in, and those coming from the Western Front would be fresh from the trenches. She walked towards the smell of salt water and, as she approached, she was amazed to find the pier busy with patients – walking wounded with bandaged heads and arms, others in wheelchairs with plaster of Paris casts or splints, all wearing blue woollen suits with white lapels and red ties, the army-issue 'hospital blues' that Iris had told her about. The men were leaning on the rail, chatting or gazing out across the water, as if they were on a day out at the seaside. This was a very unusual hospital, so different from the pavilion-style Edinburgh Royal Infirmary where Evie had done her basic training. She liked this place already, it was so vast and airy, she felt as if she had room to breathe.

Wandering back to the hospital to find a suitable spot to wait for her friend, she continued to gaze at the building until, hearing a familiar voice behind her, she turned to find Iris, slightly out of breath with a large leather suitcase in one hand and clutching a bright blue velvet cushion with the other. 'Francine made me a new one,' Iris offered, by way of explanation. 'I had to leave the other on the *Britannic*.'

'Ahh,' Evie said, making herself smile.

'Impressive, isn't it?' Iris said, nodding towards the hospital.

'It's wonderful,' Evie replied. 'I never imagined it would look so grand... I'm in love with it already!'

'You haven't even been inside yet,' Iris laughed, starting to walk purposefully, with Evie by her side, chattering on.

'I mean, I was excited to come here anyway, but then I've been for a walk and seen the pier and the park... And in your letter you said that Sister Phelps wants to make me a trained nurse. Is it really true?'

'You deserve it, Evie, after all your work on the *Britannic* and then in the thick of it on that beach... No one could fail to be impressed by your actions that day.'

They walked towards the entrance and then in through the door to the strong smell of Lysol disinfectant and a view of a broad corridor at the front of the building, which appeared to stretch the full length. Light flooded in through the arched windows and potted palms were set at intervals. A young, dark-haired army officer wrapped in a trench coat was sitting in a rattan chair and staring out at the view of the water. Something about the stillness of his posture and his unflinching gaze held Evie's attention.

'Wait here, I need to get the keys for our rooms in the nurses' quarters,' Iris said, indicating one of the wooden benches set against the wall and handing over the blue velvet cushion.

Evie duly complied, happy to sit with her suitcase at her feet and watch the hustle and bustle of hospital life go by. Busy porters in smart uniform passed with bandaged patients in wheelchairs, and a group of nurses in their grey-and-red Queen Alexandra nurses' uniforms walked briskly by, chatting animatedly, their starched handkerchief caps nodding in time. Seeing two white-coated doctors approaching, Evie didn't realise until they were close that one of them was Dr Mayhew. He looked smart in his blue tie, a stethoscope poking jauntily out of his pocket. She hadn't really noticed before, but he had glossy brown hair and he was quite good looking, for a doctor.

He was deep in conversation and she didn't want to interrupt him, but he lifted his head and spotted her. 'Evie,' he cried, as if he were greeting a long-lost relative.

She saw two spots of pink appear on his cheeks and he seemed a little flustered as his colleague nodded and left him standing there, in front of her, brushing a hand through his hair, his hazel eyes bright and alive with interest.

Evie jumped up from her seat to greet him. It certainly wouldn't have been appropriate to give the doctor a hug, but that's what she felt like doing.

'How are you?' he offered, almost shyly, looking down at the tiled floor of the corridor for a few moments before raising his head. 'I must say, you look tremendous in that blue coat, I mean it is new, isn't it...? Not that you didn't always look nice anyway... in your uniform.'

Evie took a breath – she knew she had to rescue the situation. 'I've got a post here, on one of the surgical wards, and I was hoping that I might be able to get some more experience in theatre.'

Dr Mayhew seemed to relax a little then. 'Yes, of course, I will put a recommendation forward... After the work you did on that beach in Greece, Evie – I mean Nurse Munro – you should be doing my job.' He smiled, his cheeks flushed red.

'Oh, hello, Dr Mayhew,' Iris said, joining them. 'I'd heard that you were working here. What with Sister Phelps as well, it feels as if we've got the old team back together.'

'It does indeed,' Mayhew enthused, his voice just a shade too loud. He glanced back to Evie, then cleared his throat, 'And you'll both be pleased to know that we also have two of our VADs here – Nurse Franklin and Nurse Kipling... Nurse Dooley it seems, preferred to return to another hospital ship.'

'Shame that Miriam didn't come too, but that's so good,' grinned Evie, the sentiment echoed by Iris, who then indicated that they needed to get moving.

'Oh, sorry... for delaying you,' Mayhew bumbled, reaching out to shake Iris's hand, which made Evie giggle.

'We'll see you around, Dr Mayhew,' she called back to him as she followed Iris.

The nurses' quarters were towards the back of the building. Iris was, of course, on a floor for more senior trained staff in a single room, but Evie was pleased with her shared accommodation, especially when she discovered she was lodging with her two friends Charlotte and Lucy, both of whom had started on the wards yesterday. Evie couldn't wait to be reunited with them. Her brand-new grey uniform dress, red-trimmed cape, and a starched piece of cloth that would form a handkerchief cap, were neatly folded on the bed.

Once Evie had her luggage unpacked, she shook out the dress and held it in front of her body as she admired her reflection in the full-length mirror attached to the wall. It was perfect. There would be no presentation ceremony for her, the war had changed all of that, but as her face beamed back a reflected smile, she felt so proud. She would have to consult with Iris on how to fold the cap correctly though. It needed to be sharp, regulation style.

After she'd unpacked and wandered restlessly around the room, there was a knock at the door and she found Iris, already in full uniform. 'Are you going to be working straight away?' she asked, suddenly concerned that she was going to be late.

'No, not till tomorrow morning, but I have a meeting with Sister Phelps and she always likes to see her nurses in uniform... I'll call by when I'm finished and I'll take you on a tour of the hospital.'

Evie nodded, excited at the prospect, although she'd need a map to find her way around, at least for the first week.

. . .

The next morning as she walked to the surgical ward beside Charlotte and Lucy, even though she hadn't yet done a stroke of work, Evie felt as though she already belonged at Netley.

Charlotte was chatting on as usual, telling them more about the party she'd attended at home in Cheltenham, when her brother had been back from France on leave and an army officer friend had joined them. It sounded as though Charlotte had had a romantic interlude, a brief moment when she'd been able to access a fragment of her life from the past. Evie was glad that she'd come back with a bit more colour in her cheeks, and she'd put some weight on.

Iris was already on the ward, standing with the other trained staff, ready to receive the report from Sister Phelps and be assigned duties. As she walked, Evie cast her eyes over the patients... One man was groaning out in pain, a drip bottle on a stand at the side of his bed. Evie had learned it wasn't the ones who were making a noise that were more cause for concern, it was those who lay quiet, listless. Many of the soldiers looked very poorly but a few were sat up in their beds chatting, giving some cheek. All had their regimental caps complete with badges proudly displayed on their bedside lockers.

'Some of this lot are very mischievous young men,' Charlotte whispered as they stood, still waiting for report. 'We worked our fingers to the bone, it was grim yesterday, especially not knowing any of the patients, but we had some jokes as well and managed to keep out of Sister's—'

'Nurse Franklin,' Sister Phelps frowned. 'What have I told you about chatting during report.'

'Sorry, Sister,' Charlotte called, giving Evie's hand a playful squeeze while Lucy shot her a horrified glance.

Evie was surprised at how quickly she slotted into the ward routine; it was identical to their work on the ship, except they had the luxury of space, tall windows that let in so much more light, and ready access to a much greater range of supplies. A large stove sat in the centre of the ward, with some chairs and benches for the more mobile patients set around it. Evie saw one young man with a bandaged stump where his left hand should have been and a cruel scar on the side of his face that looked as if the flesh had melted, leaving him with a clump of hair missing and a half-closed eye. He was sitting on a bench with his head down, lost in his own thoughts. Evie could see a full cup of tea going cold on the table next to him.

'Hello there, soldier,' she offered, 'are you not going to drink your tea?'

He shook his head, not even glancing up.

'It's going cold.'

His head snapped up then and he jumped to his feet, catching the table and sending the cup smashing to the floor, before marching away down the ward.

'I'm sorry about that, nurse,' said a soldier with a crooked nose and the stub of a lit cigarette at the corner of his mouth, his thickly bandaged leg elevated on the wooden extension of a wheelchair. 'That's Private Tucker, he doesn't speak and he's got the jitters.'

'The jitters?' Evie glanced up, she was already crouching to pick up the broken shards of pot.

'Shell shock... His best mate, a pal from the same fishing village in Devon, he was blown to smithereens right next to the lad. Poor sod was covered in guts and brains, you name it. And then he's lost his hand as well... so he won't be able to go back to hauling in the nets or whatever they do on those fishing boats.'

Evie felt an instant connection to the lad, and she took a breath. 'I'll see if I can find him, when I've mopped this lot up.'

'You'll be wasting yer time, nurse,' the soldier added, flicking a silver lighter and holding the flame to the fresh cigarette he held in the corner of his mouth. 'You won't get a word out of him... Many have tried, all have failed.'

Evie was soon swept up in other duties. Iris had asked her to assist with two very badly injured Gurkha soldiers who'd been admitted yesterday. One man had been rescuing the other under the heaviest fire imaginable and then they'd sustained a mustard gas attack. The soldier had dragged his brother in arms over a great distance, determined not to leave him behind. Sister had nursed many Gurkhas and as she told the story, her eyes filled with proud tears. The two men now lay side by side on the ward, helpless in their beds with inflamed eyes swollen shut and bandaged. They'd both suffered deep blast injuries to torso and legs, and their lungs had been burned on the inside by the gas. Their dressings were extensive and required intricate bandaging.

This was an ideal first task for Evie, and it felt reassuring to be working with Iris again, especially after the distress she seemed to have caused Private Tucker. She'd mentioned it to Charlotte, who'd also warned her off, telling her that the young man was on the edge of becoming violent and there'd been talk of him being transferred to the asylum block. 'That's where they have padded cells,' Charlotte had said, her eyes round. She'd also told Evie to be careful around the soldier in the wheelchair, Lance Corporal Hill – the nurses saw him as trouble, he was always playing cards and placing bets, he seemed to be sweeping up most of the more able-bodied soldier's money. Evie seemed to have made a very good start, picked out some prime patients. But she wasn't going to avoid them; she especially wouldn't abandon Private Tucker as he battled his demons.

Iris was delighted to be working with Evie too. The wound dressings for the Gurkha soldiers would have taken so much longer to complete without her ingenuity in cutting and fixing.

All her first-day anxieties seemed to be dispelling – after her work on the hospital ship, she was no longer daunted by Sister Phelps. In fact, they had a closeness now after their shared experience on the *Britannic*.

She'd also been pleased to find a letter from Miss Duchamp waiting in her pigeonhole this morning. Iris had forwarded her new address as soon as her post at Netley had been confirmed. No extravagant news from New York, it seemed that daily life was going on very much as normal and America showed no sign of joining the war yet. Marco was fine and well but Miss Duchamp was sure that he missed the ships. Iris was very sceptical on that score; all the little dog ever did on board was stay in the cabin and take an occasional trot around the deck. Anyway, what was most pleasing of all was that Miss Duchamp – Iris tried to think of her as Amelia – had repeated her invitation for Iris to visit her apartment in New York. The mere thought of it made her feel like she could breathe easier, that there would be some end to this madness. Just thinking of the Statue of Liberty and the streets of New York made Iris ache with longing.

Later that day when the next shipment of casualties arrived, Iris was put in charge of admitting the ones who were sent to their surgical ward. She chose Evie to assist and as they worked through the half dozen admissions, making sure an urgent case was flagged for emergency surgery and rapidly assessing the other men, it felt as if they were back in their stride.

When Dr Mayhew came on the ward to examine the patient who needed to go straight to theatre, Iris saw him scanning the ward as he walked. She knew what he was doing – he was looking for Evie. She'd never been sure, but there'd been hints of his infatuation on board the *Britannic*, then with the press of work it had seemed to settle. But yesterday, she'd seen his face after he'd been surprised to find Evie at the hospital. It had made her think of the time she'd seen Jack on the Olympic, the day war was declared. She'd turned and he'd been there, that flash of excitement in his eyes, the connection they'd had. She watched Evie and Adam standing together now at the bed of the new admission, sensing the crackle of attraction between them. It made her feel sad, knowing that she might never have that again, but then, at least she wouldn't be risking having her heart broken.

'Nurse Purefoy,' Sister Phelps called. 'I need three morphia injections drawing up, please.'

'Yes, Sister,' Iris called, moving swiftly, instantly focused.

When the afternoon shift duties commenced, Iris did her round of the ward, checking the charts at the end of the beds, making sure all observations were up to date. She also inspected dressings and made a note of those which would need changing. The stink of suppuration pervaded the ward, it was a constant battle to contain it and prevent their patients developing sepsis. Seeing Sister marching down the ward with her mouth set, Iris knew something was up. As she drew closer, Iris was shocked to see that Sister had tears welling in her eyes.

'I'm looking for Charlotte Franklin... She needs to come to the telephone in my office, her mother's on the line in a terrible state... I'm afraid it's Nurse Franklin's brother, he's been killed.'

Iris sucked in a breath, feeling the shock, absorbing it. 'She's behind those screens with Nurse Munro, I think they're almost finished, they've been...'

Even before she'd completed the sentence, Iris saw the screen move and Nurse Franklin's smiling face appear. She was glancing back to Evie, saying a few words to the young soldier with a bandaged head who was now sitting up comfortably against clean white pillows.

Iris swallowed hard. 'I'll bring her to the office,' she said.

Her voice felt hollow as she called across the ward. She saw Nurse Franklin glance behind to Evie and then she hurried across.

'There's a call for you, Charlotte, on the telephone in Sister's office,' Iris said gently. There was no need to say any more; the use of her Christian name and the tone of her voice caused Charlotte to clutch her chest and move immediately. Iris stayed beside her and handed her over to Sister at the door of the office. The whole ward heard the guttural scream that came. Iris felt it pierce her heart as surely as if it were an arrow.

'God 'elp her,' murmured an orderly as he passed with his trolley. The patients who were alert enough to understand bowed their heads. Iris breathed, in and out, as if she were holding the whole ward together. Seeing Evie walking towards her, with tears shining in her eyes, she took her hand.

'Go to her, she's your friend,' she said softly. 'Take her back to the nurse's quarters, she'll need to pack her things.'

Iris felt her already dulled, heavy heart ache with new sorrow as she stood for a few moments observing the ward. She thought of what Miss Duchamp had said on that final voyage aboard the Olympic about the reality of war only truly being understood by injured men and the women who had to deal with the consequences. Back then, even as the threat of war hung in the air like a living creature, it hadn't properly sunk in. But now, she felt as if the weight of it all were too much for any human to bear for this length of time.

In the next second, a young soldier who'd been gassed and had lost his sight, shouted out in distress. With a jolt, Iris's thoughts came back to her work, and she strode down the ward to the iron hospital bed where the boy was screaming, shaking and clawing with bandaged hands at the sheets. She began soothing him... soothing herself.

CHAPTER 19

When the summer came to Netley, the windows and doors were open, and the patients were able to walk the grounds or lounge in the sun.

Evie loved to do her duties in the outdoors, catching up with patients who needed medication, a wound dressing or bandage check, and she often went down to the pier where the men in their hospital blues leaned on the rail smoking, chatting, laughing together. This pier was nothing like the one in Yarmouth – so much smaller and jutting into settled waters – but still, the first time she'd walked the length of it, she'd felt her stomach clench as she remembered the wind and rain in her face as she'd waited for news of Jamie.

She could walk the pier now with ease, and in the evenings, when most of the patients were settled on the ward, she often came out here alone, resting her arms on the rail, listening to the gentle lap of the water.

This time, Iris had come to join her, but, needing to catch up on some letter-writing she'd gone back and left Evie to her own thoughts. She leaned back for a moment, stretching the aching muscles of her back, luxuriating in the warmth of the evening air.

A rustling sound behind alerted her, and then she could hear a woman's voice muttering jumbled words, sounding in some distress. Evie walked quickly back along the length of the short pier. The light was starting to fade but she could make out the shape of a woman stooping down amongst the long grass at the side of the water. She was still muttering and Evie caught what sounded like a French accent.

'Hello,' she called softly, 'are you all right?'

The woman gave a small scream, and Evie saw her face; her dark red hair was pulled back and her mouth had dropped open in a round oh.

'Do you need any help?' Evie asked gently, moving a step nearer.

The woman was shaking her head, backing away. 'I can't, I can't...' she repeated, then something in broken English about not having money.

Evie inched closer and that's when the woman stooped down to a blanket bundle that she'd placed amongst the stalks of grass. More muttered words and a strangled sob, then the woman turned and ran. Evie's instinct was to chase after her, and she lurched forward but then stopped dead in her tracks as the blanket bundle shifted and a tiny arm shot out. A baby started to cry.

Evie stood frozen, her heart thudding against her ribs.

The bundle began to writhe and the baby was crying even louder, truly protesting. Evie stooped down and picked it up from the ground, and the infant struggled against her, kicking in her arms, screaming now, its tiny face scrunched and bright pink. For a split second, Evie thought the child's top lip was cut, then she realised that it was cleft, a hare lip, just like her friend Fiona from Anstruther school. Evie gulped; she hadn't held a baby in her arms since she'd cradled her dead son. Her chest felt tight, she had to fight the panic that gripped her, but the infant was so alive, so full of fury, that it helped. Evie stood and loosened the blanket to check the small body – the child was clean and dressed in pure white cotton, its tiny hands clutching the air, wisps of dark red hair escaping from a delicate bonnet trimmed with lace.

Evie found herself starting to soothe the tiny creature. She'd always been good with Douglas's boys when they were fractious, and it came back to her as she rocked and stroked the child, starting to walk back towards the hospital. She needed to find Iris, she would know exactly what to do. Thankfully the baby had quietened before she reached the hospital. One or two passing staff gave her quizzical glances as she made her way to the nurses' quarters, but no one stopped her. Her heart was thrumming in her chest as she tapped on Iris's door.

In the second it opened, Evie said, 'I found a baby by the pier, its mother ran away.'

Iris raised her eyebrows, and appeared stunned, unable to speak for a moment. Then she composed herself, fully opening the door.

Evie felt her breath coming quick, she had a moment of pure panic, feeling the movement of the tiny body and hearing the child's snuffling breath. 'Here,' she said, pushing the bundle into Iris's arms.

Iris held the baby away from her body. 'I never did children's ward, I haven't a clue what to do with babies,' she stammered, clearly uncomfortable.

Evie had no choice but to reclaim the baby, but she was starting to feel as if something heavy was resting on her chest, making it hard for her to breathe.

Iris indicated for her to sit on the bed and tell her exactly what had happened. As Evie gave the full account, Iris nodded intermittently as she listened. 'It sounds like the woman may have run into difficulties, maybe she couldn't afford to pay for the suturing of the baby's lip or the child's father rejected her.'

'Or perhaps he's been killed in the war,' Evie offered.

Iris sighed, deep in thought for a few moments.

'I'll go and consult with Sister Phelps, she'll know what to do.'

Evie felt uneasy, imagining that Sister would be inflexible in her judgement, she might even remove the child immediately.

'Don't look so horrified,' Iris added. 'Sister is much kinder and more human than you think.'

As Evie sat and waited for her friend to return, she laid the infant down on the bed. It really was a very small baby, probably only weeks old, but it could kick its legs and it was moving its head from side to side and making cooing noises. Suddenly needing to know if the baby was a boy or a girl, Evie undid the child's napkin... It was a girl, she'd been given a girl, and for some reason it made tears well in her eyes. She'd always known that Jamie's baby had been a boy and it felt easier, knowing that this child was female. This baby girl was so beautiful and so vital, it made the sadness of her loss and the memory of her son's limp body, devoid of breath, come back to her like a noise screaming in her head. If it hadn't been for the neediness of the infant, she would have curled up into a ball and put her hands over her ears to try and blot it out.

Instead, she took some ragged breaths, let out her sobs, fought to gain back some control before Iris returned with Sister. The baby's napkin was damp but not saturated and she had nothing else, so she fixed it back with the safety pin and then picked the child up to straighten her white cotton nightie.

As she did so, something dropped down onto the bed... It was a silver necklace. When Evie picked it up, she saw an ornate pendant with an enamelled pattern of three spirals against a white background. She dangled it for a few moments, feeling the weight of it, assuming it must belong to the child's mother. The child started to whimper, and Evie slipped the necklace into her pocket, so she could use both arms to settle the baby girl.

As soon as Iris came through the door, Evie saw her shoot a glance of concern in her direction. She'd felt her hair starting to unravel as she'd rocked the baby and she was pacing the floor now, her body tense to stop herself from spiralling out of control.

'Let's have a look at the little scrap, lay the baby down on the bed,' Sister said kindly. 'And it was found near the pier, you say, left there by a young French woman?'

'Yes,' said Iris at the same moment as Evie stuttered. 'It's a girl, she's a baby girl.'

Sister peered closely at the child, checking her arms and legs and then slipping a finger gently into her mouth. Instantly the little girl started to suckle.

'It's a simple cleft lip – unilateral and incomplete,' Sister said. 'There's no division of the palate, it shouldn't interfere with her feeding, but it will need suturing of course as soon as possible. That should be easy enough though.'

Evie recalled the puckered scar that her friend Fiona had borne and she knew that it was important the operation was done by an accomplished surgeon. It would have to be Dr Mayhew. Even as she thought it, she could see his deft fingers working their magic.

'I'll take her to the nurses' sick bay for now. I'm sure that our Home Sister, Sister Baker will look after her for the night; somewhere in this hospital full of men, there has to be a baby's feeding bottle... And then, in the morning, we'll start to make enquiries around the hospital. She's a distinctive baby, someone might remember a woman visiting a patient with such a child. If nobody claims her, however, we'll have no choice but to take her to the orphanage in Southampton.'

Evie felt a stab of grief, still sharp enough to pierce her heart. She knew then that she couldn't let that happen.

She cleared her throat, spoke up, needing to buy more time. 'Can we ask Dr Mayhew to repair the lip?' Evie asked. 'I think he would make a very good job of it.'

'Yes, I agree,' Sister said, gathering the baby from the bed.

Evie made a move to accompany them to the nurses' sick bay.

'It's best if you stay here,' Iris said gently. 'We need to get our rest before work tomorrow and the child will be well cared for by Sister Baker.'

Evie felt an ache of longing in her chest. Her thoughts were whirling, she knew that she needed to follow Iris's direction.

As soon as the door clicked to, Iris took Evie's arm. 'Come on, sit down,' she said, gently pulling her down next to her on the bed. 'I think you need to tell me what's going on with this baby. Your body is shaking, Evie...'

Evie swallowed hard and for few moments she was unable to speak. Then the story of Jamie and the stillbirth came in a rush of words, spilling out of her. She had never given voice to it all before – only Rita knew the full story. Now, it was fresh in her mind and her body reacted accordingly – she wept and wailed, so much that at one point Iris's neighbour tapped on the door to enquire if everything was all right. Evie felt as if she were hawking up every piece of the pain that she'd buried deep down inside. She felt the squeeze of Iris's arm around her shoulders and from time to time she was aware of her friend sniffing and wiping at her face with her free hand.

When the telling was done, the two women continued to sit, leaning against each other until exhaustion hit, eventually laying down and sleeping together, side by side on the narrow bed, fully clothed, Iris still with her arm around her friend.

.   .   .

When the first rays of sun peeped in at the window and the birds started to sing their morning chorus, Evie opened her eyes. Iris had now turned on her side and was sleeping peacefully. Evie propped herself up on her elbow and gazed out through the curtains at a square of eggshell-blue sky. She felt drained, but her mind was clear and the one thought that she had was simple – she wanted to keep the baby. Only if the child's birth mother came back to claim her would she give her up.

When Iris woke, Evie had already gone from the room leaving a scrawled note beside the bed – *Thank you for last night, Iris, you are a true friend... Love you forever x.*

Iris wished now that she'd pressed Evie earlier, when they'd been on the ship and she'd first detected that sadness in her eyes. She'd always known there was something waiting to come out. It had been shocking to realise how much her friend had suffered, and it made tears prick her eyes just thinking about it. At least now, there were no secrets, and she prayed that the painful unburdening that Evie had undergone last night would help her.

Iris glanced at her clock, she needed to get moving or, for the first time ever, she would be late for her shift. Light-headed when she stood up from the bed, still in her clothes, she started to take some deep breaths. She would feel better once she had a wash and brushed her hair and then took her clean grey uniform off the hanger.

'You want to do what!?' Iris cried, walking beside Evie on their way to the ward.

'If no family come forward to claim the baby, I'm going to

adopt her. I went to see her in the nurses' sick bay this morning... She is so beautiful and she opened her eyes and looked straight at me...'

Iris took a breath, she could see by the determined set of her friend's chin that she was perfectly serious. 'Have you thought through the consequences? It's a huge undertaking and it will affect your career.'

'I've no choice,' Evie replied. 'She was found by me for a reason... because of my son.'

'It was random, Evie. A coincidence. You happened to be in the right place, that's all.'

Evie went quiet and Iris knew not to press the point, but she kept a gentle eye on her that morning, feeling protective still but also wanting to make sure that her friend was fully recovered, able to make the right decision. Iris couldn't grasp why a talented young woman with a promising career would consider throwing the whole lot away for the sake of a stranger's child – no matter how difficult the situation. After all, there were perfectly good institutions for orphan children. But as soon as she thought it, she felt her skin prickle. What would have happened to her, if she hadn't had Aunt Edith's home in Liverpool to go to?

Feeling irritated with herself now, Iris worked even harder and made herself double-check all the admission packs for their daily influx of casualties from the hospital ships. All seemed to be in order, and maybe they'd have time for a quick cup of tea before the patients flooded in. But no, too late, she could hear the orderlies along the corridor, the injured soldiers were coming. Within ten minutes all their empty beds had been filled, some of the men still in their dusty, bloodstained battledress. One man was groaning loudly, he needed an urgent injection of morphine. The others seemed settled, but Iris would make sure each had a full assessment; she didn't want one single detail to be missed.

. . .

When all the observations and wound checks had been done, and the men were all washed and changed, Iris saw Evie heading in her direction with a sheaf of papers in her hand – all the outstanding documentation that Iris would sort and file appropriately. But then Evie stopped dead in her tracks, and her mouth dropped open. She gazed past Iris towards the ward door.

Iris turned, and she saw another soldier; he was Royal Army Medical Corps and his uniform looked brand new. He didn't appear to be injured; the man was standing erect, and he was smiling in her direction, his dark hair slightly tousled, brushed back from his face. She emitted a small cry of disbelief. It seemed impossible. *Jack. Oh dear God.* Her chest constricted, she couldn't speak. He was just standing there, smiling. Then he removed his cap and spoke her name, in his delicious American accent. She felt a hot flush creep from beneath her collar and suffuse her face. Sister Phelps was at her desk in the office; if she lifted her head from her paperwork, she would be able to see him. Iris was certain that all the staff and the patients on the ward were holding their breath, watching what was about to happen.

'Go on, go to him,' she heard Evie urge, from over her shoulder. It was all that Iris needed, and she started to walk, indicating for him to follow her out of the ward and into the corridor.

He caught her hand and tried to pull her towards him, but she couldn't let him do that, not here.

'I'll have to see you later, after my shift,' she breathed, wanting so much to be in his arms there and then, dance with him in the corridor. 'What happened to you? Where have you been?' The questions burst out of her and for a moment he seemed unable to reply.

Iris felt her heart twist when she saw a shadow cross his face. He swallowed hard then launched into the telling of it, 'I had to jump from the lifeboat, it was heading into the propeller blades. Something caught my arm and I was bleeding, but not too badly. And I got lucky, I was picked up by an Allied battle-cruiser... and then shipped back to my mother's family in Ireland. I was in a bad state when I got there – the journey was rough and I developed a high fever. As soon as I was strong enough, I went home to New York. It took me months to get fit again. I didn't fancy going back on a ship, not for a while, so I sailed back to Ireland and joined the 5th Royal Irish Lancers as a stretcher-bearer.'

Iris pressed a hand to her heart, grasping the enormity of what he was saying: he'd been a hair's breadth from death. Holding back a sob, she reached out to him, taking his hand, just to feel the warmth of him, know that he was real flesh and blood, and he was alive. In the months that had followed the sinking of the *Britannic*, she'd pushed her feelings away, pouring everything into her work. Telling herself that whatever was meant to be, would be and if what they'd had was strong enough, he'd come looking for her. He had, he was here, and now it felt absurd that all she could think of to say was, 'I won't be free till this evening, can you wait?'

He started to laugh. 'Iris, I've been waiting all this time, I can wait a few more hours. But I'll have to be back on the last train... I'm sailing for France in the morning.'

She nodded. 'I'll make sure I'm off on time... I'll meet you outside the hospital chapel, it's just up from the pier.'

'OK,' he grinned, pulling her to him and kissing her once on the lips, right there in the corridor outside the ward. The pressure of his hand in the small of her back sent a shot of desire through her body. All her years of self-denial, of pushing away everything apart from work, the brutality of war, the futility of it, rose inside of her until she felt that she could burst with the sweet enjoyable ache in the pit of her stomach.

'See you later,' he murmured, his voice heavy, full of promise.

As soon as she stepped back onto the ward, she saw Evie and Lucy Kipling grinning in her direction and an alert patient in the bed near the door gave a whistle. Sister lifted her head and smiled. There was no way she could have known what the issue was, but she was used to the patients expressing themselves in whistles and cheers and loud banter. Iris felt her cheeks flush pink and Evie was laughing, full of joy, as she walked up the ward to meet her.

'I hope you're seeing him again,' she whispered urgently.

'This evening, we're meeting this evening,' Iris murmured, feeling young again, like a schoolgirl with a secret.

'Well, I'll come and chaperone you. Lucy was just saying that any respectable unmarried woman must never be seen alone with a young man, particularly a soldier.' Evie's brow was furrowed, her face straight.

Iris felt a moment of panic, till she saw her friend laughing.

'For goodness' sake, Iris, there's a war on, no one cares about chaperones anymore.'

That evening, as Iris stood on the shore of Southampton Water with Jack's arm pulling her close, she felt as if she'd entered a whole new world of experience. They'd found a quiet place in the grounds to kiss and to murmur words that in a different life before the war, would have already been spoken three years ago when they'd gone ashore in New York. Maybe they would have had a brief fling and then it would all have been over. But as Iris felt the warmth of his body and inhaled the dark, earthy smell of his hair when he leaned in to kiss her once more, she didn't think so. This was real, and it was better than anything she had ever experienced.

As they stood together in the setting sun, she gazed out over the gently rippling Southampton Water with its reflected hues of silver, pewter and gold, and she felt a moment of pure bliss.

CHAPTER 20

Evie had never seen Iris smile so much as when she'd left the ward. Often when her shift ended, she was deep into a final check of the observation charts, her brow furrowed as she scanned for any trace of a fever that might have been missed. It was so good to have seen her friend, for once, eager to be out through the door. It had been a long time coming but the moment had arrived for Iris to explore another side of life.

Evie heard Rita's voice in her head instantly. 'You can talk, Evie Munro.' And she was right, she'd become just the same, pushing all her energy into work. Only last night, when she'd rescued the baby, had she been distracted. She felt excited now to be going back to the nurses' sick bay to see the child again. This baby girl had got under her skin.

She'd seen Dr Mayhew about the repair of the cleft lip. He already knew about the child, Sister Phelps had spoken to him, and he'd agreed to perform the suturing early next morning. He needed strong, natural light for such dainty work, it was important that the sides of the cleft were aligned perfectly to give the best result. Evie had offered to assist. It made her cringe to think of how painful it would be for the baby, but Dr Mayhew had assured her that a whiff of chloroform would do the trick nicely.

There were no cots to be found, so the baby lay in a deep drawer that Sister Phelps had removed from the ornately carved chest in her own quarters and placed on top of a hospital bed. News had got round the hospital and already gifts from staff had been brought to the sick bay – a small, knitted teddy bear with lopsided button eyes, a pair of bootees, even a baby's rattle. It moved Evie to see the small gifts lined up on the bed. Going about the hospital today, she'd listened out for every shred of information – it seemed that one or two staff had seen a woman with dark red hair carrying a baby in the grounds but there were no reports of her being seen visiting or having any relationship to a patient. Given the sheer volume of men in the hospital and the rapid daily turnover, plus the busyness of the wards, it was easy to imagine that a visit from the French woman had been missed, so it was still possible that she was connected to one of the injured soldiers. Evie felt torn, she wanted the child to be reunited with her birth mother, of course she did, but she knew that she would be very disappointed if she had to lay aside her plans of adoption.

She hadn't mentioned the pendant to anyone yet, not even Iris, but she'd taken it from her pocket and studied it closely. She felt sure that it belonged to the child's mother, but the unusual spiral pattern didn't give away any clues and there was no inscription on the back. Evie had put it in her special box in her drawer, the one containing the single shell that reminded her of the pattern she'd left on her son's grave. After she'd told Iris about her baby boy, it felt as if the tiny ghost of him was resting more peacefully now. And finding the baby girl had to be some kind of sign, she was sure of it.

Evie arrived in the nurses' sick bay at baby's feeding time, and Sister Baker was glad of an extra pair of hands. She readily handed the bottle of diluted cow's milk over and retreated to her office to catch up with paperwork.

Sitting alone in an armchair by the window, Evie felt content as the baby suckled hungrily on the rubber teat. The child seemed to fit perfectly into the curve of her left arm and as she fed she looked up to Evie's face with bright grey eyes, one tiny hand splaying with pleasure as she gulped the milk. Small bubbles leaked out through the fissure in her lip, but it didn't hold the little girl back, she was greedy for life. Once the bottle was done, Evie sat her up and rubbed her back to wind her – like she'd done with Douglas's boys. She'd forgotten how adept she'd become at this. She loved the child already and it was hard to believe how that could happen so quickly. She hadn't dared tell Iris, but she even had a name for the baby, it had come to her during the night, as she'd woken from a dream, still drifting in that sleeping, waking state. The name had been there, waiting for her. She practised saying it out loud. *Cora,* her grandmother's name. It sent a warm glow through her body.

Evie slept better that night than she had done since the herring season. She woke early, feeling refreshed, eager to get back to baby Cora, to prepare her for the suturing.

Sister Baker had just finished the early morning feed, and she rose reluctantly from the seat and handed the baby over. It seemed that Cora had cast her spell on Sister as well. Evie washed the baby's face and changed her napkin, her heart starting to contract with pain, knowing what would be coming for her tiny patient.

A trolley stood ready, prepared by Sister Baker with a pile of swabs, a scalpel, and the finest needle and suture thread imaginable, all laid out on a sterile cloth. This would be a challenge even for someone as adept as Dr Mayhew. Evie stood rocking the baby, wanting her to lapse into sleep, but still her bright eyes were open, gazing up to Evie's face. It even looked as if she were trying to smile.

As promised, Dr Mayhew was there early. Evie had already placed a chair in front of a window with good light, and she was sitting nursing the baby in the warm glow of morning sun when he entered the room.

'All set?' he asked quietly, sounding a little nervous.

'Yes,' Evie said confidently, standing up from the chair.

He offered a tentative smile, pulling a bottle of chloroform from his pocket, and setting it down with a clunk on the metal trolley. Evie's heart jumped and the baby started to whimper. She rocked the child. 'Hush now hush,' she crooned, as the infant struggled against her.

Dr Mayhew was scrubbing his hands, she could see the set of his shoulders and the exposed curve of his neck as he stood at the sink. When he turned, drying his hands with a clean white towel, he seemed to be relaxing.

'I've not ever performed one of these myself,' he offered, 'but I've seen it done a few times and last night I revised the procedure... Let's pop the little one to sleep, and then we can get on.'

Evie felt her chest tighten. She was actively swaying from side to side, desperately trying to soothe the squirming baby.

'Hello there, little one,' Dr Mayhew said softly, leaning in to take a close look. 'She is a bonny one, isn't she? And yes, it's exactly as Sister said, an incomplete cleft which should be easy to repair.' He gently stroked the baby's face with his finger and then, smiling, he spoke directly to the child. 'Yes, you are a little beauty, aren't you... and we're going to do this operation for you and it's all going to be fine.'

His voice was deliciously warm and so soothing, Evie was able to breathe easier and the baby was already quietening.

'Now, I think the best way to proceed is... if I sit on the chair and, once we have the baby anaesthetised, you sit opposite and lay her head on my lap. That should give a good position.'

Evie took a breath and nodded.

Mayhew placed a tiny drop of chloroform onto a cotton swab, gesturing for Evie to sit down and cradle the baby. With one whiff of the anaesthetic, Cora's eyes closed and she began sleeping soundly. Swiftly, Mayhew drew up another chair and Evie laid the baby down on his lap, her head resting against his white coat. He reached for the scalpel and nimbly trimmed the edges of the cleft. Evie dabbed with a swab to absorb the bright red blood as the doctor took up his needle. 'The stitches need to go full thickness through the lip, one side at a time,' he said, 'Like this... so we can bring the sides of the wound securely together. Babies tend to do a lot of feeding and crying, and it puts a great deal of tension on the sutures, so they need to be secure.'

Evie leaned in to observe more closely, Mayhew's hands were rock steady and his fingers were so nimble that there was absolutely no mistake as to where the sutures would go. The whole thing was completed in minutes and Evie was very impressed by the clean, perfectly aligned sutures.

'It's such a good job,' she murmured, lifting her face, hearing him take a sharp breath as they both realised how close they were to each other.

She instantly drew back.

His eyes were bright, and he was looking straight at her.

The baby moved her head, gave a sleepy cry. Evie reached forward to gather her from Mayhew's lap.

The doctor cleared his throat, stood up from the chair. 'She'll always have a scar, but in time it will fade to white, it will be part of her.'

'Yes, yes, of course,' Evie said distractedly as she tried to find the best position to soothe the baby.

Once the child was settled, Evie took her across to the

makeshift cot and put her down, running a hand over the tiny head to smooth down the tufts of fluffy red hair. Aware that Mayhew had come to stand beside her she turned to him. 'I've called her Cora,' she said.

He didn't seem to have taken in what she'd just said, but his eyes were shining with intensity. It made her breath catch. He took a step towards her, so close she could smell the scent of his shaving soap. He smiled and reached up a hand to brush a stray piece of hair away from her face and when he spoke, his voice was heavy, barely above a whisper.

'I love you, Evie. I've loved you since the first moment I saw you.'

Evie drew in a slow breath. His hazel eyes were kind and alive with emotion, and she could hear his breath coming quick. Without a moment's hesitation she reached up to kiss him gently on the lips. His lips were warm and firm, and when he kissed her back it sent a shot of desire through her body.

Pulling away at last she breathed. 'What's going on, Dr Mayhew?'

'I'm not sure... but it's something we don't seem to have any control over,' he replied, kissing her again, his voice husky.

After he had gone back to his work, Evie stood beside the baby for a while longer. She couldn't stop smiling and she was aware of a warm, buzzy feeling in her chest. She gazed out through the window to a clear sky, completely losing track of time, until the door clicked open and Sister Baker's voice sounded. 'Isn't it time you were going to the ward, Nurse Munro?'

Evie gasped. 'Yes of course,' she called, rapidly firing information across to Sister about the surgery.

'Go on, go on,' Sister was saying. 'I worked on a paediatric ward for ten years, this is bread and butter to me.'

. . .

Two weeks later, once the wound on Cora's lip was properly healed, Evie spoke to Iris and Sister Pritchard about applying for adoption and she began her preparations for a visit to Anstruther with the baby. Sister had already made arrangements with the senior surgeon and the hospital administrator for provision of formal adoption certificate. Given that they were living through such exceptional times and the country was full of newly bereaved widows, fatherless children and abandoned babies, it was an easy matter to get this drawn up by the hospital.

Iris had been approving of Evie's relationship with Adam but much less so about her adopting the baby. She was coming round to it though and seemed happier knowing that Evie would be coming straight back to Netley after the baby was settled. Evie had sent a letter to Rita asking if she'd look after Cora until the war was over. She hadn't said so, but she was determined to pay for the baby's upkeep. She could afford it now that she was earning a qualified nurse's wage. Rita was a proud fisher woman, so she would have to be careful how she broached it, but she knew that the whole village were struggling for work, some of the war widows were relying on charity from the kirk to help buy food for their children.

Evie had also written to Sadie to explain the situation, knowing that as soon as the letter to Rita was delivered, word would get round the village. So, it made sense to let her sister-in-law know too. She'd been receiving regular letters from Sadie – Douglas was keeping safe, so far so good, and he'd been given a post behind enemy lines, with munitions, or at least that was what they'd managed to decipher from his cryptic postcards home. It seemed strange to have regular communication and support from Sadie; unlikely as that had seemed before the war, they now had a real closeness.

In fact, Evie was looking forward to making the journey

northward to introduce her adopted daughter, Cora Munro, to Sadie and the boys.

While Evie was away in Anstruther, Iris missed their evening chats and found herself walking the grounds, staring out across the water, feeling restless.

It was almost November and the leaves were starting to fall – before the war, she'd loved the autumn colours, going for a walk with a nip in the air. But now it meant that the soldiers would be covered in mud, suffering frostbite, more at risk of developing horrible infection, all of it adding to their misery. As the leaves drifted down, it made her feel sad, mournful, the seasons were still turning and the menace of war seemed unstoppable. Jack had written to her but hadn't been able to get leave since the summer. It made her feel like crying as she stood now at the end of the pier, feeling a shiver of cold run through her body.

Iris was still troubled by the decisions Evie had been making in such rapid succession. She prayed, for her sake, that this wasn't all a reaction to the traumas of the past. She was confident that Adam was a good, kind man, but would he be enough for Evie? Even with all her dedication to duty and keen interest in surgery, there was still a wildness about her friend, something that would make her liable to go running along a clifftop with her hair loose and blowing in the wind. Iris knew that she'd been reading too many romantic novels... but even so, she wanted her friend to find the right match, especially now that she'd taken on the care of a child. Again, all done in a whirl – typical Evie.

Then again, how could she judge... as soon as Jack had turned up in the summer, she'd been swept away by him. She'd been in such a heightened state of love and fear that she hadn't slept for nights after he'd embarked for France. She was addicted to the newspapers – seeking them out in the nurses' common room, scanning the lists of the dead. It was a grim task, but it was the only way she would know if Jack were killed. A telegram would go to his family in Brooklyn who probably knew nothing about her. In fact, all she knew of them was that Jack had two older sisters, an Irish mother, an Italian father who'd lived in Sicily and now worked for the New York City Fire Department. The 'getting to know everything' process had been impossible in the snatched moments they'd had together. That's why, now he was gone again, it had all begun to feel unreal, as if it were a dream.

Iris took a drag of her cigarette, exhaling heavily... This was the closest she could get to being at sea, standing out here in the dark, with a smoke in her hand. She imagined Jack beneath the same starry sky, in some unnamed place at the other side of the English Channel. Was he thinking of her, remembering their time together? Or was he running with a stretcher, shells bursting around him? She felt a shiver run down her spine. She'd nursed stretcher-bearers, she'd heard their stories; they were the ones who had to run towards gunfire.

Jack cupped his hands around the match as he lit up another smoke. Exhausted, standing in mud, with intermittent gunfire sounding all around, he couldn't bring himself to go into the dugout and lie down to sleep.

Last night a rat had jumped out from the blanket, scratching his arm with its claws. He shuddered again, thinking about it. He felt like scrubbing his whole body with disinfectant, but he hadn't even been able to get a proper wash for two weeks. His skin was itchy, crawling. Before this posting he'd been due to go on a week's leave, he should have been back to see Iris, but his unit had suffered so many losses, there simply weren't enough stretcher-bearers to go round. Asking and chivvying for time off didn't work – he'd tried it many times, only to see others who had kept silent be sent home. Maybe it was because he was American... nah, he fitted in well enough, the Brits loved him, and rumour had it that America were joining the allies any day now. It was just this godawful war.

Pausing for a moment, his cigarette tucked inwards to his palm, so that it wouldn't be visible to a German sniper, he lifted his face to the sky. There were so many stars up there tonight – it reminded him of those nights on the ship, out in the Mediterranean, when he'd walked the decks, hoping he might bump into Iris. Not that she'd have spoken to him even if he had... It made him smile, thinking of her attitude. He liked that spark, the strong will that guided her every utterance. She was a 'tough cookie' all right. Picking out the brightest star, he dedicated it to her, the love of his life. Taking a final drag from the cigarette he dropped it down to the muddy water in the bottom of the trench. He was bone-tired, he had no choice, he'd have to face the rats now and try to snatch some sleep.

'Stretcher-bearers!' a man's voice screamed, further down the trench.

Jack turned on his heel. Behind him he could hear his partner already stirring. He grabbed the stretcher in one hand and ran down the trench, splashing his way through water, the sound of his heart beating time to the racket of continuing fire.

'Over here,' a Tommy was shouting.

Jack knelt next to the crumpled casualty lying on his side, and he shook his arm, 'How you doin' fella?' No response, and it was only as he rolled him onto his back that he saw the chunk of skull missing from the side of the young man's head. 'Sorry, mate. He's a goner,' Jack said gently to the fella's distraught pal, who was wailing and crying, doubled over with the grief. Jack placed a hand on the soldier's arm, ducking instinctively as a bullet whistled past and buried itself in the opposite side of the trench.

'They seem to be creeping closer,' Jack's partner, Arthur, said quietly, still slightly out of breath but ready to move the dead man.

Jack and Arthur worked carefully, showing respect for the soldier's pal, giving him time to say his goodbyes, but then they had to get moving. It was strange, and Jack had noticed this many times, the dead fellas always felt heavier... Maybe it was because there was no buzz of adrenaline, no hope their man on the stretcher could be saved. Waiting for an opportune moment, between bouts of gunfire, they dodged across a section of collapsed trench to the dugout where the bodies were left. This fella was the first of the night, and it felt sad to leave him there alone, unattended, but they had no choice but to wrap him in the blanket and return to base with their stretcher. Jack swallowed hard, thinking about the rats again.

The next morning brought a welcome move to another posting, further up the line. Jack prayed they wouldn't be crouching in a trench, that there'd be access to water and he could at least get a wash. As they marched, Arthur chatted on about his lively childhood growing up in the heart of Birmingham. Jack loved to hear him talk, just for the sound of the accent. It had taken a full week for either of them to be understood by the other but now Jack found himself mixing his own Brooklyn twang with a bit of Brummy. Unlike Jack, Arthur had grown up without parents, and he'd joined a gang of youngsters and roamed the streets till he was old enough to start work in the iron-smelting industry. He was still only eighteen and he looked even younger with his boyish thatch of dishevelled hair. The life sounded hard, far different from Jack's relatively safe, comfortable existence amid his Irish and Italian extended families... and he'd had a good schooling. He hadn't made much use of it yet, but he had his eye on a job in the offices of New York harbour. That's if Iris would agree to move to America.

Along the road they met a long stream of walking wounded coming in the opposite direction, and scores of German prisoners who seemed badly shell-shocked. A fellow stretcher-bearer shouted hello as he trudged past with an injured German on his back. It had seemed strange to Jack at first, but the medical corps treated all casualties, including the enemy.

After spending the night in the barn of a ruined farmhouse, destroyed by shelling, they were on the march again. Jack was feeling better, at least he'd managed to get a wash and a shave at the cattle trough. Though the November breeze was chill, the sky was clear and the pale sun hung in the sky, marking their passing. He even felt cheery as they stumbled their way along a road pocked with shell holes. Arthur was swearing his head off as Jack, laughing, hauled him up off the dusty road for the second time.

Out of nowhere came a loud whistling and then another. Jack saw their sergeant's tin hat blown off his head and he fell to the ground. As one, he and Arthur hurtled forward, and still the shells rained around them. Others were shouting, screaming, in front of them. They were being mown down and there was nowhere to hide.

Jack took a shot to the chest and Arthur was hit in the head at exactly the same moment. They fell together onto the road. Jack lay on his back, looking up to the clear, innocent sky. He glanced to the side; a portion of Arthur's head was missing and his eyes were wide, unseeing.

Jack fought the searing pain in his chest and reached out a hand to his pal. He could hear others groaning in pain – one man shouting, 'Help me, help me.' Jack wanted to assist, but his warm sticky blood was seeping through his khaki tunic now and pooling on the dusty road. He couldn't move. He tried to shout, to call for a stretcher for the man in pain, but his voice wouldn't come. Jack felt himself drifting deeper, the light around him fading rapidly.

He lay for a few more seconds beneath the pale sun, and then with his dying breath he whispered his final word: *Iris*.

CHAPTER 21

Iris was sure that she was coming down with a fever. She'd slept badly and now on the ward in the middle of a busy morning shift her legs were heavy, her whole body ached. Last night she'd dreamt of Jack – he was calling for her, and she'd had a vision of him lying on a dusty road.

She'd woken shaking, and now the residue of the nightmare remained. She regularly had dreams about him, but none had ever been so vivid. Pushing herself as always, she got up early, made sure to get on with her work, even though she felt so exhausted she could have crawled onto one of the empty beds on the ward.

When the time came for the daily admission of injured men, she was on alert, as always vigilant for any sign of a casualty from the Irish Lancers, someone who might have news of Jack Rosetti. Only last week a nurse from another ward had come to scan the regimental caps on the bedside lockers, searching for a soldier from her fiancé's regiment. She'd screamed with delight when she'd found a man who knew him well and could give her reassurance and some anecdotes that made her man real to her again.

Iris checked every day and asked around the other wards, but she'd never found any leads on Jack. This morning she felt even more expectant, and the feeling didn't subside.

Later that day, on a short break from the ward, she walked to the pier. With Evie still away it was her usual practice to take some air as often as she could. A few soldiers in their hospital blues were leaning on the rail and they nodded and smiled. Iris pushed away the thought immediately, but she entertained the possibility of Jack getting a minor wound, a blighty as the men called it, shot in the foot or something like that. He could ask to be transferred here and then she could see him every day. She almost laughed at the ridiculousness of the times they were living through.

Leaning on the rail at the end of the pier she lifted her face to the pale sun and breathed in the salt smell of the water. November sun was always so welcome when it came. Hearing a voice behind her, calling her name, she was surprised to see the formidable shape of Sister Phelps proceeding along the length of the pier. Her expression was solemn and she held a slip of paper in her hand. Something about the look on Sister's face made Iris's stomach tighten. She held onto the rail behind her with one hand, gripping it tightly, wishing she could stop Sister in her tracks, prevent her from delivering whatever news she'd come out here with.

Sister reached out a hand to her first and then she told her it was bad news. Iris gulped in a breath, pressing a hand to her chest. The paper in Sister's hand was a telegram, and for a moment it made Iris feel certain that it couldn't be news of Jack – she'd already thought this through, the telegram would go to his family. It must be Evie or Francine or the baby. Her mind was reeling, and her ears were singing so loud she could hardly hear Sister's words. But then she heard *Private Jack Rosetti*, and a vice gripped her chest, stopping her breath. She felt as if she were suffocating. Sister was patting her, shaking her, but she couldn't get her breath. At last it came, she sucked it in, almost involuntarily, feeling that she wanted to die too, there and then. She wanted to sob and cry and wail but no sound would come, her chest was burning with pain, but it was all locked deep inside.

There was a void then, a blank, before she found herself lying on a bed in the nurses' sick bay. Groggy, she opened her eyes. Sister Baker was by the side of the bed, knitting. It reminded her of that last trip on the *Olympic* when Matron had sat with her needles at the bedside of that young woman who'd had her appendix removed. Miss Buchanan, yes, that was it... It was all a bit jumbled, but something about that time brought a flash of memory. She saw Jack, out on deck, he was wearing an ill-fitting grey jacket and a straw boater pulled down low over his eyes. She gasped with the freshness of the memory, she wanted to banish it but it was stuck, she had no choice but to see him pushing up his hat to reveal his face. Her throat tightened and tears pricked her eyes when she recalled how desperately she'd tried not to show how thrilled she was to see him... *If only she could have that time back.* It was too much to bear, knowing that she would never meet him again.

Iris turned onto her other side, pressed her face into the pillow, trying to blot out the flashes of memory but they were unstoppable, devastating. She took a breath, feeling heavy in her chest as she felt, once again, the gentle touch of his fingers on her cheek, his arm curling around her, brushing the small of her back. He pulled her close and she rested against his body, with the sound of the orchestra drifting over them. 'I wish we had some champagne,' he murmured, starting to sway from side to side with the music. Once more she felt the pressure of his body against hers as they danced. And then, unbearably, he was bending his head to kiss her on the lips. His stubbly beard scratched her chin, his lips were soft and warm, tasting of salt.

Iris felt her heart twist in her chest and she must have sobbed out loud then because she heard Sister Baker get up from her chair. Iris held her breath, squeezed her eyes shut, tried to make out that she was dreaming. Maybe she was asleep, it felt as if waking and dreaming were all one right now. Hearing Sister sit back in her chair, Iris eased out a breath, pushed her face into the pillow and let the tears flow. A surge of pain spread from the pit of her stomach, up through her chest and then out through her mouth. She was sobbing now, deep guttural sobs that racked her body. With the sobs came more tears, floods of tears that seemed as if they would never end. Sister Baker was holding on to her, as if they were both at sea in a terrible storm. Then she heard another voice – it was Evie, she'd forgotten that she was due home. Iris saw a bleary image of Evie at the side of the bed and then she felt her friend's arms firmly around her, holding her, keeping her anchored.

After the worst of the first wave of grief was over, Iris sat exhausted, her shoulders slumped, beside Evie on the bed. They were silent now. Evie hadn't even taken her coat off. Iris leaned against her friend's shoulder, feeling quiet tears running down her cheeks. Evie handed her another handkerchief and then fished in her pocket, pulling out her flask. 'Have a sup of this, it might help,' she murmured, and Iris did as she was told, feeling the strong liquor burn its way down to her stomach. She was aware of Evie shrugging her coat off then before sitting back down beside her on the bed, slipping an arm around her shoulders.

At some time during the night, Iris woke to find Evie still beside her on the bed. The curtains were open and a round, full moon was shining in the sky.

Iris slipped out of the bed and walked to the window, placing the palm of her hand against the cold glass. 'You'll always be with me, Jack,' she said out loud, 'No matter where I am or what I'm doing... you'll always be a part of me.'

Despite Evie, Sister Phelps and Sister Baker protesting loudly about her decision, Iris only took one more day off before she was back on the ward – pale and exhausted, with dark smudges beneath her eyes, but she was there, and she was doing her job. She'd explained to Evie that she had to go back, it was the only thing that would help. Evie had understood, she'd said that she'd done exactly the same after Jamie had died. And as the days drifted by, the grief didn't lessen but it became easier to keep in check.

Iris hadn't known how she'd be, seeing the casualties streaming in, the low slant of autumn sun through the windows illuminating the same khaki uniforms that Jack had worn the last time she'd seen him. But she'd made herself bear it, and now she was working as hard as she'd done before. She'd managed to find out how Jack had died, and it had helped her to know that he'd been shot in the chest and it had been quick. Seemingly, also, the reason why she'd received a telegram was that he had told his mother about her; in fact the whole Rosetti family knew about the nurse stewardess who Jack had first met on the *Olympic*. She didn't know if it made her feel better or worse, knowing that he'd thought enough of her to share it with his family, but she'd received a lovely letter from Mrs Rosetti and she'd written back to offer her condolences and tell them how Jack had been that last time she'd seen him.

As soon as her work allowed, Iris took some time off to go and see Francine. As she walked along the well-remembered street and then knocked at the door, it felt good to be greeted by the little dog who ran excitedly towards her. Barney no longer looked for Sam, but that was life and time moved on. Not that she was feeling anywhere near that stage yet. She hadn't ever disclosed any information about Jack to Francine, so there was no requirement to tell her anything of what had happened. But of course, as soon as the door opened, Francine began asking her what the matter was, and the moment she walked into the warm kitchen with its terracotta tiled floor and slid into a chair while Francine made the coffee, she felt a space inside of her open up and the whole story came out even before the coffee was poured.

Afterwards, as they sat in quiet companionship, Iris felt more at peace than she'd done for months. Resting back in her chair, with Barney at her feet and the spit of the fire, worked some magic stronger than morphia. Aware of her breath moving in and out of her lungs, she felt as if she could have fallen asleep there and then. Hearing a murmur from the head of the table, Iris turned her head, ready to speak, but Sam's chair was empty. Francine began to smile, and softly said, 'We are surrounded by ghosts, *ma chérie*... all we can do is learn to live with them.'

'Cheers, Sam,' Iris offered, turning and lifting her coffee cup in a toast.

Francine chuckled. 'He talks to me all of the time, he's always there... It helps me get through, especially with both the boys still away with the Navy.'

'I don't hear much from Jack, it's more flashes, snapshots that I see in my head. Like a collection of photographs.'

'Mmm, and you say when you met him he had a camera around his neck?'

'Yes, strange isn't it...'

'Life is strange, *ma chérie*,' Francine said, her voice suddenly melancholy. Iris heard her sigh and she pulled a French cigarette out of her pack and passed one over for Iris. By the time Francine had flicked the silver lighter, the one with the dolphin's head that Sam had given her, the moment had moved on and she rested back in her chair. Iris took a deep drag and reached down to give Barney a scratch behind the ears.

When Francine spoke, her voice was strong again. 'Now, Iris, later, if you're feeling up to it, we can pull out all of your things and find the diamond necklace that Miss Duchamp gave you... Let's both try it on!'

The necklace lifted their spirits and, as they sat at a breakfast of croissants and coffee the next morning, Iris pulled a letter from Miss Duchamp out of her skirt pocket, one that she'd received as she was leaving the hospital and completely forgotten about.

Iris smiled, neatly slitting the top of the envelope with a clean butter knife and reading it as she ate her breakfast. Amelia spoke of life in New York, now that America had joined the war. It didn't sound to Iris as if much had changed; the normal social events were going on, but it seemed that volunteer agencies and fundraising committees had been set up. Miss Duchamp appeared rather scathing of the 'do-gooder' types who were joining in, but she had given a handsome donation. She closed with a reminder that Iris must visit her apartment in New York when all the dreadful business of war was done.

Another Christmas came and went and, as the world trudged on into the fourth new year of the war, no one was confident that it would ever end. Month by month, life had become a dull repetition with more terrible news of young men's lives lost.

Iris never thought that her work would become a routine and that she would feel dragged down by it, but all the nurses were struggling now. Even Evie was battling to maintain her usual chipper demeanour. There was perhaps some slackening of casualty numbers as they headed towards the end of summer but they were all so jaded, it felt like they were losing track.

When the news came on the eleventh of November that all hostilities had ceased, Iris was delighted for the men and relieved that no more lives would be lost, but she also felt numb. As the bells of the hospital chapel rang out and whistles blew, she felt tears streaming down her face and she realised that she was crying – not just for Jack and Sam, but for all the soldiers who'd been killed or maimed. Nothing could bring back a whole generation of young men who had been lost forever. Swiping tears from her eyes, she felt Evie's arm around her shoulders, and the patients on the ward cheered for the end of the war and then more cheers for Sister and her band of nurses. Iris and Evie were both in tears now and even Sister Phelps was dabbing at her eyes with a handkerchief as, 'Hip hooray! Hip hip hooray!' echoed down the length of the ward and out through the corridors of the vast hospital.

CHAPTER 22

HMT OLYMPIC, EN ROUTE TO NEW YORK, MARCH 1919

The Southampton breeze was icy and Iris was glad that she'd worn her thick black wool coat to embark. As the giant ship began to ease out of the harbour, she stood at the side on a deck crammed with joyful homeward-bound troops. The men around her cheered loudly and threw their caps in the air. One Canadian captain grabbed hold of Iris and planted a kiss on her cheek. Normally it would have felt like an affront, but she was giddy with euphoria stoked by the excitement of departure. The same feeling sparked between the men, buzzing from one to another, impossible to resist.

'Are you a nurse?' an American soldier shouted, and when she said yes, he patted her on the back and then shook her hand vigorously. On the edge of tears, he thanked her and said, 'You nurses saved my life,' before his raucous friends thrust a bottle of beer in his hand and dragged him away.

Iris swallowed hard and turned back to watch the receding shore. Sister Phelps had told her to go to New York, stay as long as she needed; there would always be a job for her back at the hospital. Having yearned to be on the move for so long, Iris now felt some sadness at leaving. The *Britannic* and Netley hospital had been like home to her for over four years.

She'd said a tearful goodbye to Evie, who had just received some sad news from home – one of the fisher girls, Minnie McKay, had died from injuries sustained in the final week of the war, when she'd been serving as a nurse at a casualty clearing station on the front line. Evie had cried her eyes out. Minnie had been such a happy, lively young woman, even Iris knew some of the stories about her. Evie would be heading back to Scotland anyway next month, so that was good. She would be reunited with Cora, now a lively two-year-old, ably cared for by Evie's close friend Rita. Adam would be travelling with her. He'd been offered a senior surgeon's post at the Edinburgh Royal Infirmary and Evie would be one of his theatre nurses.

She'd done well for herself, Evie Munro, not that Iris had been surprised; even on the first day aboard the *Britannic*, Iris had noted her energy and potential. She'd detected a wariness in Evie when she'd told Iris about her engagement to Adam, perhaps wondering if it was too raw for her, after what had happened to Jack. But how could Iris have been anything other than delighted for them – they were perfect together and with Cora, they would be a strong, ready-made family. First though, they would be married in the tiny Anstruther church that overlooked the sea. It sounded idyllic; Iris had promised to visit as soon as she could. In the meantime she had her own business to attend to, and she didn't quite know which direction it would take her.

Back on the familiar transatlantic route, it felt strange to be travelling once more on the *Olympic*. Little trace of the luxurious liner remained within the functional troop ship that the ship had become. In a way, it helped Iris that most of the opulent fittings had been stripped out and the vessel was painted in camouflage colours. It made her less likely to expect to see familiar faces or think about Jack. The decks and the interior were dusty and dirty in places, but the shared cabin that she'd been assigned with a returning American nurse was clean enough and it was right next door to the one she'd inhabited with Roisin, all those years ago. Carla, her cabin mate, was easy company and she'd been pleased to be offered the top bunk, not knowing that Iris always preferred the bottom. They hadn't talked about their previous lives, where they'd been and what they'd been doing during the war.

Standing out at the side of the ship on that first evening to have her customary smoke, Iris's heart ached with pain when she realised this was the exact same spot where she'd turned to find Jack, making his tour of first class. Looking out to the horizon, she felt a shiver run through her body and then, in the next moment, she was sure she could hear an orchestra playing. She closed her eyes and let the imaginary music wash over her, catching an image of herself in her stewardess's uniform, bustling along a well-lit deck, picking up a murmur of genteel conversation and the rustle of a silk evening gown. Then the tinkling laughter of a young woman broke through. When she glanced sideways, she could see Carla further along the rail, standing next to a good-looking American soldier.

'Well, at least some of it's in the land of the living,' she murmured to herself, starting to smile.

As the days of the voyage went by, Iris felt a gradual unwinding of the tightly coiled lump in her chest. She must have been carrying it for a while – she hadn't even noticed it till she'd finished her work at the hospital.

By the time she disembarked in New York harbour, she was breathing a little easier, starting to take in more of the world around her. It had been years since she'd walked through the city. The buzz of activity that she'd always loved now seemed to jangle her. Not until she saw the familiar lines of Brooklyn bridge – standing so strong and beautiful – did she breathe more easily as the sights and the sounds of her treasured city started to ease her.

The spring sun had come out to welcome Iris back to New York, and she was glad that she'd changed into the pale grey suit and cream cotton blouse that she'd bought for the trip from a store in Southampton. The flattering cut of the skirt and the above ankle hemline made her feel lighter, more modern. She'd lost weight during the war, the waistband of her skirt was slack around her thin waist, and when she'd looked in the mirror to apply her powder and red lipstick, her cheekbones were much sharper than she ever remembered.

As she walked on, carrying her leather suitcase, the whole city spooled by and in the warmth of the sun she started to unwind, breathe deeply, slow her pace. By the time she was nearing Central Park, she was actively looking around her, drawing in the colours and the life of the city. Ladies with their parasols in elegant open carriages were being driven by the park, the sound of their laughter and the jingle of the horses' bridles made her feel happy.

Checking her watch, she saw that she had time to spare, and seeing the green expanse of the park waiting to be explored, she crossed over the street and entered. The sun was stronger now, the trees were in bud and time seemed to stretch out before her like paradise. Wandering through, Iris saw well-dressed ladies linking the arms of men in smart suits. An ice cream seller was surrounded by a noisy babble of children who were being shep-herded by an Italian mother dressed in black – the woman raised her voice, pulled one of the bigger boys back, the others were shouting in protest. A sweet little girl with curly black hair looked up at Iris and offered a cheeky grin. It made her smile and then, leaving behind the jostling children, she saw the calm of the lake and the lazy glide of the rowing boats on the water. She sighed with pleasure.

Seeing a statue of a beautiful angel, standing up high, on top of an impressive fountain, she walked towards it. The sound of the trickling water was so soothing. When she got close to the stone rim, she saw scattered petals gently drifting on the water and other spring flowers formed into a wreath had been laid at the edge. As she looked up to the angel, she was sure the bronze effigy moved her head. It defied all rational thought, but it made Iris's skin tingle with goosebumps. The angel, the floating petals and the gentle ripple of the water... to Iris they seemed a kind of memorial. She stood quietly, listening to the sound of the water, gazing up at the face of the angel and thinking about Jack and Sam and all those poor lost soldiers. She spent as much time as she needed and then she walked by the side of the lake, picking up the sounds of children playing, enjoying the gentle lap of the water, until it was time to find Miss Duchamp's apartment.

Making her way towards the Upper West Side, she admired the opulence of the square built apartment buildings, none of them less than twelve floors high. She easily found Miss Duchamp's address and felt a ripple of excitement as she reported to the white-gloved doorman wearing gold epaulettes. Iris half-expected to be turned away with a polite apology, but the doorman nodded and smiled and showed her through to a uniformed elevator attendant who politely took her to the correct floor.

Iris was greeted at Miss Duchamp's door by a French maid in a black dress and crisp lace cap. She started to feel a little nervous, but as she stepped through into the marble entrance hall decorated with Grecian-style statues and potted palms, she was buoyed up by the confident tap of her new leather, side-button boots.

'Iris,' Miss Duchamp called, glowing with pleasure as she swept out of her salon with Marco at her heels, barking excitedly, wagging his tail and skidding around on the shiny, polished floor. Iris had been prepared for some cooling of the intimacy that they'd shared in those final days aboard the *Olympic*, but Miss Duchamp was in tears as they hugged, and she led Iris into the sitting room where the splendour of the thick carpet and plush Italianate furnishings took her breath away.

They sipped tea and ate dainty pastries, and Miss Duchamp chatted easily about New York life and the minor inconveniences that she was forced to endure. Then she reached out a hand to Iris. 'It must have been terrible for you, working as a nurse, seeing all those awful things...' Her voice broke, she was unable to continue.

Iris took her hand and gave it a squeeze. 'It was, but doing that work was satisfying, I felt as if I could make a difference.'

Miss Duchamp dabbed at her eyes. 'I'm so proud of you, Iris, you deserve a medal.'

'Well, I'm not sure about that,' Iris smiled, 'but I am hoping for a bit of rest.'

'You can stay here, with me,' Miss Duchamp offered. 'I have a number of guest rooms.'

'No, I couldn't, honestly... I've booked into a small hotel—'

'Nonsense,' cried Miss Duchamp. 'You've just fought a war. I'm going to give you my best suite, for as long as you need it, and give instructions to my cook to feed you up. You've lost so much weight, you are thin, Iris, far too thin.'

It seemed that Iris had no choice. The maid was summoned to prepare the room and to telephone Iris's hotel to cancel the booking. She took Iris's suitcase with her.

Miss Duchamp was smiling now. 'I want you here, Iris. I have much to discuss with you and there is no time to lose.'

'Thank you, Miss Duchamp,' she said.

'Please, you must call me Amelia from now on – promise you will.'

'Yes... Amelia.'

Later, after dinner, as the two women sat with their cigarettes and a glass of brandy, Amelia fixed Iris with her sapphire eyes. Iris knew something was coming.

'I've reached a decision,' she announced. 'It was an easy one to make, given that I'm feeling my age much more now, after all this war... I won't be going back to sea, Iris, I will be spending the rest of my days here, in New York.'

'Maybe you should try—'

'No,' Amelia replied, firmly. 'I have thought very long and hard about it.'

Iris waited as Amelia took a breath and composed herself.

'I have no close family, as you know – just my feckless nephew who I only see when he needs some money. You are my only true friend, Iris, I've always trusted you...'

Iris thought she could see the direction this was going... Amelia was going to ask her to be a housekeeper or companion. It appealed... it would offer new experience.

'My nephew will inherit this apartment, he's the son of my beloved sister who died very young, so I need to honour her memory. But... the one in Paris... it has a view of the Eiffel Tower, it is my favourite place and I will never visit it again.'

Iris opened her mouth to interject, and Amelia held a hand up to stop her.

'Therefore, I have spoken to my French lawyer to make all the arrangements... I want you to have it, Iris.'

Iris gasped – she could only open and close her mouth, unable to speak at all at first. 'No, you can't... surely you...'

Amelia shook her head and then she started to laugh, glee-fully, like a child. 'It's yours Iris, it's yours already and I'm going to provide you with a lump sum to cover the upkeep, and spending money – all of it!'

Iris was stunned... she needed to take a breath. She felt a burst of excitement explode in her chest; this was the most unbelievable thing that had ever happened to her. Amelia laughed again and she got up from her seat and then Marco started barking and skidding around on the polished floor. It seemed Iris had no choice but to accept.

'I don't want you thinking that I expect something in return, Iris,' Amelia said. 'You have done so much for me over the years... You looked after me, answered all my demands, and you saved Marco that day when he broke loose on deck... All I ask is that if you are ever back in New York, you come to see me, so we can talk through old times on board the *Olympic*.'

Iris was still stunned, all she could do was nod.

'There is one more thing, Iris...' Amelia walked to a marble-topped side table to collect a familiar leather case with velvet lining. 'I want you to have the rubies.' She flicked open the lid to reveal the necklace and the drop earrings.

Iris took a deep breath, still reeling.

'We'll go through the jewellery,' Amelia announced, 'and you can take whatever pieces you want... I only wear certain things, I'd rather someone else have the enjoyment out of them.'

Iris began to feel tears pricking her eyes, she was completely overwhelmed. She composed herself enough to breathe the words, 'Thank you.'

Amelia topped up the brandy glasses and slipped another cigarette into her ivory holder, passing one over to Iris. 'We'll have this and then you get yourself to bed. You must be exhausted, and all of this will be a bit of a shock.'

A bit of a shock, Iris repeated in her head, grateful for the delicious taste of the cognac and beginning to settle with the first drag of her cigarette. And then, seeing the glee on Amelia's face, she started to smile.

By the time she was getting ready for bed her mind was already whirring with plans – she could invite Francine to Paris, and Evie and Adam and the baby... She could make a whole new life for herself there if she wanted. And suddenly, with all her heart, she knew she did want it – more than anything else in the world.

EPILOGUE

SS PARIS, EN ROUTE TO NEW YORK, JULY 1922

Iris almost didn't recognise her reflection in the ornate mirror above the dresser. With her hair pulled up into a French pleat, her neck appeared pale and slender, elegant-looking, and the ruby drop earrings were offset beautifully by the peacock blue of her silk gown. It was strange now to think back to her functional nurse's uniform and starched cap. Taking her bright red lipstick, she smoothed it over her mouth, adding the final touch to her make-up. It made her lips feel heavy, tingling with sensation.

She was ready.

A light knock at the door made her turn from the mirror.

'Some flowers for you, madame,' the steward said, handing over a stunning bouquet of pink roses. 'Thank you,' Iris smiled, slipping out the card from its tiny envelope... As expected, they were from Miss Duchamp, wishing her a safe journey on this, her annual trip to New York. Iris arranged them in the plain glass jug that she always brought in her trunk, aware of the busyness of the stewardesses and the shortage of vases.

This time her trip would involve a visit to Evie, Adam and Cora. The family had moved to New York after Adam had been

offered a senior post at the Bellevue Hospital. Iris couldn't wait
to see them; it had been a year since they'd last met up in
Anstruther – Evie full of life as ever and Cora an adorable five-
year-old, with dark red curls and a mischievous grin.

Iris had been so busy this year, with alterations to the apartment in Paris, and Francine had been over to stay for an
extended period, and now it was summer already. Miss
Duchamp had seemed more frail during her last visit and
Marco's legs were weakening. She wanted this trip to go well, to
be just as positive as the other yearly trips had been, but she
knew that it was only a question of time before her elderly
friend's health began to deteriorate. It had made her feel sad last
time, to see Amelia struggling to catch her breath when they
took their customary walk in Central Park. Iris had offered to
stay on, to nurse her, but – stubborn as ever – Amelia had
refused point-blank, reminding her that she was very capable of
making her own arrangements.

Iris gathered her evening bag and did one quick check
around the cabin to make sure she was leaving everything spotless and tidy. She loved travelling on board the *Paris* because
the staterooms had square windows that gave a view of the sea,
and of course the haute cuisine was superb.

After dinner in the first-class dining room, Iris made her way to
the side of the ship, walking delicately in her heeled velvet slip-
pers. The soft brush of her gown against her silk-stockinged legs
sent a trill of pleasure her body. As she leaned out to
watch the meandering trail of white spray at the side of the ship,
the gold bangle on her left wrist knocked gently against the
wooden rail. Breathing in the salt air, she closed her eyes,
savouring this moment. Even though it had been some years
since she'd worked as a stewardess, she never took for granted
the time that she now had free from the responsibility of

tending to other people's needs, having to snatch respite whenever she could. Leaning further out, the drag of air mussed her carefully coiffed locks. It made her feel giddy.

Hearing a sound, she straightened up and glanced behind her. She was sure she'd heard a voice, and it had sounded familiar. Her skin began to tingle with sensation.

There was no one there. *Strange.* Maybe it was her mind playing tricks, but this had happened to her before when she was crossing the Atlantic. Feeling the reassuring weight of the ruby necklace against her skin she gripped the rail to ground herself. Drawing in another deep breath of sea air to steady the full beat of her heart, she remembered what Francine often said about being surrounded by those who had passed and learning to live with them. It made her wish she'd brought the pink roses from her cabin so she could strew them in the wake of the ship, to pay tribute to all her ghosts.

Here we go again, she thought, hearing another voice to the side of her. But when she sneaked a glance, she saw a living person, a man with silver-streaked brown hair was leaning on the rail, he was wearing an expensive-looking linen suit and a blue shirt, open at the neck. She heard him strike a match and then she smelt fresh tobacco smoke. She was sure that he'd just moved closer.

'Do you mind if I share the view?' His manner was very direct and his voice French, deliciously accented.

She turned with a polite smile. 'Of course I don't mind, this is for all passengers.'

As he stepped closer, she felt a tiny vibration of something between them.

'I saw you in the dining room, earlier,' he said. 'Is the other woman at your table a friend or a relative?'

'Oh neither, we are both women travelling unaccompanied.'

Iris saw the warmth in his eyes deepen.

'How about you?' she asked, boldly. 'Are you with anyone?'

'No, my wife died many years ago. I have business interests in New York, I'm on one of my regular trips... May I introduce myself? My name is Lucien Becker,' quickly adding, 'German father, French mother,' when he saw her puzzlement. 'I am very pleased to meet you... And you are?'

'Iris Purefoy, Miss Iris Purefoy,' she said, reaching to shake his hand.

As they continued to chat, time slipped by and neither of them noticed the sky darkening and the lights of the ship coming on behind. Their murmured conversation, punctuated by laughter, rose effortlessly to the full moon that hung low over the flat, limitless ocean. Feeling a slight nip in the air, Iris ran both hands over her bare arms.

'I can see you are a little chilly, I think it's time we went back inside to the cocktail bar. I believe the barman does an excellent Manhattan...'

'Yes, I've already tried many of them, and the Tom Collins is also very nice,' Iris smiled, linking his arm as they strolled together back down the deck towards the sound of the orchestra playing and the passengers still revelling in the first-class dining room. It was a perfect evening for making a new acquaintance, and Iris hoped that this one would last for much longer than a single voyage.

A LETTER FROM KATE

I want to say a huge thank you for choosing to read *The Sea Nurses*. If you enjoyed it and want to keep up to date with all my latest releases, just sign up at the following link. Your email address will never be shared and you can unsubscribe at any time.

www.bookouture.com/kate-eastham/

My inspiration for *The Sea Nurses* came from the true account of a White Star Line stewardess, Violet Jessop, who not only survived the sinking of the *Titanic,* but had previously been involved in a collision on board the *Olympic*, when the ship took on water but stayed afloat. Then, training as a wartime nurse during the First World War, she was on board the hospital ship, *Britannic,* when it struck a naval mine and sank to the bottom of the Aegean Sea. Reading Violet's memoir, I was impressed by her resilience, independence and sense of adventure. I also became more aware of the work of the giant ships which steamed backwards and forwards across the Atlantic before the advent of the airlines and passenger flights that we now take for granted. Intrigued by the glamour, the work of the often unrecognised victualling crews, the sense of freedom and the opportunities these people made for themselves to travel and open up new experience, I was captured.

Expanding my research to other women who lived and

worked by the sea, I was unable to resist the stories of the vibrant, hard-working herring girls who gutted and packed fish during the season every year from Berwick down the east coast of England to Yarmouth. Evie Munro came fully formed, bursting with energy, ready to step on board my hospital ship alongside Iris. I loved the contrast of their very different personalities and backgrounds, all interwoven with a common bond – a love of 'life on the ocean wave' and the solace that only the sound and the smell of the ocean can bring. It made me yearn to stand at the rail of ship, breathe in the salt air.

Another aspect of the story that also intrigued me was the wartime repurposing of the giant luxury liners, particularly those of the White Star Line. The *Britannic* was sister ship to the *Titanic*, almost identical but set to be even more luxurious. Once war was declared she was stripped out and re-fitted with hospital beds and operating theatres. The pantries where luxury food would have been stored held medicines and equipment. It felt sad, given that the *Britannic* never got to carry passengers in peacetime, but it was also pragmatic and heroic for the ship to work as part of the war effort.

Writing the horrors of war from a nurse's perspective, I am in awe of those women and men who have served throughout time and across the world. I hope that *The Sea Nurses* can convey some of that experience and make it more accessible to a wider audience.

As for Iris and Evie, their story is set to continue as their world rushes headlong towards the Second World War. Watch this space for details of a sequel...

I hope you loved *The Sea Nurses*. If you did, I would be very grateful if you could write a review. I'd love to hear what you think, and it makes such a difference in helping new readers discover my books for the first time.

I love hearing from my readers – you can get in touch on Twitter. Thank you!

All best wishes to you and yours,

Kate Eastham

 twitter.com/eastham_kate

ACKNOWLEDGEMENTS

Heartfelt thanks to my brilliant editor, Kathryn Taussig, and the amazing team at Bookouture for making this book happen. Without you my nurses would have been forever at sea.

I'd also like to thank my agent, Judith Murdoch, for her unwavering support and encouragement.

And, as ever, I am grateful to my wonderful family who sustain me through all things with their energy, enthusiasm and wicked sense of humour.

Lightning Source UK Ltd.
Milton Keynes UK
UKHW012009200622
404701UK00004B/688